W9-BUP-794

OUT

OF

THE

BLUE

OUT

OF

THE

BLUE

SOPHIE CAMERON

ROARING BROOK PRESS · NEW YORK

To my grandmothers

OUT

OF

THE

BLUE

PROLOGUE

THE FALL ONLY LASTS A FEW SECONDS. A QUICK FLAILING OF her limbs, hair rippling like ribbons, and then it's over—almost kind in its quickness, some perverse mercy of gravity. It's only later, when I replay the scene in my head, that the seconds begin to slow. They stretch and fracture, each one splitting into countless freeze-frames. I see her hands grapple at the air. I see her legs kick against the invisible tide dragging her toward the ground, a flicker of recognition before she closes her eyes. I see things I couldn't possibly have seen. Not from where I was standing. Not when she was falling so fast.

But I see them anyway, over and over: in the hazy moments before sleep, in the hypnotic blue glare of the TV screen. I remember them each time I see another news report, another viral video. Sometimes, I imagine alternate endings to the story: touches of magic, last-minute miracles. I picture how things might have gone if I hadn't been there. If I'd left just a few minutes earlier. If I hadn't been alone.

It doesn't make any difference. One way or another, the crash always comes.

ONE

ANOTHER BEING FALLS AS WE'RE DRIVING INTO EDINBURGH.
Not here—that would be lucky, and luck doesn't run in the Mackenzie family.

"Number eighty-five!" Rani shouts. "Just landed two minutes ago!"

She leans between the front seats, waving her phone like a newsboy hawking the evening paper. On the screen, a slim, copper-colored woman lies slumped over a pile of broken wood and burst watermelons. Golden blood trickles out from under the debris, tracing shimmering lines in the dust.

"Where is that?" I ask. Perry, our West Highland terrier, raises her head off my lap for a look, then gives a disinterested *ruff* and goes back to bird-watching through the car window.

"Malaysia again," Rani says. "Some market near Kuala Lumpur."

At least the Falls have improved my sister's geography; she was still calling it "Koala Lumper" last month. She taps the screen and a pixelated video stutters into action. The Being is only visible for a second before the crowd swoops. Tourists form a heaving scrum around the body; a woman emerges red-faced and grinning, clutching a handful of feathers. My stomach churns. I've seen dozens of clips like this—everybody has, by now—but they still make me want to throw up.

Dad's head swings between the video and the rain-spattered windscreen. "Is it badly damaged? Masculine or feminine?"

It. Always "it," not he or she, and "masculine" or "feminine" to describe how they look—as if the Beings were a style of jeans or a Spanish noun. The papers talk about them the same way; it's their way of making them seem less human. It's Dad's way of rationalizing his obsession with them.

"*She's* a woman, if that's what you mean," I say. "Besides, she's not just damaged, she's dead. No one could survive a fall that far."

"We'll see." Dad gives me one of those infuriatingly patronizing smiles that he does so well, and I have to physically bite my tongue to stop myself from snapping at him. Behind us, Rani keeps tapping through photos on Wingpin or 247being or one of the other hundred or so apps she's downloaded.

"This one looks young." She nudges her glasses up her nose. "Like, seventeen or eighteen."

"You're judging by human standards, though, pet," Dad says. "We don't know how time affects their bodies yet. It's possible that a Being who looks twenty in our terms could be a hundred, maybe even a thousand years old."

He launches into yet another speech about yet another theory, and yet again, I don't give a crap. Ever since the first Being fell almost eight months ago, our house has been like the Michael Mackenzie Center for Really Boring Theological Research. I can't even remember the last time he asked if Rani had lunch money or if I'd done my homework. He's too busy cutting articles out of newspapers, sticking pins and Post-its onto maps, chatting with Wingdings—a not-so-polite term for angel chasers—in Germany and New Zealand and Japan.

"At the moment it's difficult due to the different chemical composition of their teeth, but scientists think they may be able to calculate their ages by the end of this year . . ."

He natters on and on, getting so caught up in his tales that he misses the change of the traffic lights and a pissed-off lady in a 4x4 beeps her horn at him. Rani nods and "mmms" and "uh-huhs" along. I'm pretty sure that even she, eleven-time winner of Daddy's Girl of the Year, can't *actually* be interested in the levels of linoleic acid in the Beings' fingernails, but she puts on a good act.

I stick my earbuds in and gaze out of the window, nodding along to imaginary music. (My iPod ran out of battery just before we passed Pitlochry, but I've learned it's easier to pretend I can't hear Dad's ramblings.) Outside, the drizzly city streets pass by in a blur. Seagulls swoop across the pale gray sky, on the hunt for food. Perry whines and scratches at the door.

"Almost there, Per," I murmur, stroking the white fur of her back. "Just ten more minutes."

I know how she feels. We've spent five hours in Dad's stuffy

Renault Clio, stuck in traffic on the A9 from Inverness to Edinburgh. It's a shitty way to spend the summer holidays, but neither of us had any choice in the matter.

In hindsight, I should have known something was up when I woke to the smell of pancakes last Saturday. It was the first time Dad had cooked in months; ever since the Falls started, we've lived on a diet of microwave dinners, cereal, and takeaway pizzas. Just as Rani and I had finished drenching our plates in maple syrup, he gave a nervous cough.

"How would you two feel about going down to Edinburgh for a few weeks? I think . . ." He was trying to sound casual, but I could tell from his hesitation that I wasn't going to like what he had to say. "I think I could catch a Being there."

My food went cold as I listened, openmouthed, to his plan. He'd done some "research" (i.e., chatting with other Wingdings on CherubIM), and based on the fact that southeast Scotland has had the highest number of Falls in the world, had "come to the conclusion" (made a wild guess) that another one was due to land in Edinburgh "within the next few weeks" (at some point in the future, or possibly never—he'd figure out the details later).

"Think about it, girls," he said. "We'd finally be able to find out where they're coming from and why they're falling."

I put up a fight. Dad pretended to listen, but when I finally ran out of reasons why this was the stupidest idea since chocolate teapots, he just smiled and ruffled my hair.

"I know it's a long shot, Jaya," he said, "but I really need to do this."

The car glides through a puddle, splashing the windows with

murky rainwater. My phone buzzes. I know it won't be from Leah, but my heart leaps with hope all the same. Instead, I find Emma's name on the screen.

Look what sad sausages we are without you! Attached is a photo of her and Sam pretending to cry, their frowns hidden behind curved hot dogs. The sky above them is bright blue, perfect weather for a barbecue. They're only two hundred miles away, but suddenly the space between here and home seems infinite.

I'm tapping out my reply when Rani pipes up with another update. My sister is on constant Being-watch. She could tell you when and where each one fell, what he or she looked like, sometimes even how much their blood and feathers sold for. Personally I think there's something kind of creepy about an eleven-year-old trawling the internet for news of dead bodies, but Dad finds it useful.

"Listen to this," she says. " 'Today's news means that seven Beings have now landed in Malaysia. The only other country to have hosted as many Falls is Scotland, also with seven; Russia has seen five, and Algeria four.' "

I twist in my seat to face Dad. "What if you got it wrong? What if the next one falls in Malaysia? I mean, they've had just as many, so it's just as likely, right?" I kick my right foot onto the dashboard, jab a toe at the sealskin-colored sky. "Maybe we should be on our way to Kuala Lumpur right now. At least it'd be sunny there."

"Malaysia's a lot bigger than Scotland, Jaya," Dad says, swatting my shoes away. "Plus, the Falls over there have been scattered all around the country, whereas here they've had seven within thirty miles of the city. There's no comparison. If I'm going to catch one anywhere, it'll be in Edinburgh."

I grit my teeth, trying to still the anger bubbling up inside me. He's so stupid. This whole "plan" is so ridiculous. You can't catch a Being. You just can't. They fall at unbelievable speeds. They've smashed through buildings, turned highways into craters. One caused a mini tidal wave when she fell in the South Pacific, and another killed a woman when he landed on her in a town square in Armenia. It's not a bloody *Looney Tunes* cartoon: you can't stick a trampoline under them and spring them back to safety.

Nobody knows when the next one will fall. Sometimes three will tumble down in one day, and sometimes weeks will go by before another appears. There are scientific and religious institutions pouring billions into working out a pattern, but they haven't even come close to finding one. It's not like Dad, former sales and marketing manager for Tomlinson Cigarettes, now stay-at-home layabout, is going to be the one to crack the code.

He makes a right turn onto a brightly lit street of shops and restaurants. Outside Pizza Express, a man in a kilt and tinfoil wings is playing something that sounds vaguely like Robbie Williams's "Angels" on the bagpipes. Dad sings along, drumming his fingers on the steering wheel. Rani joins in for the chorus. They belt it out together, carefree and off-key, the excitement crackling off them like static. A dash of pity simmers with my anger. He really thinks he can do this.

He actually thinks he's going to catch an angel.

TWO

THE FLAT THAT DAD HAS RENTED IS A DUMP. THE KITCHEN IS Barbie-size, the bathroom walls are cloudy with damp, and the living-room carpet looks like somebody's gone all Jackson Pollock with a bottle of red wine. Behind the smell of chemical lemon cleaning products, there's a stubborn undercurrent of beer, weed, and takeaway pizza.

"I rent it out to students during term time," says Shona, our landlady for the next few weeks. "Gives the place a youthful energy."

She fixes me with a wide mulberry smile. She's white, fiftysomething, and looks just like an aubergine: skinny on top, round on the bottom, and purple all over. Baggy violet trousers, an indigo blouse, hair the exact shade of grape juice. At first I thought it might be a cult uniform, but then she told me I had "aggressive red tones in my aura," so I think she might just be a bit odd.

"I'm sure you'll be comfortable," she says as she leads us back to the living room. "It's small, but the chi flows very well."

"It's great," Dad says. He hasn't noticed the scowl on my face, or that Rani has pulled the collar of her T-shirt over her nose to block out the smell seeping from the sofa. "Reminds me of my uni days."

For Dad, this flat is yet more proof that his angel-chasing plan is destined to succeed. Just a few days ago, he was frantically searching hostels and campsites—with the festival a couple of weeks away, most accommodations in Edinburgh have been booked for months. Shona's place was, too, until one of the acrobats she'd rented it to broke his ankle tripping over a paving slab and the duo had to cancel.

"And it's just a few hundred feet from St. Giles' Cathedral!" Dad said as he eagerly sent off the deposit. "Being number eight fell there on New Year's Day, remember? That has to be a sign!"

Now, in the living room, he goes to the window and pushes it open. "You can see it from here! Look, Ran, see the scaffolding?" He twists back to look at Shona, a stupid grin on his face. "If this doesn't help my research, I don't know what will."

Shona nods gravely. "Aye, I find the atmosphere in this part of the city very vitalizing. It's sure to inspire you." Her eyebrows— also purple—rise slightly. "So, is it just the three of you?"

I shoot her a dirty look. This again. I'd noticed a split second of confusion in her eyes as she opened the door, wondering how my pale, blond father could have two brown daughters. It quickly faded as she worked it out, but now she's looking for the missing part of the set. It happens a lot when we we're out with Dad, sometimes accompanied by a bunch of nosy questions. I've always hated when people do that. Since Mum's accident, it's felt even worse.

To my relief, Dad changes the subject without answering. Soon they're talking about his research and about the trip that Shona's taking to a silent retreat in Italy next week. I leave them to their small talk and wander off to the room that Rani and I will be sharing for the next few weeks. Cucumber-green walls, gray metal bunk beds, three dried-up ferns in one corner. My heart sinks a second time as I dump my bag on the floor.

"I call top bunk!"

Rani scrambles up the ladder and dives onto the bed, tossing her spindly legs into the air. She's barely hit the mattress before she whips out her phone again.

"Guess what? They think number eighty-five could be the sister of the Being who fell in Greenland in April. Look, they're like twins!"

She holds out the phone to show me, but I swat it away and go to the window, gazing down at the bustling street five floors below us. I miss my room back home already. It's one of the few places in the world where I can escape the news, photos, adverts, nonstop mindless 24/7 chatter about the Beings. Not much chance of that here.

"Number eighty-five also landed at the same longitude as the Being in Laos." Rani taps on another link, ignoring the fact that I'm ignoring her. "Isn't that interesting?"

I bump my head against the windowpane. Raindrops race down the glass, sketching ghostly rivers over my vision. "Fascinating, Ran. Utterly fascinating."

It poured last time we came to Edinburgh, too. That was two years ago, during the Fringe, the huge arts and theater festival that happens here every August. Never one to be put off by a "bit of drizzle," Mum dragged us all over town watching all the street artists: a cappella groups and contortionists and hip-hop dancers, acrobats and fire-eaters and a tightrope-walking violinist, all scattering flyers like wedding confetti. My hair went frizzy, Perry smelled like compost, and Rani kept moaning about her wet trainers, but it was sort of fun.

"A city of spirit and spectacle," as Mum said. She was always saying stuff like that. Dad used to call her "my poetess," then laugh when she'd go off on a rant about the term being sexist.

This time round, Edinburgh is full of fake angels. Performers dressed head to toe in gold are dotted around the street, reenacting the Falls in stilted clockwork dances. Two little girls skip past Starbucks, plastic halos bobbing over their heads, and tour guides lead groups of Wingdings to and from the cathedral. The spectacle goes on, but the spirit has darkened. It's all just a way to squeeze money from dead Beings now.

"Jaya!" Rani shouts suddenly. "Jaya, look!"

I spin around. "*What*, Rani? What now?"

She points through the second window. I follow her stare—and my heart drops. Across the street, twenty, thirty, forty people are emerging onto the rooftop of the flats opposite ours. It's them. The Standing Fallen.

They look just like the groups on the news: a mix of ages, all dressed in stained shirts, ragged sweaters, jeans far too ripped to be fashionable. Most of the men have uncut beards, and the women's hair lies long and lank around greasy faces. One of the members, a short, squat man holding a loudspeaker, tiptoes across the ridge. He hops nimbly onto the chimney as the others inch toward the roof's edge, forming a line behind the rain gutter.

I've seen scenes like this on TV dozens of times, but it's different this close up. I'd imagined fear on their faces, panic in the air. The members slither a little as they creep over the wet tiles, but most of them don't look scared. Beneath the dirt, their expressions are cold and blank.

"Jaya!" Rani grips the edge of the bunk bed. "They have *kids* with them!"

My mouth goes dry. She's right: there's a boy of around thirteen up there, and a younger girl, maybe seven or eight. Unlike the adults, they're obviously terrified. The girl has her eyes squeezed shut tight, as if making a wish, while the boy stares at the crowd gathering seven stories below. His legs are shaking so much, I'm sure he'll slip. A small woman holds one of their hands in each of hers, but she doesn't comfort them. She doesn't even look at them.

"I'm going to get Dad." Rani slides down and runs out of the room. The man by the chimney switches his loudspeaker on. It gives a sickening squeal, but he doesn't flinch.

"Sinners." His voice is loud but calm, more a statement than an accusation. "For nearly eight months, angels have fallen from the skies. Not for millennia has the Creator sent so clear a sign of his wrath—but does Man repent? Does he scrub his soul of spite and greed, devote himself to a higher cause? No. He picks like a vulture at the bodies of angels, hungry for naught but blood and gold."

I tell myself to turn away, just like I do when they come on TV, but my body won't comply. Though their displays make my stomach churn and my head spin, there's something about the Standing Fallen that forces me to keep looking. I've watched and rewatched the videos. I know the speeches by heart.

The man on the rooftop pauses for effect, just like all the leaders do. It's hard to tell how old he is. His beard hides one half of his face, and the other is coated in a thick layer of grime.

"We represent no one church, no one religion," he says. "We are only a reminder: a reminder of the evils of greed and godlessness, the unwavering arrogance of the human race. We are a reminder of your *sin*. No good awaits man on earth now. Our only chance at redemption is to eschew earthly pleasures, to degrade our bodies as we have degraded this planet, to sacrifice our lives as so many have been sacrificed in the ruthless race for so-called progress . . . to repent and prove ourselves worthy of the freedom of the afterlife."

Somewhere in the distance, a siren begins to wail. Someone on the street below is screaming. Tears are running down the little girl's face; the boy tries to talk to her, but the woman snaps at him and he shrinks back. The speaker carries on, seemingly unfazed by the ruckus he's creating.

"We are the Standing Fallen." His voice swells with pride, though I'm sure it's not supposed to. "As the Beings tumble, we take to the rooftops. We climb to remind you of the precipice upon which you teeter. We stand to remind you of how far you, too, could fall."

In perfect unison, the followers place one foot on the rain gutter. My head spins. They won't go through with it. The Standing

Fallen have put on displays like this on Seoul skyscrapers and Caracas tower blocks; they even made it to the second floor of the Eiffel Tower back in April. They've tiptoed over cliffs and swung from scaffolding. They've threatened to jump countless times—but so far, they haven't actually done it.

I know all that, but it doesn't stop the sinking feeling in my stomach, or the pulse pounding in my ears—

The weightlessness in my legs—

The storm spinning in my head—

The last thing I see, before my eyes close and I hit the floor, is the boy on the roof bowing his head and beginning to pray.

THREE

IT WAS OUR 9/11, OUR PRINCESS DIANA, OUR JFK. YOU'D always remember where you were when you heard about Being No. 1.

He landed on a street corner in Shanghai, 10:46 p.m., 7 December. An Italian tourist caught the whole thing on camera. He'd only meant to take a photo of his wife, but he pressed the wrong button and ended up creating the most-watched video on the internet. (Forty-six billion views, according to Rani's latest update.) Though I've tried to avoid it, I've seen the clip so many times I can close my eyes and replay it in my mind, frame by frame.

First, a spot of silver appears in the smog-orange sky. It hovers for a moment, then quickly grows bigger, plummeting earthward faster than the eyes can follow. Voices start to shout in Mandarin, Italian, English: it's a shooting star, a meteor, a tumbling sun come to crush us all! But then the light twists and elongates, and two streaks of silver spread across the sky. Wings.

Broken wings.

If you pause the video at two minutes, thirty-one seconds, you can see the man's face. There's none of the noble peace you'd expect from an angel: he looks young and frantic and scared to death. He spins toward the skyscrapers, wings beating hopelessly. Even when he's only a heartbeat from the ground, you're sure he'll somehow take off, back toward the heavens and to safety—but then, with an earth-shattering blast, he smashes face-first into the pavement.

Tires squeal, horns blast, a cloud of dust mushrooms into the air. The chaos begins.

For days it was all anyone could talk about. We swapped stories like football stickers, each hoping to find the shiniest. Sam and Marek were playing Xbox when one of Sam's gamer buddies sent him a link. Emma's Mormon cousins in the States posted a rapturous status on Facebook about it. Dad was watching the eight o'clock news, no doubt washed down with his fifth G&T of the evening.

Mum didn't see it. She'd been dead for ten days by then.

I was at Leah's house. She was cutting off my hair.

That's what I remember most about that day. Not her mum hammering on the bathroom door, shouting about something we absolutely had to see, or watching that first blurry clip on her phone—I was sure it was a hoax, anyway, so I wasn't paying that much attention. What I remember best are Leah's fingers trembling as she picked up the scissors, and the quiver in her voice as she asked me for the hundredth time if I was *sure* I wanted to do this.

"Oh my God, Leah, *yes*." I tugged on the hem of her T-shirt. "Come on! It's just hair. It grows back."

"I don't know, Jaya," Leah sighed. "I've never cut anyone's hair before. I don't think the Princess Jasmine doll I had when I was seven counts."

"Fine." I spun her mum's kitchen scissors around my finger. "If you don't do it, I will, and then you'll have to shave my head to cover up the mess I've made."

"All right, all right!" She snatched the scissors back. "Fine, I'll do it. Just don't blame me if you're handing over eighty quid in Toni and Guy tomorrow, okay?"

I remember the tightness in my throat as she made the first few cuts. I remember the locks slipping past my knees, curving like strokes of ink on the bathroom tiles. It was my childhood, that hair. It was bedtimes and bath times, messy French plaits and too-tight braids the summer we went to the Bahamas. It was Mum's hands: washing and combing and tying, winding the tresses around her fingers or stroking them as she read me a bedtime story. It was the sleek black veil of her hair, too, and my grandmother's when she was younger, and all our Sri Lankan ancestors before them. That hair was my history, and now it was gone.

I didn't regret it. But it didn't feel as good as I'd hoped it would.

Leah was right, as it happened: it turned out years spent scalping your Barbies didn't make you a good hairdresser. I walked home with an NYC cap on my head and a nervous flutter in my stomach. Mum would have found it hilarious (I could almost hear her cackle: "What have you done to yourself? You look like the ne-glected love child of Noel Fielding and Edward Scissorhands!"), but Dad was a different story. Dad would be Concerned.

He came running into the corridor as soon as I pushed open the door to our flat. My heart was pounding. I tugged the cap off quick, like a bandage, but he didn't even blink.

"Did you hear what happened?" he asked. "In China? Did you see the news?"

His eyes were red, like they had been for most of the past ten days—a combination of gin and tears—but this time there was something different. They were bright. Hopeful.

"This has to mean something," he kept saying as he paced around the living room, stopping every few minutes to rewatch the video on his laptop. "It has to be a sign. It has to."

It took him two hours and twelve minutes to notice the mess on my head. Being Fever had already kicked in.

Rani wakes me up the next day with the latest Being Bulletin: an-other angel landed off the coast of Alaska early this morning. A fisherman and his son spotted him bobbing facedown in the water, his wings like storm-torn sails, and rowed out to bring him back to shore. It sounds just like a dozen other Falls, except for one thing. Both the boy and his father swear that, just as they were hauling him onto the boat, the Being said something. It wasn't any lan-guage they recognized—it sounded more like music than words—but it was something like speech.

"By the time they pumped his lungs and checked his pulse, he was dead." Rani leans over the top bunk and shows me a photo on her phone. "If they're telling the truth, the Being must have survived the Fall!"

I rub my eyes: the blur on-screen becomes a man, middle-aged with metallic red skin. He's lying on a pebble beach, his wings patchy where his "rescuers" have helped themselves to feathers. By now the Alaskan authorities will have flown his body to a lab. They'll slice him open, marvel at how his heart is so like ours though his blood is golden, how his bones look almost human yet are light as a bird's. They'll scan his face through an ever-growing database of the dead, trying to find the person he could have been before.

So far, they haven't found any matches. I never really believed the theory that the Beings were once human, but I don't see why they shouldn't be treated like people.

"Listen to this, Jay." Rani starts scrolling through links on CherubIM. "'Reports suggest that the Being has only one broken wing, whereas all other bodies have had both severely damaged or, in a few cases, ripped off entirely.'"

I yawn and check my phone. No messages from my friends. Still nothing from Leah.

"Absolutely enthralling, Ran," I mutter. "I can hardly contain my excitement."

She ignores the sarcasm. "'At this early stage we can only speculate, but experts suggest that Being number eighty-six may have been able to slow its descent with its one functional wing, allowing it to land safely on the water.' Isn't that amazing?"

I pull the phone from her hand. "Hello? What? Oh my God,

Ran, news just in! Experts have now confirmed that I really don't give a crap."

"Ha-ha." She scowls and snatches it back, rolling her eyes. "I'm just trying to keep you informed of world events, Ja*ya*."

Before I can think of a suitably snarky reply—something about not needing life lessons from a girl who was still watching *Dora the Explorer* two years ago—there's a tap on the door. Dad pokes his head in.

"Morning, girls." His eyes are slightly bloodshot, and his T-shirt is crumpled. I wonder if he's been to bed, or if he was up all night doing research. "How you feeling, Jay?"

My cheeks burn as I remember my fainting spell last night. I'd woken to find Dad and Rani crouching over me as Shona looked on, her mouth a purple pout of concern. Dad sat me up and told me to put my head between my knees. "Probably just dehydrated," he said, patting my shoulder. "It was a long journey."

Shona clicked her tongue. "Very negative energy, that Standing Fallen lot. I'm not surprised it's having such an overwhelming effect on you, hen. I'll bring you up some quartz, maybe a bit of amethyst—very cleansing for the aura."

Outside, two fire engines were pulling up beside the flats. We watched in silence as the firefighters unfolded their ladders and led the members of the Standing Fallen off the roof. The adults' faces were impassive as ever, but the little girl was sobbing, and the boy melted with relief as a fireman lifted him away from the rain gutter. Nobody had jumped, nobody had slipped. Not yet.

Dozens of religious cults have popped up since the Falls began. Hundreds, probably. Guild of Gold is the largest, and Fourth Age the most deadly—countless suicides all across America, and some in Europe. But it's only the Standing Fallen that make me feel like this: small, and light-headed, and totally powerless.

"Fine," I say now. "Just felt a bit woozy."

Dad nods in agreement. "I'm heading down to Roslin to check out the spot where number thirteen fell," he says. "Anyone fancy coming?"

Rani leaps off the bed, demanding to go to McDonald's for breakfast. For a moment, I almost feel like I'm back in my bed up north, and that Dad's asking us if we want to come to the supermarket or for one of those pointless drives that he used to like so much. I'll walk out to the car and Mum will twist around from the passenger seat, hand me the iPod, and say, "Pick a tune for us, John Peel" like she always did. But then, like a punch in the gut, I remember: I'm not, and he isn't, and she won't, she can't, she's gone.

I don't bother to answer. After a moment, Dad drums his fingers on the door frame lightly. "Okay, Jaya, see you later. There's some money on the kitchen counter if you need it."

He waits another moment, then sighs and shuts the door. His disappointment lingers long after he, Rani, and Perry have left the flat. I don't know what he expects of me. I can't play happy families. I can't pretend everything is normal, that I don't spend every waking minute wishing I could go back eight months and make things right.

I bury my face in the pillow as my eyes start to prickle. Nothing is normal anymore. He's just too busy chasing angels to notice.

FOUR

DAD WASN'T THE ONLY ONE TO LOSE THE PLOT AFTER THE Falls started. No matter what you believed in, there was something undeniably sinister about angels falling from the sky. In the first few weeks, after a second and then a third Being had landed and even the most devout atheists had to admit that this probably wasn't a hoax, the whole world spun off-course.

The mail stopped coming. For me, that was the first clue that things were about to change—that George, our ever-punctual postie, had sacked off work to spend what he thought were the last days with his family. Buses didn't turn up; bins overflowed when no one came to collect them. Shops and restaurants lay in the dark for days. There were rumors about tourists arriving at hotels like ghost towns, cancer patients walking into graveyard-still hospital wards. Half our teachers gave up, too. Duty, it turns out, doesn't mean much when you think the world might end tomorrow.

For many, their first reaction was to run. Houses all around the country sat empty, their owners having fled for London or Warsaw or wherever they had moved away from, back to the people they had left behind. Between the near-constant coverage of Falls in Malawi, Nicaragua, Algeria, the news would occasionally jump to shots of mile-long traffic jams or crowds jostling in train stations. Commercial flights had all been postponed—no one wanted to take the risk of an angel-aircraft collision thirty thousand feet above the earth.

After that, the price of petrol skyrocketed. Banking systems blacked out as people frantically tried to snatch their savings, and the stock market crashed as hard and fast as the Beings themselves. Looting flared up like an angry rash, infecting cities all around the globe. (It was kind of amazing seeing the things people would steal, even in the face of Armageddon—as if you could take micro scooters and thirty-two-inch TVs to the afterlife.) Christmas was only a few weeks away, but turkeys and pigs in blankets were left to rot on supermarket shelves. Instead, people stocked up on tinned foods, toilet paper, batteries, flashlights, warm sweaters, sturdy shoes . . . anything that might help them survive the weeks ahead.

Through all of this, between news reports and TV shows that nobody was watching anymore, government announcements urged everyone to keep calm.

"It is still unknown where these Beings are falling from, or what their doing so signifies." They named them "Beings" because "angels" seemed too religious, too obvious—calling them angels would have been admitting the world was ending, and inciting the very panic they were trying to avoid. "We urge the public to avoid drastic action and to await further information as it becomes available."

For those of us who bothered to show up, school was an eight-hour debate on if, when, and how the Rapture was going to happen. The remaining teachers did their best to distract us, but it never worked—there was always somebody having a panic attack in French or storming off in the middle of PE, ranting about the futility of netball when we'd all be dead in a week anyway.

The rest of us made jokes about it.

"I think it'll happen on Christmas Day," Emma said at lunch one day. "In the middle of the Queen's Speech. She'll be sitting there, all smart in her pearls and whatnot, and then the screen will start shaking, like they've put Buckingham Palace in a tumble dryer. There'll be corgis flying about, footmen screaming—"

Marek chucked an M&M at her. "The Queen's Speech is pre-recorded, genius. I think it'll be aliens. They'll come on New Year's Eve, when people are drunk and don't have their wits about them. Just as we're counting down to midnight, BOOM—they'll zap us into dust and turn the country into a water park."

"It'd never be as dramatic as that," Leah said, scoffing. "It'll happen on some random day of the week, probably a Tuesday. We'll be sitting in history, writing about boring Liberal reforms or whatever, and the ground will open up and swallow us whole. The end."

"You're probably right," Sam said through a mouthful of tuna baguette. "Mrs. Maciver would still expect you to hand in your homework the next day, though."

But the weeks trickled on, and though Beings kept falling, nothing else happened. The sky didn't cave in. The earth didn't split in two. Jesus didn't rock up on a golden chariot, ready to whisk away the good and the pious to the afterlife. Neither did Marek's extraterrestrials. For most people, there's only so long panic can hold out. And after so much madness, we were all desperate for monotony.

So the airports reopened. Buses started running on time. The council sent out emails saying it would not, under any circumstances, accept any more school truancies. Most people returned to their jobs; George showed up a few days after New Year's with a sheepish grin and a handful of very late Christmas cards. Some of those who had left town to be with their families came back, laughing off the terror they'd felt just a few weeks ago.

By the end of January, life had returned to something resembling normality. It was the world as we'd known it, only with the occasional winged person falling out of the sky.

But not for everyone. Some people joined cults. Some found religion. A few poor souls even killed themselves, a desperate attempt to reach an afterlife they felt had been proven to exist. The papers were filled with tragic stories about lives wasted. They never got easier to read.

Other changes were less drastic. Some people quit their jobs to spend more time doing what they loved, for example. Dad said he'd handed in his notice to look after Rani and me, that he needed a job with shorter hours and more holidays, but that was bullshit. If there's one thing a sort-of apocalypse is good for, it's showing you what really matters in life. For Dad, that was getting rich, chasing angels.

I didn't need the Falls for all that. My own personal apocalypse had happened when Mum died. In all the chaos the Beings had created, everyone else had forgotten.

There's no TV in Shona's flat—no doubt it'd interfere with the cosmic vibes or whatever. Instead, I while away the morning watching vlogs and scrolling through Tumblr, playing music full-blast to drown out the bagpipes and the ranting preacher outside. I check the BBC and the *Guardian* websites for the latest news on the Standing Fallen. There's a video of last night's display on the rooftop, plus others in Luton, Cardiff, Bexhill-on-Sea, dozens across Europe and the States. I refresh my Twitter, my long-neglected Facebook.

Still nothing from Leah.

I know she won't get in touch. It's been four months since she and her mum moved to Stirling, four months since anyone's heard from her. Emma's lost hope, and Sam and Marek act like she never existed, but I keep waiting. It's different for me. Even if we were on and off, even if we never gave a name to it . . . she was my first girlfriend. I can't just forget about her.

Not even if she's forgotten about me.

I amble around the internet for a few more hours, but at half past twelve, hunger finally drives me out of the flat. Despite the rain, the street is still full of Wingdings. Tour groups swarm around the cathedral, selfie sticks bobbing in the air. The queue to see the spot where Being No. 8 fell through the roof snakes right across the square, and dozens more tourists clamor around the merch stalls lining the road. Each one is heaped with tacky souvenirs: postcards, candles, tote bags, mugs, tins of shortbread, all emblazoned with illustrations of angels midfall. Some are even selling tiny vials of gold liquid meant to represent Beings' blood. Just as I ask myself who would possibly spend their money on such a thing, a woman in a tartan bonnet picks one up and hands the seller a tenner for it.

Outside Starbucks, a huge TV screen is playing footage of the Scottish Falls. I've seen it all before: No. 42 floating in a river; No. 33 plummeting between two tower blocks; No. 46 smashing into the motorway, sending cars spiraling off the road. Between clips, the film cuts to interviews with witnesses.

"Ah wiz pure terrified! Ah wiz just walkin' tae work when ah seen this spot of light in the sky . . ."

"I'd been reading about the Fall in Kazakhstan that morning, but it didn't click at first—I thought it was a shooting star, maybe an asteroid."

"And the sound when she hit the ground, it was so loud! I think I'll never stop hearing this in all of my life."

"It came out of nowhere, man. It was just so . . . out of the blue."

A sudden blast of pop music drags me away from the screen. Farther down the Royal Mile, a queue of fifty or sixty people has gathered on the pavement opposite the Storytelling Centre. As I walk toward the crowd, I see a couple of girls in skimpy white dresses and glittery wings scurrying along the pavement, handing out flyers and shouting over the music.

"Welcome to Celeste's, the UK's first Being-themed restaurant!"

Two more angels stand by golden-gates doors, writing down names on clipboards shaped like harps. The walls of the building are baby blue, both inside and outside, and decorated with fluffy white clouds. One of the waitresses, a skinny girl with platinum-blond curls, flips her hair and pushes a flyer into my hand.

"Heavenly hour from two to four, Sunday to Thursday!"

One side of the paper shows a cartoon of a female Being with a silver halo and red lips, winking as she bites into a burger. The other lists the menu: halo bagels, cherubim chips, "angel" wings. Just your average diner food, only with silly names and at ridiculous prices. My stomach growls. I'm starving, and the "Erelim omelet" does sound pretty tasty, but I wouldn't be seen dead eating in a place like this. As I turn to leave, a voice cuts through the girls' sales pitch.

"Don't want burgers, chips, and Sprite—we want decent Beings' rights!"

Half the queue turns to stare. Two kids, both about my age, come stomping along the pavement, each with a placard over their shoulder: a short, very skinny white girl with wavy brown hair, chanting into a plastic megaphone, and a boy who, though blond and less pale, can only be her brother—he has the same heart-shaped face, the same slightly upturned nose.

"Celeste's has no morality! Don't profiteer from tragedy!" the girl shouts, raising her sign into the air. It's shaped like a pair of wings and shows a businessman trampling over the body of an angel, chunky pound signs twinkling in his eyes. "This place is an abomination, down with Being exploitation!"

The boy cups one hand around his mouth. "Novelty Being restaurants are demeaning to angels and humans alike," he says, forgoing the rhymes. He seems a bit nonchalant compared to his sister. "I mean, come on, guys, there's a Nando's up the road if you want chicken wings so badly."

While the waitresses huddle on the top step of the restaurant, wings trembling as they discuss how to handle the situation, the kids walk up and down the queue, trying to talk to the people waiting to get into Celeste's. Most shake their heads; some tell them to piss off. Almost everyone groans at the terrible chants, but nobody leaves. The girl doesn't seem discouraged, but the boy puts his placard down and starts taking photos of the scene instead. When his sister notices, she flaps her own sign at him and hisses at him to concentrate. The boy rolls his eyes, slides his phone into his pocket, and shouts something halfhearted about fair treatment of Beings instead.

For a moment I'm almost tempted to pick up his placard and join in: they're vocalizing every thought I've had about how people treat the Beings, about how horrible and unfair and exploitative it is. But before I can, a short man with a shaved head and a wonky nose steps out. He exchanges a few angry whispers with the girls, then shakes his head and stomps down the steps. The boy's eyes widen. His sister smirks.

"Right, you two. Piss off," the manager snarls. "You're not being funny, you're not being clever. Stop making prats of yourself and go home."

"We're on the pavement." The girl drops her placard and puts her hands on her hips. Her dress, dark green and decorated with tiny white birds, ripples in the breeze. "It's not private property. We can stand here all day if we want to."

The man grits his teeth. I flinch—it's like watching a Great

Dane squaring up to a Chihuahua—but the girl doesn't seem fazed. The boy steps forward, his arms crossed.

"We have every right to peaceful protest." His voice quavers a little, but he looks the manager in the eye. "Call the police if you want, pal. It's not like they can arrest us."

"Oh, aye?" The man's eyes bulge. "We'll see about that, you smug wee shit."

He fumbles for the phone in his pocket, so fast he drops it to the pavement. There's a collective "eesh" from the crowd. The manager's hands twitch into fists, but he just snatches it up and storms back into the restaurant while the kids snigger. One of the angel waitresses waits until he's past the golden gates, then runs up to the protesters.

"Can you just go? Please?" She's wringing her hands like damp cloths. "This is our big launch. He'll be unbearable if it doesn't go well. If you really have to do this, could you come back tomorrow?"

The boy's expression softens, but the girl's hands are still firmly on her hips.

"No. Sorry, but this is important. We're trying to get you to realize that the Beings are *people*. It's sick, treating them like this, as if they were just—"

Whatever the next word is, it catches in her throat. Her chest heaves, and she coughs. Not your usual cough, but a great, tearing sound that sends tremors through her whole body. A few people in the queue turn around to stare; the angel waitress takes a hasty step back. Her brother leans in, passes the girl a tissue, and whispers something to her. It takes a minute for the coughing to ease off, but eventually she wipes her mouth and shrugs.

"God, whatever." Her voice is hoarse, but she rolls her eyes like it never happened. "We'll let you have your stupid launch. This isn't right, though. Not by a long shot."

The waitress thanks them and runs back inside, teetering in her white heels. The pair shoulder their placards, the girl sneaking in one last chant before they leave: "Hope your business belly flops, exploitation has to stop!"

As they turn toward me, her eye catches mine. I realize I'm still holding the restaurant's flyer in my hand; I don't want her to think I'm just another Wingding, so I crumple it and give her a double thumbs-up. My cheeks flare—*a double thumbs-up?* What am I, Borat?—but the girl just grins and salutes in return. She's kind of cute. Really cute, actually.

They walk right past me, and there's a moment when I could say something—strike up a conversation, let them know that I find all this Wingding crap as awful as they do. But by the time I've fished a half-coherent thought out of my brain, they're already rounding the corner, laughing about something, their placards bobbing in the air.

FIVE

THE NEXT MORNING, I WAKE UP TO FIND THE FLAT EMPTY AND Shona, dressed in plum jeans and a satin violet shirt decorated with green flowers, knocking on the door.

"Smoky quartz!" For a second I think she's speaking German at me, but then she pulls a large, shiny oval the color of dirty dishwater from her pocket. "Removes negative energy from the aura. Always works for me. And this one"—she holds up a jagged lump of amethyst, a perfect match with her lipstick—"will draw in divine energy to protect it."

"Eh . . . thanks?" She pushes the stones into my hands. They're lighter than I imagined. "Um, what do I do with them?"

"Just pass them over your body, like so." She moves her hands around her chest, stomach, and legs in large sweeping motions, like she's rubbing cream into her skin. I must look unconvinced, because she adds, "I know it sounds like nonsense, and who knows, maybe it is. But if it works, if it makes you feel better, does it really matter?"

"I guess not. I'll, um, give it a go," I say. "Thanks, Shona."

"No problem, hen. Let me know how you get on."

I begin to say good-bye, but she pulls a set of keys out of her pocket and holds them out to me. "Another wee thing—would you mind popping in to water my bonsai tree after I head off to my retreat tomorrow? I'm just downstairs at number four. I'll leave instructions."

"Um, sure. How long are you away for?"

"Two weeks. Two perfect, silent weeks." She closes her eyes and gives a happy little shake of her shoulders. "You should try it, hen. It's fabulous, really centers you."

I give a vague "mmm" and thank her again for the crystals before she heads back downstairs. It's kind of nice that she cared enough about my dodgy aura to bring them up. Even if I have no intention of using them for anything other than paperweights.

Then again, I might as well be on a silent retreat with the amount of talking I do over the next couple of days. My friends back home are too busy with their summer jobs to chat much, and though I wander down to Celeste's a few times, I don't bump into the protesters again. As for Dad and Rani, they spend all their time visiting Fall spots around the city: the crater where No. 33 fell in Sighthill, the river where No. 42 washed up in May . . . It's like a treasure hunt, each trip another step toward the final prize.

If I weren't so against Dad's whole Being obsession, I might have gone with them just for the company. Instead, I spend my first few days in Edinburgh bored and alone in my room, watching the latest

Standing Fallen displays online and refreshing Leah's profile pages for updates that never come.

I'm scrolling through her Instagram feed when Dad and Rani arrive back from checking out an angel statue in the National Museum on Wednesday evening. The last photo on her account is of Emma and me at the beach, taken back in March. Emma's doing her best Kardashian pout; the corner of my mouth is twitching into a smile, but I'm not quite looking at the camera. My eyes are on Leah.

She stopped speaking to me a few days after that. No argument, no explanation; she just stopped acknowledging that I even existed. It wasn't the first time—Leah was forever stressing about "us," though what "we" were changed as often as Emma's nail color—but it had never been so abrupt, or so extreme. Still, I didn't think it was anything more than another freak-out. Sam and I even put bets on how long it would last: he said Friday, I said Tuesday lunchtime.

We never found out who won, because on Monday Leah didn't turn up to school at all. The next morning the worries started to creep in, and by Wednesday I couldn't concentrate for the sickly feeling in my stomach. I made Emma skip second period and come to Leah's house with me to find out what was going on. Her dad flung the door open barely a second after I'd knocked.

"Oh. Hi, girls." His face flooded with disappointment. "Leah's not here. Kirsty's . . . Kirsty's moved out, gone to her sister's down in Stirling. She took Leah with her."

"Oh. Right." My initial reaction was relief, followed by confusion—why hadn't they told anyone? When I'd asked at the school reception, they said they hadn't heard anything. "Well, will they be back?"

Mr. Maclennan swallowed. There was a long strip of stubble over his Adam's apple that he'd missed shaving. "I don't know, Jaya. I didn't think she'd actually—I don't know."

He mumbled something about needing to make a phone call and quickly shut the door. And that was it. There was no note left for me from Leah, no emails or messages since. I must have called her a hundred times, but she never picked up. Her online profiles lay unchanged; eventually, her phone started going straight to voice mail. Stirling might as well have been Saturn.

My phone vibrates in my hand, making me jump. The notification scrolls along the top of the screen: *BREAKING: Glasgow chapter of Standing Fallen stage "protest" on top of high school.*

I click on the link; after a moment a video flickers onto the screen. Dozens of tiny figures are stretched along the roof of an empty school building somewhere in the city, holding hands like paper-chain people. I recognize some of them from past protests on the news. There's the fat man with the acne scars, his stomach lolling over the waistband of his baggy jeans. The tall redhead who was a grown-up Princess Merida a few months ago now has dark shadows circling her eyes and hair hanging to her shoulders in lank, greasy tresses.

The camera zooms in on the leader. He's an emaciated white guy, maybe midthirties, with strawberry blond hair, cauliflower ears, and almost no chin. He's standing by one of the chimneys, screaming into a loudspeaker, just like the guy here in Edinburgh did the other night.

My head begins to spin again. I feel like I'm going to fall, though I'm lying on the bottom bunk with nowhere to go but through the mattress. I hate seeing them teeter there, knowing just one gust of wind could send them tumbling. I know I should just stop watching, but I can't. It's a compulsion. Rani's addicted to tracking the Falls; I'm addicted to tracking the Fallen.

On the screen, the sirens are growing louder and louder. The group raise their arms, their own broken wings, like a troupe of actors accepting applause. The leader screams something about the arrogance of the human race, and—

The video cuts out. Not just the video: the whole screen. My phone, medieval piece of junk that it is, has run out of battery.

I toss it aside and roll off the bottom bunk. "Rani!"

She and Dad are in the living room, working on their research. After just a few days, Dad has managed to transform the place into a madman's laboratory: there are pin boards covered in notes, a fringe of Post-it notes stuck to the sofa and chairs, books on Zoroastrianism and weather patterns and aerodynamics spread like stepping-stones across the carpet. It's like the guy has never heard of Microsoft Office.

"Can I borrow that?" I ask, while Rani swipes at the screen. "Mine's just died."

"I'm busy, Ja*ya*." Her tone makes me bristle. Whenever she's acting as Dad's research assistant, she talks to me like I'm five years younger than her and not vice versa. "Why don't you just charge it?"

"I need to watch something *now*, genius. Come on, Rani, I'll just be a minute."

"Jaya! This is important! They're about to release the results of

Being number eighty-six's autopsy! This could tell us whether he was still alive or—"

She starts to explain, but I cut her off. My need to watch this video feels more urgent than usual, almost desperate. I turn to Dad.

"Can I jump on your laptop quickly? It'll just take a minute."

He keeps on typing, staring zombielike at the screen; I have to shake his shoulder to get him to look up. He spins around, so annoyed that I actually take a step backward.

"*What*, Jaya? Can't you see I'm busy? Your music videos or vlogs or whatever can wait until tomorrow."

And I don't know why, but that's the thing that finally makes me snap. I kick the wall, leaving a muddy smudge on the off-white paint. Rani drops her phone into her lap; Dad spins in his chair, his mouth open. Before I can stop myself, all the anger that's been bubbling up inside me for weeks, even months, comes spilling out of my mouth.

"This is ridiculous! You're totally delusional! There's absolutely *no* chance you can do this, you do realize that?" I kick over a huge leather-bound book so hard it sends shooting pains through my foot. "You've given up your job, ruined our whole summer, our whole lives, and for what? For the tiny, impossibly small chance that a Being *might* just happen to fall out of the sky at the right moment? It's not going to happen!"

Dad's cheeks turn red, but he doesn't shout. Instead, he closes his eyes and takes a long, deep breath. It's such a Mum move, it actually makes me feel a bit sick.

"I'm trying to make things better," he says calmly. "I'm trying to make things right again."

"*How?* By getting some big cash prize? If you wanted to be rich so badly, why didn't you just keep working at Tomlinson? Oh wait, yeah, you're 'looking after' us," I say, adding air quotes with my fingers. "Hardly. Rani and I don't need you; we'd be fine on our own. You barely act like a parent, anyway."

"Don't you—"

He stumbles over his words, breaking off midsentence. He looks . . . wounded. There was a time when a look like that would have had me apologizing in a nanosecond, but not now. I storm out of the room and grab my rain jacket and the dog leash from the coatrack.

"Come on, Perry."

The dog leaps out of her basket, tail wagging happily. I let her run out onto the stairwell, then slam the door behind me. I half expect Dad to shout at me to come back, or at least to ask where I think I'm going, but the door doesn't open.

Outside, people speed past with their heads bent and their hands in their pockets, or shielding their heads with handbags. The drizzle has turned into a full-on downpour and the sky is turning from pale gray to charcoal, but I don't care. I turn away from the cathedral, surrounded by its usual orbit of tourists, and instead walk down the Royal Mile. I pound the pavement with my trainers, imagining I'm stomping all over Dad's stupid research, stamping on his laptop. Crushing his notes and algorithms and time-wasting theories into pulp.

I turn past the Parliament and toward Arthur's Seat, the hills tucked behind the city center. Last time I came here, it was full of people: tourists taking selfies, couples lounging on the grass, walkers in ugly boots and warm fleeces. Now the hills are practically empty: just one very dedicated photographer, taking pictures of a ruin perched on a low crag overlooking a rain-spattered duck pond. I follow a steep path in the opposite direction, stopping halfway to find a stick to throw for Perry. She bounds through a puddle and races after it, then sprints back with it for me to chuck again.

By the time we reach the top of the hill, the rain has eased off and we're both panting hard. I sit down on a rock and Perry slumps to the ground, her tongue lolling. Below us, the city looks like a toy town. I reach into my pocket for my phone before remembering I left it at home, so I try to commit it to memory instead. Windows glow in the twilight, the pinpricks of streetlamps swirl like golden galaxies. Church steeples and towering monuments pierce the skyline, standing sentry around the illuminated castle. And for the millionth time since last November, I wish Mum were here.

Mum wouldn't have put up with this Wingding crap. She cared about stuff. She cared about our littered seas, our burning forests, the species being wiped from the planet. She cared about the African towns being used as dumps for Western gadgets, the factory workers in Asia paid pennies to make our clothes. I'd seen her crying over photos of drowned refugees, and over people's refusal to help them. There were times when all the bad in the world seemed to overwhelm her, and times when she couldn't avoid being part of it. But she never resigned herself to it.

There was a time, back when they were students, when Dad had that much passion, too. Mum would sometimes talk about the eighteen-year-old she'd met at university, the one who joined the

Socialist Workers Party and got the sleeper train down to London so he could go to Carnival Against Capitalism, but I always felt like she was describing a different person.

I heard them arguing about it once, just after he'd accepted the job at Tomlinson Cigarettes. Mum didn't say anything about it in front of Rani or me, but their arguing woke me up that night.

"We'll be living off other people's lung cancer. How can you be okay with that?" Mum was hissing—I had to creep from my bedroom to the top of the stairs to hear her properly. "What's happened to you, Mikey?"

"I grew up, Sonali!" Dad sounded more exasperated than angry. "I grew up and realized that the world just isn't perfect. There is no fair, equal society lying dormant under all this injustice, waiting for a student protest or peaceful demonstration or some stupid online petition to wake it up. I realized that, actually, money *can* bring you happiness, and, you know what, that I *would* rather have a nice life than nice principles, and—"

Mum cut him off with a cold laugh. "Wow. Nice. Great example you're setting for the girls there, Michael."

I don't know what she would have thought about the Beings, but I know she wouldn't have let him turn our lives upside down to go chasing one. I close my eyes. I wish I could turn back time, back to that morning in November, change every choice I made that day. There's no way Dad would have dragged us on this wild-goose chase if she were still here.

Somewhere in the distance, thunder starts to rumble. Raindrops slip over the edge of my hood, landing on my nose. I wipe my eyes and try to swallow down the lump in my throat, the knot of guilt in my chest that's been there since November. When I look up, the sky has slid from dark gray into black, and the anger that drove me out of the house has morphed into a tired sort of sadness.

"Perry!" I shout, getting up to go home. "Come on, let's go!"

I hear her rustling around in the bushes, then the soft scuffling of her paws on the grass. I clip the leash back onto her collar and hurry back down the path, only I must take a wrong turn somewhere, because suddenly I'm in some sort of clearing, rocks on one side and trees on the other, with absolutely no idea what direction I'm going in. There are streetlights glowing in the distance, but the Parliament has disappeared from sight.

"Shit." It's dark. Really dark. The moon is hidden behind murky black rain clouds, and I don't even have my phone to use as a flashlight or, more importantly, to call for help. *Don't panic*, I think, but my pulse is starting to race. I stumble forward, scraping my hand on a rock, when something appears in the sky.

It's barely visible at first: just a smudge, a tiny ripple of movement. It lasts only a split second, and at first I think I imagined it, but then something shifts in the clouds, and a dull pink dot forms against the blue-black sky. It slips toward the earth, falling at breakneck speed, so fast my eyes can hardly keep pace.

I start to run, but it's coming closer, hurtling like a comet toward me, and though I've seen scenes like this a hundred, a thousand times, I don't realize what I'm looking at until it's just ten or fifteen meters away, until it spreads its wings and comes plummeting toward the hill.

Another Being, falling right in front of me.

SIX

I WAIT FOR THE CRASH. I WAIT FOR BONES CRACKING, A neck snapping. My eyes are scrunched shut. My hands are clenched so tight, the handle of Perry's leash digs into my skin. There's a noise that sounds like fabric ripping, another of wood breaking. I wait for that aching *thwunk*, the sound of a body breaking against the earth.

It doesn't come.

And then Perry begins to bark. She runs off, yanking on the leash so hard I almost fall into the bracken. I open my eyes and see a bulky shape stuck in a tree on the edge of the hill, just a few hundred yards away. My mouth goes dry. Images swirl around my head: dull eyes, a smashed skull, blood seeping into the ground. I don't want to see that. I cannot, cannot see that. Not again.

But for some reason I keep running. Perry bounds ahead, a white blur against the dark grass. I run full speed after her, sprinting until I'm just a few meters from the tree.

The shape shifts.

I freeze.

It's *moving*. It—he? she?—flounders between the leaves, thrashing and kicking. The tree's trunk groans, and with a strangled yelp, a Being slips through the branches and comes tumbling down to earth.

And this time, for the first time since the Falls began, the Being is alive.

She's not like any of the others I've seen (or what was left of them, at least). Her skin is a shimmering shade of rose gold, and her hair falls in dusky pink tangles around her shoulders. She's young, maybe eighteen or nineteen in our terms, and small but muscular, like an athlete or a ballet dancer. Her cheekbones are sharp, her lips thick, her eyes the color of garnet in the dim light—eyes that are wide and twitchy, darting around the hill and up to the sky before settling on me.

We stare at each other, this angel and me, both of us too shocked to move. Her eyes flick past my shoulders, over the place where there should be wings but aren't. Her mouth twists in disgust; mine opens and closes a dozen times, but I can't form any words. I don't know what to say. I come in peace? Welcome to earth, population seven billion?

"Um," I say. "Hello."

My voice breaks the spell. A fault line of fear shudders through her and she scrambles backward, scraping her wings against the gnarled tree trunk. She screams something in a language I can't understand, though it hardly sounds like a language at all: more like whale song and waves and high-pitched pipes, all blended together with the volume turned up.

"Shhh! Shhh!" I stumble forward, my palms up. "It's okay!"

I try to think, but my mind is full of white noise. I should help her. I should hide her. I should get Dad, let him know he was right. (Oh my God, Dad was *right*—he's going to be unbearable when he finds out.)

The Being grabs the lowest of the tree's branches and hauls herself up on trembling legs. She teeters for a moment, but then her knees buckle and she slumps to the ground. I move forward to catch her, but she screams and swings a punch at me. I duck, and a great ripping sound tears through the air.

My breath catches in my throat.

Her right wing is torn down the middle, its pinkish feathers littering the ground. The left, however, is perfect: a vast sail of feather and sinew, curving in a slick arch three feet above her head. Even in the darkness, the fibers of the feathers glisten like oil on water: countless shades of pink, speckled with tiny hints of azure and turquoise and teal.

The Being's face contorts in pain as she beats the wings together. There's another light tearing sound, as if she's ripped through gravity, and she begins to rise. She beats them a second time, creating a gust of wind so strong it sends me staggering backward, my hair whipping around my face. Relief radiates out of her as she floats upward: six inches, a foot, a meter . . .

But then she starts to wobble. The wings move faster, but instead of taking her higher, she just spins in a jerky circle, arms and legs flailing like she's treading water. She falls back to earth with a bump, then gets up and tries again. And a third time, and a fourth. I can see the panic begin to set in. There's no way to escape. She's trapped here, on earth, with me.

My brain is a swamp, but one idea keeps bubbling up to the surface: I need to get Dad. He came here to find a Being. Now that I've done his job for him, we could probably go back home. I could get back to my friends, back to the village and my own room—

The Being lands with another dull thud. This time, she doesn't get up. Her lip quivers, her eyes close, and she starts to cry.

"No, shhh! It's okay, you're okay!" I reach out a hand toward her, but the Being flinches and pulls away. The noise swells, her sobs growing louder and louder until Perry starts to howl along. The Being looks up, so surprised she forgets to keep crying, but then her entire body begins to tremble. Wherever she comes from, they clearly don't have dogs there.

"It's okay! She won't hurt you."

They say dogs can sense fear, but mine doesn't notice the Being's. Perry climbs onto her knees and curls up in her lap, just like she would with Rani or me, then gives a lazy *woof* and starts licking at the scratches on the angel's thighs. Thousands of pounds' worth of Being's blood, being eaten by my dog. If the Wingdings could see this. If *Dad* could see this.

Then something happens. The Being sniffs. She puts her hand on Perry's haunches, then snatches her fingers away as if she's been scalded. After a moment, though, she touches Perry's back. She strokes her fur, her expression veering from fear to wonder.

As I watch, my thoughts of handing her over to Dad slowly curdle into sickly shame. It would be the simplest solution, but I can't bring myself to do it. Everything about her, from her eyes to the tentative way she strokes Perry, is just too human. Dad might sell her to science, and I know better than to think those researchers would treat her kindly. They'd probably slice her open like a lab rat, pull her wings apart to find what makes her fly, maybe even try to inseminate her to create half-angel babies or some weird shit like that. The cults would be worse. She'd probably end up as a pet for some billionaire's bratty kids, or as a sort-of-human sacrifice.

I can't let that happen. I have to help her. Not because I found her, not because it's my destiny or any crap like that, but because she is, quite obviously, a person. She deserves to be treated like one.

And that means getting her out of here.

I squint into the darkness. I need to find somewhere to hide her, and fast: other people are sure to have noticed the streak of pink in the sky as she fell, and it won't be long until they head up here to investigate. This part of the hills is stark, with hardly any trees or bushes for cover. I remember the ruined building on one of the lower peaks, where I saw the photographer taking pictures on my way up.

The Being wipes her hand across her nose, still crying softly.

"We have to go." I point toward the other side of the hill and mime running. "You're not safe here. Not safe! Bad! We have to go!"

Her expression stays blank. Slowly, I edge my hand toward her and slide my fingers into hers. The touch of her skin is soft as mist, like she's hardly there at all. Our hands only meet for a split second before she snatches hers away, but she grabs the lower branches of the tree and reluctantly pulls herself to her feet.

It's a slow process. The Being is limping, and her right wing is drooping so low it almost brushes the grass. The sky is pitch black now and it's hard to see where we're going, although her skin glows like dying embers in the darkness. My stomach flutters with nerves. It'll be a miracle if we can make it to the other side without anyone spotting us. Then again, it's a miracle she's alive at all—maybe a second one isn't too much to ask.

As we follow the path toward the foot of the hill, the rotting building comes into view. I pull the Being back and crouch down by some gorse bushes. The ruin is just a shadowy lump before the glittering skyline, but there's the tiniest bit of movement around it: the outline of a couple, kissing in the darkness.

"Shit!"

I fall to the ground, pulling the Being down with me. She spreads her wings flat, or as flat as she can given the state the right one is in. The feathers tickle the nape of my neck.

A voice comes floating out of the darkness. "Did you hear something?"

"You're imagining things. Not scared of the dark, are you?"

The girl laughs and pulls the boy toward her. There's some shuffling and lip smacking as they kiss again. My pulse is pounding so loud, I'm sure they'll hear us. Footsteps crunch on the stones, but then there's silence. I poke my head over the bushes. The couple have disappeared.

"Come on," I whisper. "We're almost there."

We scramble up a steep, rocky slope, the Being grunting a little as the stones dig into her bare feet. The ruin is much more exposed than I realized. It's perched on a low peak overlooking a pond, clearly visible from the road; three of its four walls have crumbled away, and the only one that's left has several large windows gaping through it. There are cigarette butts scattered on the grass, an empty beer bottle smashed in the corner, the initials *HW + DR* chipped into the stone. I kick the rubbish out of the way, clearing a space for the Being on the ground. She starts to copy my movements, thrusting her right leg back and forward like a broken football player in a FIFA game.

"No! Look, like this."

She follows my lead as I ease into a crouching position. The night air is starting to nip at my skin, but I shrug my arms out of my hoodie and put it around her shoulders. (Not very successfully, given the pterodactyl-size wings attached to her back.) She's completely naked underneath. Until now, I hadn't even given it a second thought.

Past the pond, headlights sweep across the road. I press myself against the wall, my heart in my mouth. The car glides by, disappearing around the corner and past the Parliament.

"That was too close," I murmur. She can't stay here, but there's no way I can walk her back to our flat without her being swamped by a hundred Wingdings en route. Even if I could, there's nowhere in the flat for her to stay—I can hardly stick her in the bottom bunk and hope Rani doesn't notice.

"I'll come back," I tell the Being. "I'll go home and get you some clothes, and then we'll figure something out, okay?"

It's far from ideal, but right now it's all I can think of. I tell Perry to stay, pull the hoodie back over the Being's shoulders, and sprint back down the hill. This is a dream. This is madness. This is really, *really* damn ironic.

But I don't have time to think about why it's happening, or what it all means. There's only one question on my mind:

Where the hell am I going to hide an angel?

SEVEN

THE ANSWER COMES TO ME ON MY WAY HOME. OR RATHER,
I come to it: number four, Shona's flat. The key is still upstairs, in
the pocket of my gray jeans, waiting for me to let myself in and water
her plants.

Think, Jaya, think. Shona said she'd be in Italy for two weeks.
If she left on Monday, then that gives me eleven full days, maybe
more if she wasn't including travel time. I sprint up the final flight
of stairs, my chest swelling with excitement. It's like a sign—a gift
from the gods, if there are any, or at least from a hippie and her
bonsai tree.

The lights in the hallway are still on when I push the front door
to number five open. Dad stomps through from the living room,
looking tired and pissed off in equal measures. Oh shit, he knows.
How does he know? Can he smell the Being on me? Do they have
a smell?

"Where the hell have you been? It's half past twelve!"

My face is frozen with shock. Somehow, I manage to mutter an apology. I kick off my very muddy trainers, mentally crossing my fingers that he won't notice Perry isn't with me. "I just went for a walk."

"For *three* hours? In the rain?" His eyes flick over my damp hair, my grass-stained jeans. "God, Jaya, look at the state of you. You'd better take a shower before you catch a cold."

There are times when Dad is so absorbed in his research I could set myself on fire and he wouldn't notice, but the whole Concerned Parent act is much more annoying. It's just so fake. Even in the years before Mum died, he barely paid any attention to us. Not since he started his last job, anyway. Before, when we lived in a smaller house in the village and he worked in a music shop, he was always around. He'd pick us up from school and take us into town to go ice-skating or to Milo's Diner for peanut butter milk shakes.

That stopped after he got the job at Tomlinson. After that it was all business trips and conferences, phone calls in the middle of meals and nights when he wouldn't come home till ten o'clock. It felt like we stopped being enough for him.

There's no time to argue, though. I have to get back to the Being.

"Okay, sorry," I say. "Won't happen again."

I try to push past him, but he puts a hand on my arm. "Wait, Jaya, I . . ."

For a second, I'm shocked by how old he looks. His hair has gone from sandy blond to almost entirely gray in the past few months, and time has carved deep lines around his eyes and mouth. He's only thirty-six, but he looks a good decade older.

"Look, pet, I'm sorry about earlier," he says. I grit my teeth. Why do parents always decide it's time for a heart-to-heart at the worst possible moment? "I know you weren't keen on coming here, and I know you must miss home, but I just really, really need to do this. I can't explain it. I feel like it's the only thing that gives me any purpose."

My eyes start to sting. *You could try being a dad for once*, I think. *Maybe that could give you purpose.* The words bubble into my mouth, but I swallow them down.

"I understand," I say, though I really, really don't. "I get it. It's fine."

"Thanks, love. Listen, I think I worked out when it's going to fall." He beams. "I have to double-check, of course, but I think it'll be on the fourth of August. Less than two weeks! I'll have a few things to sort out afterward, but if all goes well, we might be able to head home after that."

That feeling comes back—that weird mixture of exasperation, anger, confusion, and pity.

"Awesome, Dad. Well done." I slip under his arm and push our bedroom door open, ignoring the hurt look on his face. "I'm going to take a shower. Night."

Rani is fast asleep, one skinny arm slung over the edge of the top bunk. Leaving the door open a crack for some light, I tiptoe toward the wardrobe and find Shona's key in the pocket of my jeans. I change into a dry T-shirt and hoodie, then stuff my backpack full of clothes and shoes for the Being: leggings, jeans, cardigans, shirts, baggy things to fit over her wings.

When I sneak back into the hallway, I hear the muffled

commentary from a news report coming from Dad's laptop. I creep toward the door, pausing as the floorboards creak beneath my feet, and then slip outside. The street is even busier now. People are spilling out of pubs, singing and giggling and having top-volume arguments about politics or the meaning of the Falls.

I pull my hoodie over my head and run down the road, ignoring the shouts of "Where's the fire, hen?" and "Run, Forrest, run." By the time I arrive back at the ruin, my legs are aching and my chest is tight. My head spins with relief when I see the Being and Perry, still tucked up behind the wall where I left them.

"I'm back!" I pant. "I've found somewhere we can go, somewhere safe."

For a second I think I see a hint of relief in the Being's eyes, but I'm probably just imagining it. I drop to my knees, rummage through the clothes in my bag, and pull out the biggest top I can find—an oversized knit sweater that belonged to Mum—a pair of patterned purple leggings, and my running shoes. The Being looks at me in total bewilderment.

"Here, like this."

She looks perplexed, but folds her wings flat against her back, wincing a little as she bends the right one into her shoulder, and I pull the sweater over her head. Despite being so large, her wings are surprisingly compact: at their smallest, only the tips stick out behind her neck. I take my jacket off and tug it over her arms: it's a bit of a tight squeeze, but with the hood up, it doesn't look too suspicious.

Her skin is the real problem. It shimmers in the light, like the smooth inner side of a seashell. If only Emma were here—she has the cosmetic equivalent of a first aid kit on her person at all times, but I only ever wear eyeliner and the occasional dab of lip gloss. Hopefully people will be hurrying along with their heads down, too busy to take notice of a couple of girls running through the rain.

"Come on," I say, stretching my hands out. "We have to go."

After a long moment's hesitation, the Being takes them. I pull her to her feet and steer her toward the road.

Somewhere in the darkness, a car screeches to a halt.

The noise makes us both jump. I crouch behind the wall of the ruin, pulling the confused Being after me. A car door opens, then slams; faint footsteps move across the tarmac. Two voices, one male and one female, cut through the silence.

"Where do you think you saw it?"

"About there—must have been just off the path."

"Any chance it's alive, you think?"

"Nah, man. Too many rocks up there. It'll have smashed its head open soon as it landed."

Two tall figures walk across the car park. They start up the steep path, in the opposite direction from us. I wait until their voices have faded away, then slowly move out from behind the ruin. If these people noticed the Fall, others might have, too.

We move down the hill, as slowly and quietly as possible, both stumbling a little on the sharp rocks. The Being is still limping, so I slip my arm around her waist and help prop her up. I can feel the mass of her wings, sturdy yet soft, through the fabric of the jacket.

"You can do this," I whisper. "Just stay calm."

Perry runs ahead, stopping every so often to give the Being an encouraging push at the ankles. As we reach the pavement, footsteps scuffle on the gravel path high above us.

"I'm telling you, I saw something!" The woman's voice, loud and high-pitched.

"Must have been a bird, love."

"What bird falls that fast, Gordon? Wait, look—" Her voice dips into whispers, then shouts out louder than before. "Excuse me? Girls? Can we talk to you a second?"

Fear jolts through me. My legs are telling me to run, but I force myself to keep walking, to pretend I haven't heard, though I can't help picking up the pace a bit. The footsteps behind us are moving faster now. As we reach the Parliament buildings, I hear a car engine rev.

"Quickly!" I break into a jog and pull the Being into an alley just off the Royal Mile. The car, a red Honda, crawls past; a round-faced woman with short black hair stares out from the driver's seat, then disappears from sight. A second car zips past, then a third. The Being lets out a strangled yell. It takes me a moment to realize what's scared her: these beasts of red and black and silver metal, wheels roaring as they turn the corners, enormous eyes gleaming.

"Don't worry, we're almost there," I whisper as she clamps a hand to her mouth. "Not much farther to go."

The Royal Mile, to my relief, is still busy. People pass in twos or threes while we stagger up the street, but they're all too engrossed in their own conversations to pay us any attention. Eventually, we arrive at the crossing opposite our flat. As we start toward it, my heart gives another leap: there's a red Honda parked outside Starbucks, directly opposite the entrance to our flat. The dark-haired woman steps out, squinting as she scans the crowd, followed by a guy with a beer belly squeezed into a green T-shirt.

I grab the Being's hand and pull her into a throng of boozy guys stumbling across the road. One is wearing a tutu and a T-shirt with a picture of himself and the words STEPHEN'S STAG DO printed on the back. His friend, a chubby guy with a tattoo of a dog's paw print on his upper arm, lifts his chin at us and asks where we're off to. His breath smells like beer and cigarettes. The Being's nose crinkles.

"Um, just heading home," I squeak. "My friend's not feeling too well."

"Yeah? One too many, eh?" The man squints at the Being. His eyes widen. My blood feels like it's frozen over, but he blinks and shakes his head, trying to focus. "What's up with your face, love? Is that sunburn? Looks like Gav in Gran Canaria. Ha, Gav! Check out this bird's tan—"

Before Gav, or any of his less drunken friends, turn around and notice that there's no amount of tanning that can turn your skin a metallic rose gold, I pull the Being down Cockburn Street and make a U-turn through one of the narrow side streets connecting with the Royal Mile. The couple are still standing by their car: the woman staring hawklike around the street, the man rolling his eyes behind her back.

I slink out of the street and creep toward the entrance to our block. As I usher the Being into the stairwell, her face crumples into a confused frown. The steps, I realize—she's never seen steps before.

"Like this," I say, showing her how to bend her knee and push herself up. "Quickly, we don't have much time."

The Being hesitates, then slowly staggers up the first flight, Perry nudging her forward with her nose. By the time we reach Shona's place on the fourth floor, my hands are trembling so much I can hardly get the key into the lock, but somehow I manage to open it. We tumble inside, and I bolt it shut and slot the chain into place.

"Thank God." I lean against the door, letting out a long breath. "That was intense."

Shona's living room is just how I imagined it: a dozen china elephants on the mantelpiece, decorative Indian throws draped over the sofa, lingering smells of incense. I pull the blinds down so the neighbors across the road can't see in and switch on only one light, a small desk lamp. I pat the sofa for the Being to sit, but she doesn't move. Her lower lip is quivering. Out of nowhere, she opens her mouth and begins to sob again. The noise is so loud, the elephants on Shona's mantelpiece start to tremble.

"No, no, no!" I jump up. "Shhh!"

I look around, but there's no TV to cover up the racket. I put the radio on instead: a Nirvana song comes leaking out of the speakers. I turn the song up full volume, crossing my fingers the neighbors— or worse, Dad—won't come and complain. The Being breaks off midwail. She blinks, stares at the radio, then gingerly takes a step toward it.

"It's a box, and music comes out of it," I say dumbly. We studied how they work a few years ago, but right now I can barely remember my own birthday, let alone explain how radio waves function. It doesn't seem like she'd understand me even if I could. "Look, you can make it change like this . . ."

I turn the knob and it crackles through the stations: a weather forecast, some light jazz, somebody shouting about the council. The Being hiccups. She touches the button and gently twists it from right to left, blinking in wonder as the voices slide in and out of earshot. After a few minutes, she leaves it on Radio 1. Sia is playing.

"Good choice," I say, as she gawps at the speakers. I turn the volume down, leaving it just loud enough to cover the Being's footsteps as she paces around the room. Her right wing drags along the floor, leaving thin trails of golden blood over the carpet.

"Are you hungry?" I ask, though by now I've stopped expecting an answer. "Let's get you something to eat."

She watches me as I walk to the kitchen. I pull Shona's cupboards open, expecting health foods and whole grains and vegan snacks and other generally unpalatable things. Instead, there are spaghetti hoops, chocolate digestives, multipacks of salt-and-vinegar crisps. A wall-to-wall stock of junk.

Next issue: what the hell do angels eat? I grab a box of Tunnock's Tea Cakes, a pack of Cheetos, and, in the name of healthy eating, a tangerine from the fruit bowl. When I go back to the living room, the Being is perched on the edge of the sofa, nervously prodding the orange fabric. Perry is stretched out beside her, beating her tail against the embroidered pillows. The angel's eyes keep darting around the room, flitting from a framed drawing of Buddha to an old copy of the Yellow Pages to the purple lampshade above her and back again.

"Here you go. It's food," I add, seeing her blank look. I make a hand-to-mouth action. "You, um, you do have food where you come from, don't you?"

It's hard to tell from her reaction. She spits out the crisps, refuses to even touch the tangerine, and attempts to eat the tea cake wrapper and all. I pry it out of her hand and peel back the foil.

"You have to take the cover off. See?"

She lifts it to her lips and slowly sinks her teeth into the chocolate. Her eyes brighten ever so slightly. She shoves the rest of the biscuit into her mouth, then scoffs down a second one, and a third. I run my hands through my hair.

"I am eating biscuits with a fallen angel." I try to let the words sink in, but they might as well be Russian. "This is too weird. This is so, so weird."

My own stomach is rumbling, but I'm way too jittery to eat. Everything feels heightened. Shona's embroidered pillows are psychedelic bright. Taylor Swift comes on the radio, and the melody swirls like warm chocolate sauce in my head. My finger brushes the edge of the Being's feathers, and the tips tingle.

Maybe she's having some weird effect on me. Or maybe this is what life is supposed to feel like. Maybe this is what it always felt like, before I became numb to it.

The song comes to an end. A lilting female voice begins to speak. "And now for the news, at two a.m. . . ."

Two a.m.?! I leap up from the sofa. The Being starts and almost chokes on her biscuit. Before I leave, I show her Shona's bedroom (the bed receives a blank stare) and the bathroom—an even blanker stare, followed by a lightbulb moment in which her eyebrows rise and she shakes her head in amazement.

"I need to go, but I'll be back in the morning," I promise the Being. "First thing. As soon as I wake up."

She stares at me from her spot on the sofa. I kneel in front of her, so her eyes are level with mine. There's a ring of chocolate around her mouth, and her eyes are blurry from crying.

"It's going to be okay," I say, and though I know she doesn't understand, I'm sure I see a hint of relief flicker over her face. "I'm not going to let anything happen to you. I promise."

And though I have no idea how I'm going to manage it, I'm determined to keep my word.

EIGHT

IF YOU'D ASKED ME A FEW DAYS AGO TO GUESS WHAT IT would be like to hang out with an angel, I probably would have said warm. Cozy. I mean, I wouldn't have expected harps and halos or anything, but I'd figure it would be a bit ethereal. All pastel colors and soft filters and kooky camaraderie, like a dream sequence in a Michel Gondry movie. Wise words and kindly smiles, that sort of thing.

As it turns out, it's actually kind of stressful. To start with, when I hurry downstairs at six a.m., I find the Being trying to jump through the window. Not out of, *through*. She takes a run up toward the window, like an athlete about to perform a long jump, and slams her arm against the double glazing. There's a loud thud and she staggers back, clutching her bicep and groaning. Perry runs around her ankles, delighted at this strange new game.

"Stop it!" I grab the Being's wrist and pull her back. "You'll hurt yourself!"

The Being wrenches my hand off her arm, and I let out a scream. She's much stronger than she looks—it feels like my hand is about to be ripped clean off my wrist. She spins on her heels, her teeth bared, and hisses something in that weird, musical language of hers. Any trace of cherubic innocence is gone; right now, she's more wolf than angel.

"It's okay!" My hand is throbbing. When I pull it back, there are half-moon marks where her fingernails have dug into my skin. I hold my palms out toward her, like I did last night. My heart is pounding. The shock of yesterday's Fall has worn off: she is bared teeth, claws poised, garnet eyes blazing.

"It's me, Jaya . . . I found you, remember? I hid you. I'm trying to help you."

She snarls something in reply. Beneath the scowl, I can see she's trying not to wince with pain. The skin of her upper arms and shoulders is already bruised deep purple from trying to break through the glass, and her right wing is bent back so far it looks like it might rip right off. As she tries to beat her wings together, her face wrinkles in agony. Golden blood is smeared across the walls and on the sofa, and there are pinkish feathers scattered across the carpet. I feel a sudden stab of guilt. I should have wrapped it up for her last night.

"Let me find a bandage," I say. "Just sit down, okay?"

I go to the bathroom, moving slowly so the Being doesn't freak out again. There's a box of first aid supplies under the sink, including two rolls of bandages. I find three packets of painkillers in there, presumably for the days when Shona's crystals just won't cut it, but I decide against giving them to her. It'd be just my luck to find the world's only living angel and kill her with a couple of ibuprofen.

The damage is worse than I realized. There's a huge gap in the wing where loads of the smaller middle and outer feathers have fallen out, and the tissue around the edges is all bloody and inflamed.

"Jeez." I wince. "Okay, this might sting a bit . . ."

Her moans are so loud that I have to turn the radio up, just in case Dad and Rani hear through the ceiling. The blood seeps through the bandage, turning it a dull gold. The Being picks at the corners, sniffing at it in distaste. Still, it does seem to help. The pained expression on her face relaxes a little, and she stops snarling every time I try to come near her. It'll take a while for me to build any trust, I know, but it feels like a first step.

The morning passes in a blur. Everything is foreign to her. She tries to eat Shona's incense, cuddles the bonsai tree like a baby, keeps peeking inside the radio to see where the voices are coming from. Even furniture is a confusing concept; at half past nine, I go to the shop to fetch some breakfast and come back to find a stack of kitchen chairs piled like the makings of a bonfire on the table. She tries to climb to the top of the stack, but they slip off and she tumbles to the floor, landing on her bum with a thump.

She looks so bewildered, I burst out laughing. The Being stares at me for a moment. Her head drops into her hands, and she starts to cry. My heart swells with guilt and worry.

"Sorry, sorry." I kneel beside her and try to take my hand in hers, but she pulls it away. "It's okay. You're okay."

But she's not. Of course she's not. Since the Falls began, there have been hundreds of articles written about what the angels' arrival might mean for us: the Rapture, an apocalypse, the crumbling of heaven . . . but I haven't heard many people wonder what it means for the Beings themselves. Perhaps their countries are falling apart. Maybe they're being cast out from their homes or killed in some sort of mass genocide. It could be that the Falls are actually leaps of faith, that the risk is better than what awaits them up in the sky.

"Please don't cry," I say, though I know it's like using a cloth to soak up a flood. "You're safe here, I promise."

I don't try to take her hand again. Instead, I gingerly pat her head. This close, the thing that leaves me breathless isn't the glittery sheen of her skin, or the enormous wings sprouting from her shoulder blades; it's how human she looks. Her face stretches and crumples with the same expressions; her hands shake like ours do, and her eyes fill with the same confusion or fear.

There are differences, though. Her skin is so much softer, impossibly soft, and her hair feels different from mine—kind of waxy, like fake flower petals. I can sense her shoulders stiffen as I touch it, but she doesn't pull away. Her strange, musical moans fill the room, almost drowning out the radio. It's a good thing there's a bagpiper playing an earsplitting version of Bryan Adams's "Heaven" outside, because otherwise I'm pretty sure half the street would be able to hear her, never mind Rani and Dad.

"Come on," I say. "Let's get you something to eat."

She doesn't like the croissants or the instant porridge pots I brought back for breakfast, so I raid Shona's cupboard and find some more biscuits: Party Rings, Digestives, and half a pack of Ginger Nuts. I help her unwrap the Party Rings and pick out two pink-and-yellow ones. For the first time that day, a tiny smile spreads across her face.

"Good, right?"

I make myself a cup of tea and sit in what I'm guessing is Shona's favorite seat: an ancient, sagging armchair covered in worn purple paisley. The Being leans back against the sofa, wincing as her bad wing rubs against the fabric. The clothes that I dressed her in last night are now scattered across the floor. My leggings are ripped in two; the neck of Mum's sweater has been stretched so wide it'd fall right over my shoulders.

I'm pretty sure if I were hanging out with a naked girl who I'd only just met under any other circumstances I'd be (a) mortified (b) probably confused (c) possibly turned on, if she was hot (okay, more than possibly). With the Being, it's like . . . nothing. I mean, I definitely don't feel the urge to tug my own clothes off or anything, but it's also not weird or embarrassing. If anything, my skinny jeans and Years & Years T-shirt start to feel a bit ridiculous.

"Where did you come from?" I keep asking her. She doesn't reply, of course, but images float into my mind. I picture places with clouds for ground, houses spinning in orbit like satellites, entire towns floating across the blue. Invisible cities, impossible worlds. It's like trying to imagine a color that doesn't exist, but it still sends thrilled shivers across my skin—knowing there could be a whole other universe waiting for us to discover.

Unless she really did fall from the afterlife. Golden gates and fluffy clouds, angels playing harps and salted caramel Häagen-Dazs for dinner. I mean, angels come from heaven—any four-year-old could tell you that. In a way, it's the most obvious answer.

It's also the one idea that I haven't really allowed myself to think about before. Not properly, anyway.

The morning after the first Being fell, Elsie Jackson, a mousy girl who ran the Scripture Union group at school, ran up to me and Sam in the corridor on our way to French. Her eyes were shining with tears.

"You must be so happy!" she squealed. I stared at her; we'd never spoken beyond *Can I borrow a pencil?* but suddenly she was squeezing my hand in both of hers. "Now you *know* you'll get to see your mum in heaven."

Before I could process what she'd said, she'd started reciting Bible passages at me: "'And I saw the holy city, new Jerusalem, coming down out of heaven from God, prepared as a bride adorned for her husband . . .' See? She's with the Lord now, Jaya. She's at peace."

Apparently Elsie hadn't considered that my mum was technically a Hindu, though not a practicing one, or that she might have had an abortion or committed adultery or done any one of the hundreds of things that void your ticket to heaven, at least according to some Christians. Elsie wasn't that kind of person. She was terminally nice: the sort of girl who could see the good in a serial killer. If she was telling me this, it was because she really thought it would help me.

"Maybe your mum saw him," she added as she shifted her

backpack onto her shoulder. "The angel. Maybe they crossed paths on her way to the stars."

Sam bit his lip until she'd turned the corner, then burst out laughing. "Poor Elsie," he said, shaking his head. "She's going to be so disappointed when it turns out it's all a publicity stunt for Samsung or something."

But Elsie wasn't proved wrong; if anything, Sam was. Even the staunchest atheists had to at least consider, once three or four Beings had landed and the general consensus that the Falls were a hoax was starting to fade, that there might be something beyond the grave. Attendance at religious buildings suddenly skyrocketed; the waiting lists for christenings and blessings stretched from weeks to years; online shops ran out of holy water.

For people like Elsie, who had always had one eye on the afterlife, it was a confirmation of what they'd always known: that this world was just a stepping-stone to whatever came next.

For me, it was just confusing. I'd never been religious—even with angels falling from the sky, I felt some scientific explanation had to come sooner or later. But as much as I tried to shrug it off, I couldn't get that image out of my head: Mum and the angel crossing paths, like two cars passing on a lonely highway in the night.

I'm rubbish at keeping secrets. It always feels like having a bunch of balloons trapped in my rib cage: they swell and swell, and eventually it's either pop them or suffocate. The first time Marek told me that he fancied Jennie Zhang, back when we were twelve, he swore me to secrecy. I lasted all through double English and the first half of chemistry, but by history I'd traded it for a rumor that Emma had heard about Kelly Hislop's cousin and a packet of Starbursts. I don't know how I'm going to keep the fact of an angel from Dad and Rani.

Luckily, they don't even seem to have noticed that I've been gone all day. They're sitting on the living-room floor, surrounded by maps and books and scribbled notes. I lean against the door frame, trying to look natural and failing miserably.

"Oh, hi, pet," Dad says, forty-eight seconds (I count them) after I say hello. I begin to ask what we're having for tea, but he holds up a finger. "Hang on, I think I could be onto a breakthrough here, don't want to lose my flow."

Among the papers, I catch a kaleidoscope of broken angels: glassy eyes, smashed limbs, heads surrounded in halos of golden blood . . . a tragic family photo album. It makes my head spin to think how easily my Being could have ended up like these poor creatures. Just another sad, dead person, smeared on the front of the Sunday papers, ripped apart for her feathers—

Feathers. My stomach flips. Feathers floating around the hillside last night, glints of pink in the dim light. Feathers that would fetch hundreds or thousands of pounds online, the only clue that another Being had fallen.

Feathers that I left for anyone to find.

NINE

MAYBE THE WIND BLEW THEM AWAY. MAYBE I'LL FIND THEM in the corners of the gutters, or tangled in the gorse, or tucked into bird nests in the bushes. That's what I tell myself as I pace around the ruin, looking for hints of pink against the grass. Because I've checked the spot where she fell, I've followed our route across the hillside, and the feathers are gone. Every single one of them.

"Crap, crap, crap." I kick the broken beer bottle against the wall of the ruin. "You absolute idiot, Jaya."

At the foot of the hill, two people are sitting on a bench by the pond. They look up in unison as the glass shatters against the stone, then go back to watching ducks fight over scraps of bread. Perry snuffles around by the gorse, following some invisible trail. For a moment I have this vision of her leading us back to whoever took the feathers, breaking into their house and disposing of the evidence, like a less stoned version of Shaggy and Scooby-Doo, but then she yawns, pees on a bush, and comes padding back to me.

"Oh, great work, sniffer dog," I mutter, rubbing her head. "No job at Heathrow for you."

I slump down onto a rock and rip out a handful of grass from the earth. There's a dull dread gnawing at my insides. I know it wasn't just the wind. Some of those feathers are huge, twice the span of my hand, and such a distinctive color; leaving them lying around was like writing *an angel woz ere* across the hill in giant neon letters. Somebody's sure to brag on Wingpin or CherubIM about finding them, and then Dad and loads of other Wingdings will put two and two together and realize there's an undiscovered Being somewhere in the city. It's only a matter of time before someone comes after us now.

I need help, but I don't know who to ask for it. Marek wouldn't believe me, Sam would freak out, and Emma can't keep her mouth shut—it'd be all over Twitter in five minutes.

I could trust Leah, if I knew where she was. Leah was always the one people went to with their problems. Every time we were at a party you'd find her in the bathroom with whoever happened to be in tears that night, nodding like a priest as they spilled out their confessions. We always said if Leah ever wanted to blackmail us, we'd be totally screwed: she knew everybody's secrets.

She had quite a few of her own, too. There was that time we got lost on the school trip to Paris, when she held my hand as we walked around the Catacombs, when she said it was just because those leering skulls were creeping her out and I knew she was lying. There was the first time we kissed, in the bathroom at one of Sam's parties: Leah leaning back against the sink, my hands gripping the ceramic. There was the day she came over to watch a film and Rani was at gymnastics and Dad, by some miracle, had dragged himself off CherubIM and went to do a food shop, giving us a whole hour alone in my room. There were other times we slept together—just a few, but each one a step, I thought, to something proper. Something with a name.

But then there were all the days she stopped talking to me, the times she acted like there was nothing between us, the night she kissed Joseph Macrae right in front of me. There were all those words: labels that we didn't need but that wrapped themselves around us, suffocating whatever it was we had.

Though I never wanted them, they became my secrets, too. My friends all know that I'm gay, and I hated having to keep our relationship hidden from them, but I forced myself to do it until Leah was ready. I was sure that in a few months she'd come out, and that all this sneaking around would seem cute and silly in hindsight.

It does seem kind of silly now. Especially given the other secrets she must have been keeping. Maybe if she hadn't been so stressed about what was going on with us, she would have talked to me about what was happening between her parents. Maybe she would have warned me that her mum was planning to leave. I still don't fully understand what was going on, but it must have been bad if she can't even call to tell me about it, even now.

Suddenly, Perry starts to bark. For a second I think she's proved me wrong and tracked down the feathers, but then I notice the pond: a few dozen ducks and a couple of swans glide elegantly over the water, sending ripples over the reflection of the ruin. Before I can grab the leash, she bounds off and races down the hill.

"Perry, no!"

The two figures by the water's edge look up as this streak of white comes zipping toward them. One of them, a fair-haired boy, lifts a camera and takes a photo just as Perry plunges into the water. The ducks explode into a horrified chorus of quacks; the swans skate by, beaks tilted gracefully in disapproval.

"Perry!" I shout. "Out! Now!"

She pads over to the edge of the pond and climbs out, looking very soggy and a bit sheepish. I lean down to grab her collar, but she slips out of my grasp and shakes herself dry, splashing me and the people on the bench. They groan and laugh, covering their faces with their hands. I spin around to apologize, but the words catch in my throat. It's them, the protesters—the kids outside Celeste's restaurant on Tuesday.

"Sorry," I stammer. "She's obsessed with birds. Thinks they're her friends."

"Don't worry about it." The girl smiles. "I'm a bird fan, too. I mean, I wouldn't jump in a pond for them or anything, but they're pretty awesome."

I laugh. Probably a little too loud, but I don't think I've properly laughed since I came to Edinburgh. There's something almost nostalgic about it, like rediscovering a forgotten favorite song on your iPod.

The girl cocks her head to one side. "Do I know you from somewhere? You look really familiar."

"I think I saw you the other day, actually," I say. "Protesting, I mean. Outside that restaurant."

"That's it!" She gives me a double thumbs-up. I feel my cheeks burn, but I return her grin. If she's teasing me, it's not in a mean way. "We went back yesterday, but the guy called the police on us for real. I was all up for chaining myself to the railings, but Calculus here was too chicken."

She nods to her brother, who shoots her a dirty look. His eyes are the same color as his sister's—warm brown, surrounded by a ring of mahogany—but while his don't really stand out, hers look almost black against her pale skin. It's pretty.

"Sorry for not wanting a criminal record." His fingers are still poised around his camera, ready for the next picture. "I don't really fancy spending the rest of the holidays in juvie."

His sister rolls her eyes. "You're such a drama queen. You know all they'd have done is taken down our names and told us to piss off." She sticks out her hand for me to shake. "I'm Allie, by the way. This is Calum, my twin."

"Jaya," I say, "and this is Perry. After Katy Perry. My sister has shit taste in music."

They laugh. It's not actually true (I got Perry in the height of my "Teenage Dream" obsession when I was ten and named her myself) but, whatever, it feels good to make somebody laugh.

"I'm with your sister. 'Roar' is one of the best pop songs ever written." Allie pushes herself off the bench and hops toward the edge of the pond. She's bone thin and short, three or four inches smaller than me, but somehow she doesn't look it. It's the way she holds herself—like she's about to give a speech, or break into a ballet dance. "So, do you live here?"

She treads around the edge of the water, spreading her arms like a tightrope walker. The sleeve of her sweater falls down, revealing a tattoo on her right wrist: a blue-gray rose, outlined in navy ink, with two petals falling toward her elbow.

"No. Well, for a wee while. My dad's working down here for a few weeks." The lie feels awkward, but they'd be disgusted if they knew the real reason we came to Edinburgh. "How about you?"

I've never been very good at chatting to people I don't know. I usually make friendships like the old masters painted landscapes: slowly, with lots of color and details. I don't rush in, but they're beautiful, and they tend to last.

But with Allie, it's easy: she's so friendly, so open and smiley, that it brings out the more talkative side of me, too. She tells me they're seventeen—though Calum's just finished school and Allie has one more year left, like me, as she had to repeat a year for "some boring health shit"—that they live in Edinburgh, and that they've spent the whole summer so far protesting what she calls "Being exploitation sites." In addition to Celeste's, they've picketed outside the merch stalls by St. Giles' Cathedral, a nightclub called Broken Wings, even a theme park outside Newcastle with a roller coaster called the Fall.

"So far our success rate has been about 0.001 percent," Allie admits. "We've only managed to get a few people to walk away. The ones who think like us don't go to these places, and the ones who do just don't give a shit. They don't see the Beings as living creatures."

"I know what you mean," I say, thinking of the Being back at Shona's. "Nobody is thinking about why they're falling, what that could mean for them."

"Yes!" She throws her hands into the air. "That's exactly what I said. God, it's so nice to meet someone who gets it."

There's a click. When I look around, Calum has his camera pointed at Allie and me sitting on the bench, catching us mid-conversation. He's much quieter than his sister; he's only spoken a couple of times, to add a few details to a story or rebuff one of Allie's exaggerations, before turning back to his camera, framing the fluid movement of the ducks and the colors of the setting sun on the water.

He smiles awkwardly and digs his hands into his pockets. "We should get going," he says to Allie. "I want to take some more photos before it gets dark."

Allie nods seriously. "Yeah. You do that, Calico. The world really needs more pictures of sunsets." She stands up, smooths her skirt out, and smiles at me. "Nice to meet you, Jaya."

"You, too," I say. "Good luck with the protests."

There's a pause. I want to suggest we hang out, but I don't want to come across too keen. I don't know how things are done here. Back home, it's easier to get talking to strangers—there are so few of them in our village, it's kind of natural to be curious—but obviously things are different in the city. After a beat, I've left it too long: the opportunity's gone. We awkwardly say our good-byes, and they walk off toward the car park.

This time, I actually do kick myself, right on the shin. I'm such an idiot. Who cares if they thought I was weird? At least I would have had someone to talk to other than my Wingdinger family and my dog.

Unless.

"Hey, wait a second."

They turn around. I blink at them, my mind wrestling with my tongue. I shouldn't tell them this. I've only just met them, and I don't know if I can trust them, but then they're obviously pretty passionate about Beings' rights, so surely they wouldn't—

I'm already saying the words.

"I think I know something you might want to take a photo of."

TEN

"HOLY SHIT."

"Jesus Christ."

"Rufffff!"

Perry leaps onto the sofa, curling up on the Being's lap. The Being's gaze flicks from Allie to Calum and back to me, her expression a mixture of fear, panic, and amusement. The twins stare from the doorway, their faces frozen in shock. I grin and flop onto the sofa beside the Being, like it's no big deal. Like I've been hanging out with angels all my life.

"You hungry?" I ask the Being, and her eyes light up when I hand over the box of Tunnock's Tea Cakes that I stopped to buy on the way back to Shona's. "Remember to take the wrapper off this time," I add, grinning.

Her smile is a little hesitant—but she's not freaking out and trying to jump out the window, so that's something. She rips into the cardboard, her audience by the door forgotten, and pulls two biscuits from the packet. Calum runs his hands through his hair.

"This is unbelievable." His camera hangs heavy around his neck, forgotten. "This is un-bloody-believable."

"How did she . . ." Allie's mouth opens and closes, the words snuffed out by shock. Her face has gone from cream to bone white behind her freckles. "Where did you—how—what the *hell*?"

They sit down on the carpet, kneeling in front of the Being and me like little kids at story time. Their expressions rotate between shock and sheer wonder as I tell them the story, but they still look as if they can't quite believe me—as if they expect the Being to pull off her wings, wipe the metallic sheen from her face, and admit that it's all a hoax. I don't blame them, really. If I hadn't seen her tumble from the sky myself, I probably wouldn't believe it, either.

"What are you going to do?" Calum asks once I've finished explaining how I smuggled her back to the flat without getting caught. "Are you going to hand her over?"

Allie gives him a light punch on the shoulder. "Of course she's not!"

"I didn't mean to the Wingdings," he snaps, rubbing his arm. "I'm not saying you should sell her for her blood or anything, but there are research centers who would take her. Apparently there's one just outside Manchester," he adds, looking at me. "They could help her. They might be able to work out why they're falling, too."

"No one knows who's running those centers," I say. "There's no telling what sort of weird experiments they might do to her; she could end up with ears on her back, or her hands and feet swapped over. Or the cults might be behind them—can you imagine if the Standing Fallen got hold of her?"

Calum shrugs. "What other option is there? She can't stay here forever."

"Can we stop talking about her like she's not here?" Allie says loudly. She flushes and crosses her arms. "Sorry, but I hate when people do that. Just because she's not speaking, it doesn't mean she can't understand us."

"You're right. Sorry," I say. I give the Being an apologetic smile, but she just stares and unwraps another tea cake.

"Do you think she does understand you?" Calum asks me, before quickly turning to the angel. "Sorry, I mean, do you understand us?"

The Being wipes the marshmallow from her mouth and blinks. After a moment, I clear my throat and reply for her.

"I don't know. Sometimes I think she does, but other times it's like she can't hear me at all. She seems to like the radio, though."

As we talk, Calum's fingers edge toward the button on the top right of his camera. I promised him a good picture to get them here, and Allie was intrigued enough to go along with it, but looking back, I really shouldn't have: the flash might freak the Being out, and if somebody happened to flick through his camera and see the photos . . . Calum has obviously had the same thought, because instead of framing a shot, he slips the camera into his backpack without a word.

"Can I take a look at your wing?" Allie asks her suddenly. "Maybe I can help. I mean, I don't have any experience in angel anatomy, but neither does anyone else on the planet."

Playing an awkward game of charades, I gesture at the Being to lean forward. Confusion flashes through her eyes, but she slowly copies my movement, allowing Allie to see the damaged wing. Her face contorts in pain as Allie peels back my shoddy bandage work.

"This is pretty bad." Allie's face is suddenly serious. "It looks like she's been mauled by something. She must have lost a ton of blood, did she?"

I nod. "Perry licked most of it up, and I think the rain must have washed away whatever was on the ground. I didn't keep any of it for myself."

Allie gives me an approving nod. "How many feathers did she lose?"

My insides jitter at the mention of her feathers. "I'm not sure. Maybe a third of them? It looked like a lot, anyway."

Something begins to buzz. The Being starts, looking around for the noise. Allie reaches into her satchel, pulls out her phone, and swipes the call away. Calum begins to say something, but his sister glowers at him and he shuts his mouth with a snap. After putting the phone away, she pulls out a small purple notebook with a pen clipped to the spine.

"What's that?" I ask as she flips through the pages.

"Her oh-so-secret notebook." Calum's voice rises two octaves. " 'Dear Diary, today I skived off English and made out with Filip Rutkowski behind the Sainsbury's on Middle Meadow Walk and—' "

"Piss off, Calum. What are you, twelve?" Allie rolls her eyes, but she's grinning. "It's not even a diary. I just write stuff in it. Nothing exciting. Anyway," she says, turning back to the Being. "What are we going to call you? If you can't tell us your own name, maybe we should give you a new one."

I blink. Stupid as it sounds, I hadn't even thought of naming the Being. It would be like trying to name the rain. "Um, I dunno. Any suggestions?"

"Nothing cheesy," Calum says firmly. "Nothing like Angelique or Celeste or whatever. Something normal."

"Arthur?" says Allie. "She fell on Arthur's Seat, after all."

"That's a guy's name, you knob. You might as well call her Gavin, or Steve."

"I know, but you could call her, like, Arthurette or whatever. Arthurella. No, Arthurina!"

"That's even worse." Calum chucks a scrunched-up tea cake wrapper at his sister, then pauses. "How about Teacake? Seeing as she likes them so much."

Teacake. It's the sort of thing that Rani would have suggested, but coming from Calum, it sounds quirky rather than cute. I look at the Being: her garnet eyes and the sharp curve of her wings, still regal despite the damage the Fall has caused. Her name should be majestic. Something that soars and sweeps. Something wild. I would have named her after a bird. Goshawk, or Starling, or Kite. This sweet, sugary, artificial word shouldn't suit her.

But it does.

Somehow, it's sort of perfect.

"Teacake," I say, looking at her. She licks the last of the marshmallow from the biscuit. "That works."

Allie nods. "More of a Caramel Wafer fan myself, but I like it. Nice one, Calamari."

She gives him a high five, then holds her hand up for Teacake to slap; she looks at it, her head cocked to one side, then reaches for another biscuit. After a moment, there's another buzzing sound. This time, it's Calum who pulls out his phone. He and Allie exchange a look.

"We really should go, Al," he says. "It's late. They'll be getting worried."

Allie's shoulders heave. "God's sake, Calum. We're not five years old. Besides, I've got the car."

"I know that, but it's me who'll get the—"

"All right, fine!" She gives me an apologetic look as they get up to leave. "Sorry. Our parents are like something out of a Jane Austen novel. They'd send me out with a chaperone if they could."

She turns to Teacake, who has picked up one of Shona's elephants and is turning it around in her hands. She blanches when she notices us looking at her and shoves it back onto the mantelpiece.

"So, what are we going to do?" Allie asks her as she slips her feet back into her shoes. "You can't stay here forever. How are we going to help you?"

I hold back a smile at the "we." This isn't my secret anymore, and it's not only my problem. It's ours. She's *our* responsibility. If this were a superhero movie, this would be our origins moment—we'd be on the brink of a high-power training montage set to "Eye of the Tiger."

"I'm not handing you over," I tell Teacake, folding my arms. "I don't trust anyone else. All the adults I know would trade you for a reward. I mean, look at the crowds outside," I say, turning to Allie and Calum. "No one cares about the Beings. Not really."

The twins nod. Even Calum, who half an hour ago sounded like he was ready to ship her off to the nearest lab for a few shiny pound coins. It's harder to betray something with a name.

There's a heavy silence as each of us thinks. Finally, Allie puts her hands on her hips and nods.

"You're right. We can't trust anyone else." She pushes her hair behind her ears, suddenly businesslike, and looks at Calum and me. "There's really only one thing we can do."

"What?" I say dumbly.

"If there's nowhere safe for her here on earth . . ." She turns back to Teacake and gives her a nod. "We're going to have to get you back home again."

ELEVEN

CALUM AND ALLIE ARE ALREADY WAITING ON THE FRONT
step when I sneak downstairs the next morning. For two people
who look so alike, their moods couldn't be more different: Calum
has bedhead and blurry eyes, while Allie is already bouncing on the
balls of her feet.

"I've got a plan! Well, kind of." She waves her purple notebook
at me as we walk up the stairs to Shona's. "It's more of a rough
sketch than a proper blueprint, but it's a start."

"You don't waste any time, do you?" I say, as I unlock the door.
"It's not even nine o'clock yet."

Calum lets out a long, slow yawn. "Allie's a morning person,"
he says. "And an afternoon person. And an evening person. It's annoying as hell."

Inside, the radio is blasting pop music from the living room. I
start to say hello, but the words fizzle out on my tongue. Teacake

is sitting cross-legged on the dining table, her head bent and her hands resting on her knees. The bandages that I wrapped around her have fallen to the floor, grubby and golden, and her wings have unfolded.

They look bigger here than they did on Arthur's Seat: so tall they curve at the ceiling, so wide they brush the walls that cage her. The edges of the feathers glow in the morning light, deep fuchsia and hot coral. Beneath my nerves and excitement, I feel an ache of sadness. There's something overwhelming about it, seeing this sparkling, ethereal creature trapped in some pokey little living room. An eagle in a budgie's cage.

The others feel it, too. There's a long moment of silence, and then Allie lets out a cough. Teacake looks up and twitches her wings together—something I'm starting to recognize as a greeting. Only the left one moves; the right still drags downward, hanging about six inches lower than the other.

"Morning, Teacake," Allie says, suddenly shy. "Here, got you some breakfast."

She reaches into her tote bag and pulls out a box of Jaffa Cakes. Teacake's eyes brighten, and the atmosphere with them, as she sees the pictures on the packet. Still coughing, Allie passes a second box to me.

"Have you eaten? I'm starving," she says. "Make us a cup of tea, Calabash?"

Her brother mutters something about not being her intern, but goes to put the kettle on anyway. Allie disappears to the bathroom; I can hear her coughing through the walls as Calum putters about in the kitchen. Remembering what she said about not talking about

Teacake as if she wasn't there, I start to tell her that we're going to try to help her get home, that Allie has a plan.

"Home," I say. "Up there, where you came from."

I point to the ceiling. Teacake licks a spot of chocolate from her lower lip and follows my finger with her eyes. I realize that, beyond the layer of plaster and timber, my dad is probably sitting directly above her, trying to work out when she'll fall. I brush the thought away. We're doing the right thing.

After a few minutes Allie comes back into the living room, wiping her mouth on a tissue. Her face is even paler than usual. Calum passes her a mug of tea; she takes a long gulp, finishing half in one go.

"Are you all right?" I ask. "That sounded bad."

"Yeah, fine. Just got something stuck in my throat." Her voice is still hoarse. "Anyway, let me tell you what I was thinking."

She goes toward the table and, using a mixture of words and hand gestures, asks Teacake to turn around. Teacake eventually understands and swivels toward the window, showing us the outer edge of her wings. The damage is much more obvious from this angle: the feathers of the right wing are greasy and matted with blood, like those of a bird caught in an oil spill.

"We need to fix this," Allie says, "so she can fly home again."

Moving her hands over the bloody area, taking care not to actually touch the feathers, she explains her idea: birds. She'll move the wing back into place with a sort of splint, and then we'll use birds' feathers to replace the ones she lost when she fell—a sort of feathery skin graft, to help the healing process along and allow her wing the movement it needs.

"Our dad's a total bird nerd. He's the one who got me into ornithology," she says. "I found a ton of books at home to help us out, and we can look up the rest online."

Calum unzips his backpack and tips the contents onto the floor. Hardbacks and textbooks fall to the carpet: *The Big Book of British Birds*, *Introduction to Veterinary Anatomy*, *Integrated Principles of Zoology*, even *Inventions of Leonardo da Vinci* . . . a dozen or so in total. Allie starts flipping through *Eagles and Birds of Prey*, pausing at a detailed illustration of a hawk's wing.

"It's just a case of working out what type or size of feathers will be best," she says. "And I . . . well, I'll try to attach them somehow. I want to be a surgeon, so it'd be good practice."

"Yeah?" I say, glancing up from the page. "What kind of surgery?"

"Transplants," Allie says. "I like the idea of creating a positive outcome from something negative, you know? Like, when a person dies in an accident—it's tragic, of course, and nothing can make up for it, but their death can give someone else a second shot. I really like that."

My smile wavers. Mum's organs were donated after she died. Her kidneys, her liver, her pancreas. Sometimes, afterward, I'd think about the people out there, alive thanks to some tiny part of her tucked inside their bodies, and it made me feel sort of proud. Other times it made no difference at all.

"That's really cool," I say. I wish I had my future mapped out like that. I have no idea what I'll do when school ends. Between the accident and Leah disappearing, the Higher exams I sat back in May were a total write-off.

"Well, we'll see," Allie says. "It's a lot of studying. Might not happen. How good would 'angel surgery' look on my university applications, though?"

We start brainstorming places where we might be able to find birds' feathers: parks, gardens, the beach. As we talk, Teacake clambers over the back of the sofa and onto the coffee table. Her wings slide against the walls, dislodging photo frames and pushing ornaments to the carpet. The right one catches the edge of the door frame, making her grimace with pain. It seems unlikely that we'll be able to fix it before Shona gets back, which means we only have ten days to come up with an alternative hiding place.

Allie opens her mysterious purple notebook and begins jotting down ideas. I pull one of the books on birds toward me and flick through it. Teacake, who has landed back on the dining table, leans forward to look at the illustrations, knocking a china elephant off the mantelpiece in the process.

"Did you sleep up there, Teacake? On the table?" Allie looks at me. "Did you not show her the bedroom?"

"Of course I did," I say, bristling a little. "She just prefers being up there."

"Maybe she's trying to climb higher," Calum says. "Like how some churches have steeples, to bring people close to God."

I remember the way she tried to pile chairs on top of the table yesterday, and the way she tried to climb on top of them. Maybe Calum's right, in a way. Maybe she's trying to get home.

Allie snorts in response. "Aye, right. She wants to get back for a barbecue with Jesus and Marilyn Monroe."

"She might!" Calum says. "Like, don't get me wrong, I'm not

going to get baptized or start going to church or whatever—but, come on. There are *angels* falling from the *sky*. That has to mean something."

"Not necessarily, Calamitous," Allie says. "My faith is in science. It's only a matter of time before they work out where they're coming from and why this is happening."

Calum flicks the edges of the da Vinci book. "Allie, are you actually saying that you're sitting in the same room as an angel and you haven't even *considered* there might be a God or an afterlife?"

"Look, I'm not saying I'm *right*. I don't think I have all the answers to the meaning of life; I'm not that bigheaded," she says, grinning. "But no, the Falls haven't convinced me that there's more than this, and I think it's because I don't need to be convinced. If this world is all there is, I'm fine with that."

They look at each other. Something passes between them, but it's just a flash of something too fast for me follow.

"Anyway, maybe you'll learn to speak English, Teacake," Allie says. "Then you can tell us yourself."

We glance over at her as she slides off the table, her wings sloping toward the floor like two shimmering veils, and kneels beside Calum. Fumbling with the corners a little, she beings to look through the illustrations in the da Vinci book: a crossbow, a tank, his famous flight machine. I try to read her expression as she turns the pages. There's no sign of recognition, but there's also no obvious confusion, no real surprise.

"What about you, Jaya?" Calum asks me. "Where do you think the Beings are coming from?"

I take a long sip of tea. After eight months, I still have no idea how to answer that.

In the weeks after the Falls began, particularly after my run-in with Elsie Jackson, I couldn't shake the feeling that Mum's death was connected to the Beings' arrival. It felt like a sign—though of what, I couldn't say. For the first time, I wished I'd been brought up with a religion to lead me to one conclusion or another. Maybe it could have been the ship to steer me through the storm.

Though he'd always been an atheist, Dad bought a ton of books on religion as part of his research: Islam, Judaism, Christianity, Sikhism, Buddhism . . . every major religion, plus a few others that I'd never even heard of. One rainy afternoon, while Rani was at a dance class and he'd fallen asleep on the sofa, I found myself flicking through his books on Hinduism, looking for stories about angels like the ones crashing down to earth.

I couldn't find them. They don't exist in Hinduism, at least not the same way they do in Judaism or Islam or Christianity. The Bhagavad Gita talks about spiritual beings that act in angelic ways, but they're mostly said to appear in human form; some have a negative influence, and others work to help people achieve greater levels of enlightenment. Guardian angels, perhaps, but not the winged beings that were falling from the sky.

I liked reading about them. Regardless of what Mum did or didn't believe, the religion was part of her—and my—culture, our history. It made me feel closer to her, somehow. But it didn't bring me any clear-cut answers. I knew that the timing of the Falls and Mum's death was just a coincidence. Thousands of people around the world died in the days leading up to the first Fall; it couldn't be connected to all of them.

Sometimes, though, I still find myself wondering.

"I don't know," I say. "Maybe we'll get an answer, or maybe we won't . . . Either way, right now I just want to focus on getting Teacake back to wherever she came from."

To my surprise, a rare smile flickers across Teacake's face. Her wings rustle; it sounds like the song of waves on sand. And though I might not be sure if I believe in any gods, I find myself praying that Allie's plan works.

TWELVE

WHEN DINNERTIME COMES AROUND, WE RELUCTANTLY SAY good-bye: Allie and Calum have had three missed calls each from their mum, and there's nothing much in the flat for me to eat. Before we leave, we pull the mattress and duvet from Shona's bed and lay them out on the dining table. If Teacake's going to insist on sleeping up there, we can at least try to make her as comfortable as possible.

"So, see you around ten," Allie tells me, as she slides her feet back into her trainers. We've made plans to go to the Botanic Garden tomorrow to start our feather search. We tried to explain this to Teacake, pointing out illustrations in Allie's books. She seemed slightly more interested in those than she was in the da Vinci drawings—she stroked the inked birds with her finger, leaned in to sniff the pages—but there was still no recognition. Nothing that reminded her of home, as far as I could tell.

I stay with her a little longer after the twins have gone. I set out a dinner of biscuits for her on the coffee table, then turn the radio until I find a song she seems to like. I'm starting to get to know her tastes a little now. Her sweet tooth extends to music as well as food: she likes bubblegum pop, things with high-pitched vocals or fluttery percussion.

"I guess you must have music where you come from," I say, as she nods along to the radio. The few words I've heard her speak have sounded so much like singing, it's the one thing about her world that I feel fairly sure of.

She wrinkles her nose and sighs in reply, making a sound like long grass rustling in the wind. Though she's much calmer around me now, I can tell that being trapped in Shona's apartment is starting to get to her. She's clearly not used to lazing around eating biscuits and listening to music all day—her arms and legs look too strong for that, and her good wing rarely stops twitching. Whatever's going on in her world, she's clearly anxious to get back to it.

At eight o'clock, my stomach starts to rumble and I reluctantly get up to leave. Teacake flutters her wings good-bye, making the tips brush against my forearm. I leave the flat with the same slightly disoriented feeling you get when someone wakes you up mid-dream. It's strange: the closer I get to her, the more unreal she seems.

Rani runs into the hallway as I walk back to the flat. "Where have you been all day?" she asks, not bothering to swallow her mouthful of soggy cereal. "Did you not get my text?"

I haven't even looked at my phone. That's a first. "Just out," I say, shrugging my jacket off. "I met some people. I've been hanging out with them a bit."

Her eyes light up. "Can I come with you tomorrow? Dad's going to Perth to work on the formula with some other Wingdings. They'll be doing math stuff all day. It'll be *so* boring."

"No!" My voice comes out sharper than I intend. Rani blinks, surprised. "I mean, doesn't he need your help? You're good at math. You got full marks on that trigonometry test a few weeks ago, didn't you?"

She gives me a withering look. "Don't patronize me, Jaya. Dad's not drawing triangles. This is, like, proper serious algebra. Probably Higher level or something."

I try not to laugh. She looks so young, with her Adventure Time pajamas and her long hair in messy self-made plaits. I forget she's only eleven sometimes. Her part-time job as a theological researcher has made her seem years older. She wipes the milk from her lips and gives me a pleading look.

"*Please* can we do something tomorrow? How about the dungeons? It's just down the road."

There's a flutter of guilt in my chest. I haven't spent any time with Rani in ages. It's been months since we had a movie marathon or played Bananagrams and painted our nails. She hardly ever asked; she was always too busy helping Dad with his research.

But I didn't ask, either. If I'm honest, I used Dad as an excuse to avoid her. Spending time with Rani was just another reminder of everything that had changed. No chance of Mum coming in with a plate of cinnamon buns, picking through Rani's nail varnishes and asking for a manicure. No chance of Dad sticking his head around the door to tease Rani about whichever boy-band member she liked that month. Spending time with Rani would have meant pretending everything was okay again, or acknowledging that it wasn't. I wasn't ready to do either.

"Another day, Ran—" I start to say, but I'm interrupted by Dad's shouting from the living room.

"Mate, it's nonsense! It must be! They must have faked them somehow. There's no way they can be real."

My stomach lurches. "What's he talking about?" I whisper to Rani.

She trickles the last of the milk into her mouth. "Dunno. This is, like, the fourth phone call he's had in the past hour."

I ease the living-room door open. Dad is standing by the window, pinching the bridge of his nose with his thumb and forefinger.

"Tell you what, I'll try to look up the IP address, maybe we can track down whoever the seller is," he says. "Honestly, though, I think it's a waste of time. Chances of them being real are one in a million. Less, even."

A muffled, panicked voice keeps babbling on the other end of the line. Dad listens to whatever the person has to say, then mutters a grumpy good-bye and slumps onto the sofa. He's wearing the same T-shirt he had on yesterday, with the same tomato soup stain below the collar.

"What's going on?" I ask, stepping into the room.

"Och, nothing important." He shakes his head, and he sounds more exasperated than angry. "Some Being's feathers have appeared online, and the seller says they were found in Edinburgh. A few of the other enthusiasts are worried that we might have missed the Fall."

When I find my voice, it doesn't sound like my own. "That's not possible, though, is it? Someone would have seen something."

"That's what I said." He gives me an appreciative nod. "It'll just be some idiot with bird feathers and spray paint trying to con us out of a few grand. I don't know why anyone's taking it seriously."

The guilt in my chest tightens. *I'm doing the right thing*, I remind myself. *I'm doing the right thing.* I chant the words in my head as I make pasta for dinner, as Rani nags me about doing something tomorrow, as I lie in bed listening to a busker bleating out "Angel of Harlem." *I'm doing the right thing.* Teacake is more important than Dad's plans, more important than the uneasy feeling stirring in my stomach. Saving her is what matters.

But behind my words, there's another niggling voice telling me that the "right thing" may not be the right thing for my family—and if that's the case, I don't know if it's the right thing at all.

THIRTEEN

SOMETIMES, WHEN SOMEONE DIES IN A BOOK OR ON TV, THE people left behind say they can't believe the world keeps on turning. They can't understand how there are still people driving to the supermarket or queuing at the post office; that there are still cereal bowls in the sink and piles of laundry at the foot of the stairs.

I never got that. The drive back from the hospital felt like being in a foreign country. The garden where Mum had spent so many hours planting and pruning now felt strange and savage. Our house seemed both bigger and smaller, as if the walls had been lined with fun-house mirrors. Her famous pineapple and cherry scones, still on the cooling tray, had become inedible; I didn't think I'd ever eat again. Her perfume was still lingering in the bathroom, but it smelled stronger than before. Sweeter.

Even weeks afterward, once we'd had the ceremony and scattered her ashes in the Ness, after Ammamma, my grandmother, and the rest of the family had kissed our foreheads and gone home to London, "back to normal" was never what it had been before. The lack of her was in everything: in the overgrown grass, in the cookbooks gathering dust by the microwave, in the sunny spot in the living room where no one stretched out to read anymore. Everything was different, as if her leaving had shaken up the world's atoms. And I only had myself to blame.

I get the same feeling when I arrive at the Botanic Garden the next day. The weekend's rain has been replaced by bright sunshine, and the place is packed: little kids playing hide-and-seek, students reading on the lawns, couples wandering between the flower beds. I keep catching glimpses of our last trip here as I walk through the garden to meet Allie and Calum. Mum kneeling by the edge of a flower bed, trying to take a photo of a gray squirrel. Perry chasing a terrified Chihuahua across the lawn, being chased in turn by its irate owner. The garden hasn't changed, but it's not the same place it was a few years ago. Not with these ghosts floating by the pond or between the trees.

Rani asked if she could come with us again this morning. I almost wish I'd said yes, instead of sneaking out of the flat while she was talking Wingding stuff with Dad. Most of my memories are these little scraps, threadbare and worn at the edges. Maybe together she and I could patch them into something bigger, something that would give us a bit of comfort.

Not all the changes are bad, though. Now there's Calum, wandering around the trees in the Arboretum. And there's Allie, waving a feather at me as I walk up the path. She's even dressed for the occasion: her skirt is patterned with tiny blue birds, and there are feather earrings dangling above her shoulders. She looks cute. More than that—kind of gorgeous, actually.

"We're off to a good start!" She reaches a rubber-gloved hand into her bag and pulls out three long, white plumes. "We've found all these already."

"Nice!" I raise my eyebrows at her as Perry bounds ahead to say hi. "Go on. What kind of birds are these from?"

She clears her throat. "These specimens hail from the *Larus argentatus*," she says in her best David Attenborough voice. "Commonly referred to as a seagull. Bit gross, but they'll do the job. Though Mr. Hypochondria here is convinced we're all going to get bird flu and die."

She waves the feathers at Calum, who scowls and swats them away.

"I'm just being realistic! Birds are manky, they're teeming with diseases," he says, taking a miniature bottle of hand sanitizer out of his jacket pocket. "Plus, Teacake's immune system won't be able to cope with the germs here on earth. I'm surprised she can deal with Perry, or us."

My eyes widen; I hadn't even thought about stuff like that. Allie waves her hand dismissively.

"Och, she'll be fine. We'll just need to sterilize them really well before we attach them to her wi—" She breaks off as a woman edges past us with an enormous double buggy. "Her, um, winter coat."

I grin. "Don't you mean her windowsill?"

"Wait, wait, wait," Calum says. "I thought we were repairing her windmill?"

We pace around the Arboretum, throwing out more words

beginning with "win" as we search. After just twenty minutes, we've found four blackbird feathers, two blue tit, two sparrow, and three more seagull, all in that one area of the garden. Perry bounds between the trees chasing birds, her tail wagging happily. For the first time this year, I feel properly summery. It's so hot that soon I have to take my sweater off, and every so often we take a break to stretch out on the lawn and soak up the sun.

There's just one thing spoiling my mood: I can't get Dad's phone call out of my mind.

"Are you okay?" Allie asks me as she stoops to pick a blackbird feather off the grass. "You've gone a bit quiet."

Though I don't really want to admit to making such a stupid mistake, I end up telling them about what I was looking for the night I met them by the duck pond near Arthur's Seat. Calum's mouth falls open.

"What were they saying about them?" he asks, ignoring Perry's nudges to throw the stick again. "Were they trying to sell them? Did the message come from a company, or just some random person, or—"

"I don't know," I say, holding my hands up. "My dad thought it was a hoax. He's totally deluded when it comes to this stuff, though."

"What? Your dad's a Wingding?" Allie says. "You never told us that!"

Her eyes narrow, and I find myself mirroring her expression. "The first time I saw you guys, you were protesting a Wingding restaurant. If I'd told you, you might have thought I was the same. And I'm really not—I hate all that stuff, I don't want anything to do with it. I mean, I hid Teacake from him, didn't I?"

Allie crosses her arms. "But is that why you came down here?" she asks, her expression stormy. "For him to go Being-hunting?"

I nod. "He created some algorithm that told him that another one was going to fall in Edinburgh this summer." My cheeks burn. It's embarrassing talking about this, especially to Allie. "He figured he might be able to catch it, and here we are."

"So, he was right?" Calum's eyebrows rise. "Only you found Teacake before he could? That's kind of unbelievable."

I hadn't thought about it like that. "I guess," I say. "It must have been a lucky coincidence, though. The Falls are so random, there's no way he could have actually worked it out."

"Maybe not," Calum says. "But if somebody's found the feathers, it won't be long until they come after Teacake."

Allie shrugs. "Look, even if someone did pick them up, so what? They've got no other leads. As long as no one saw you, they won't be able to find her. Don't blame yourself," she adds. "I mean, you witnessed a *Being* fall out of the *sky*—it's amazing you were thinking clearly enough to hide her, let alone her feathers."

She smiles, my Wingding connection forgiven if not forgotten. "Let's try the pond," she says. "We might find some duck feathers or something."

We move around the garden, searching between azaleas and under bushes and along the edge of the water. Soon we have about fifty feathers, all different shapes and sizes. It's not enough to fix Teacake's wings, not by a long shot, but it's a start.

At half past eleven, Allie declares a snack break and sends Calum—who rolls his eyes but complies—to the café to get us ice creams. She and I head to the Chinese Hillside, taking a seat in the pavilion overlooking the pond. A starling is balancing on the edge of the wooden barrier; it leaps off as we come closer, sending Perry chasing after it. Allie watches her white tail go bouncing across the grass and grins.

"Wish we had a dog. My mum would never let us. She's worse than Calum, paranoid about germs and—"

She breaks off, coughing. It sounds worse than yesterday, almost as if her lungs are being used as punching bags. I make a move to tap her on the back, more as a token gesture than anything, but she shakes her head. Eventually it eases off, leaving her red-faced and wheezing a little.

"That sounded bad," I say. "Have you seen a doctor about it?"

"Aye, I have. Don't worry, it's not as bad as it sounds." She wipes her mouth on a tissue, then pulls two fruit-and-nut bars from her tote bag. "Want one of these? They're not as rank as they look."

She's changing the subject—I can tell, I've done it enough to Rani recently—but I take the energy bar. "So, your dad," she says. "What was he planning on doing with the Being when he found it?"

"I have no idea. Sell it, maybe." I sigh. "Before the Falls started, he was always working late or on business trips. I don't know if he thinks this is an easier way to make money, or if he's just swapping one obsession for another. Maybe both."

Allie screws her nose up sympathetically. "Our parents are a bit like that," she says. "Well, they're not Wingdings or anything. But they're always so distracted—work, our exams, exactly where I am and what I'm doing . . . Sometimes I just want to plonk them down with a bottle of vodka and tell them to chill the hell out."

"I don't think that'd help my dad," I say, laughing. "If the Wingding stuff is anything to go by, he's got a bit of an addictive personality."

She smiles. It's the sort of smile that takes over her whole face: dimpling at her cheeks, crinkling at her eyes. I get that lurching feeling in the pit of my stomach—like someone's grabbed me by the ankles and flipped me upside down. I haven't felt like this for ages. Not since Leah and I got together.

Almost immediately, that upside-down sensation turns to guilt. Though I haven't seen her since April, Leah and I never properly broke up. We were never officially going out, either. But that doesn't mean it didn't count.

"Well, even if you came here for your dad to go Being-chasing, I'm glad you did." Allie glances down at the wrapper in her hands, folds it into quarters. "For Teacake, I mean."

The tips of her ears have turned pink. Before I can reply, Calum appears, three fast-melting ice creams balanced between his hands. As I take one of the cones from him, I picture myself snuffing out that flicker of guilt between my fingers. Leah's moved on with her life. Here, hundreds of miles from everything that's happened over the past eight months, maybe I can start to do the same.

FOURTEEN

OVER THE NEXT FEW DAYS, OUR FEATHER HUNT SHOWS ME more of Edinburgh than I've ever seen before. We take the bus down to Portobello Beach and collect plumes from seabirds lying on the sand. We search the trees in the Meadows, ignoring the curious looks from Frisbee players and families having barbecues as we pick sparrow and chaffinch feathers from the long grass. Each time, I wish we could have brought Teacake with us. It feels wrong for us to be enjoying the air and the wide-open sky when all she gets are small, square glimpses of blue from the window of the flat.

But the Fringe Festival is just a few days away, and the city's so busy it's far too dangerous for Teacake to go out even for a minute. The rumors about the pink feathers have spread, too. When we go back to Arthur's Seat, we find Wingdings all over the hill, whispering to one another and scanning the grass. We probably look just like them, picking through the bracken and briar along the paths, but I still can't help worrying that one of them is watching us.

On Tuesday, we find a huge haul under a bridge near the Parliament—the result of some poor seagull colliding with a windscreen—and Allie decides that we finally have enough feathers to repair the wing. We arrange to meet at the flat again the next day; we've spent so much time there that I've now started thinking of it as Teacake's place rather than Shona's.

When I go downstairs the next morning, Teacake is asleep on the table, her good wing curled around her body like a blanket. She's turned the radio to a folk music station, all guttural vocals and nimble fiddles. Outside, the buskers and bagpipes have been joined by clunking, drilling noises as stages are set up on the Royal Mile. Between the Wingdings and the festivalgoers, the next few weeks are going to be utter chaos.

Somehow Teacake sleeps through it all, her eyebrows knit in a tight frown. Now and then her hands twitch, and sometimes she mumbles words in her low voice that sound tense and panicked. Whatever she's dreaming of, it's not all white clouds and golden gates.

A loud bang comes from a truck outside: Teacake wakes with a start and a scream. She leaps onto all fours and spins around, blinking wildly. I scramble to my feet, babbling that it's all right. Her eyes are still wild, but she takes a breath and sits back. She pushes her tousled hair out of her face and rolls back her shoulders, making her wings ripple like pink-dappled waves.

"Morning," I say, holding my palms up. "Did you sleep okay? You looked like you were having a nightmare."

I try to mime sleep, closing my eyes and resting my head on my hands. Teacake opens her mouth. Her lips move silently; she puts her fingers to them, as if tracing the shapes they're making. For one breathtaking moment, I think she's going to speak—but instead, she just tilts her head back to look at the ceiling, at the dull white plaster hiding the sky.

"You must be so homesick," I say quietly. "There must be people waiting for you. People you're missing, too."

As if on cue, the radio starts to play some wistful Gaelic tune. Teacake turns toward it, drawn in by the emotion in the song. I try to picture what she's thinking of: what her home might be like, the friends and family she might have left behind. Soon, I find myself thinking about Leah's dad.

He flits into my mind a lot these days. I think about him alone in that house, where his wife and Leah used to be. I think about the empty chairs at their kitchen table, the silence behind the bedroom doors. Loss is mathematical: two-thirds less washing, two-thirds fewer dishes, two-thirds fewer footsteps thundering down the stairs. Subtract music blaring through the walls. Subtract eyeliner smudges on the towels. Add silence. Add more silence.

I've done those sums. The results are always greater than you think they'll be.

Teacake turns to look at me. She puts her fingers to her mouth again and murmurs something I can't make out. Even if we can't communicate, I feel like there's something we have in common: loss. I have some faint idea of how she's feeling, at least.

I start laying the feathers out on the carpet for when Allie and Calum arrive: soft downy ones and semiplumes on the left; long, elegant flight feathers on the right. A few minutes later, there's a knock at the door. I open up to find Calum standing on the step, red-faced and panting, with Allie on his back. Her skinny arms are wrapped around his neck, her trainers dangling in midair, and she has a tube sticking up her nose.

"Oh my God, are you okay?" I ask. "What happened?"

Allie gives a weak smile. She's wearing pajamas: baby-blue trousers decorated with clouds, paired with chunky high-tops, a navy duffle coat, and a striped blue-and-white scarf. Calum is dressed in jeans and a hoodie, but his hair is sticking up on one side and there are deep bluish bags under his eyes.

"I'm fine," Allie says. "Had a bit of a bad night, that's all."

"Mind if we chat inside?" Calum asks in a strained voice. "You've got about three seconds before I drop you."

I move back to let them in. As Calum shuffles past, I notice he's holding Allie up with one hand and dragging something with the other: a small green cylinder on a sort of metal trolley. He hurries into the living room and gently lowers Allie onto the sofa. She looks exhausted: her face has gone from its usual chalky color to a sickly gray-white, and her normally neat hair is pulled into a scruffy ponytail.

"Don't worry," she says, letting out a cough. "It's not as bad as it looks."

I have about a hundred questions, but before I can ask any of them, Teacake leaps onto the coffee table. She bounds toward the kitchen, ruffling my hair up with her good wing, and begins rummaging through the cupboards and drawers for biscuits. She comes back chewing on a cracker, but it doesn't go down well: she pulls a face, makes a sound like a plug draining, and spits it out. I get up to check the cupboards, but Shona's supply of sweets has finally run out.

"Maybe you should try some vegetables or something, Tea," I say, picking through the tins in the back of the cupboard. "I'd feel pretty bad if we gave the world's only living Being type two diabetes."

"Well, I'm not having mushy peas for breakfast," Calum scoffs. "I'll go to the shops and get us something."

He heads back out, leaving me alone with Teacake and Allie. I know I shouldn't be, but I'm acutely aware of the tube up her nose. Before I have a chance to say anything, Teacake leans across the table and tugs it out to examine it. Allie laughs and prizes it out of her fingers.

"See, you should be more like her. It's just an oxygen tube," she says, as she fits it back into place. "Why are people always so terrified of bringing it up? I am aware it's there. You'd have to be pretty stealth to get one of these up somebody's nose without them noticing."

I realize I'm gawping and close my mouth. "Um, can I ask . . . ?"

"I have cystic fibrosis." Seeing my blank expression, she explains. "It's a chronic genetic disease. My lungs and pancreas produce this thick, sticky mucus that clogs my airways, so it's hard for me to breathe. I had a double lung transplant for it when I was fourteen, though, so I'm a lot better now."

She says this like she just got a tooth pulled out. It takes a moment for the words to sink in. A double lung transplant. The scope of that knocks the words out of me. I have no vocabulary for something that big.

"Wow," I say finally, and it sounds even more inadequate than it felt in my head. "Is it still serious?"

As soon as I've asked, I realize what a stupid question that is, but my knowledge of cystic fibrosis ends at . . . well, it started about thirty seconds ago. Allie pulls something from her bag: a yellow plastic pillbox, the kind Ammamma has in her bathroom. Behind the cover are dozens of tablets, red and white and green.

"This is cyclosporine—it's an antirejection drug. Voriconazole—that helps with infections. That's a painkiller for my spine, these are protein supplement pills—I can't process food properly, that's why I have to eat so much. That one's just a vitamin . . ."

She introduces them like they're old friends. There are antibiotics, anti-ulcer medications, pills for pancreatic enzyme replacement therapy. Pills for problems that I didn't know existed. Teacake picks up a small green capsule and holds it to the window, watching the light shine through the plastic.

"Wow," I murmur, prying it out of her hand before she eats it. "So, all that's for one week?"

Allie bursts out laughing. "A *week*? That's for one day. I'm like one of those coin-operated attractions the Victorians used to have. I don't usually need the oxygen now, it's just because I've got some crappy infection. But without all this, I'd just shut down."

She pretends to collapse, like a robot going into meltdown. There are dozens of thoughts swirling around my head, but I can't find any form for them. The image in my head that I have of Sick People doesn't fit with the loud, opinionated, bossy girl I've gotten to know over the past week.

"I'm really sorry," I say. "That must suck."

I cringe as soon as the words leave my mouth: it sounds so half-assed, so flippant. Allie just shrugs.

"It is what it is. I mean, don't get me wrong, it's not exactly a day out at Disneyland. All the side effects suck. Missing school sucks. The fact I can never, ever forget about it sucks—I have to do about a billion tests every day."

She pulls one of her energy bars from her bag, peels off the wrapper. "But my life is so much better than it was before the operation. The main threat now is infections. I've got basically no immune system: I need to be really careful around pets, and I can't even eat sushi. But most days I feel like a superhero, compared to what it was like before."

I rummage around for something to say, something meaningful, but my mind has gone blank. For the first time since I met Allie there's an awkward silence, broken only by the rustling of Teacake's wings and a lively ceilidh tune on the radio. Allie curls up on Shona's sofa, her hands deep in the pockets of her duffle coat, and gives a world-weary sigh.

"See, this is exactly why I didn't want to tell you," she says. "I'm not ashamed of having CF, I'm not hiding it. But it's not the most important thing about me. It's not *me*."

"Of course," I say quickly. "I totally get that."

"Sometimes I just don't want to think about it, you know? No one ever, *ever* lets me forget about it. Every time I plan to do something, it's 'Are you sure you're feeling up to it?' or 'You won't forget your meds, will you?' If it's not my mum and dad, it's Calum, or teachers at school, or even my friends. To everybody else in the world, I'm Allie-the-girl-with-CF." She traces the pattern of an elephant on one of Shona's pillows. "It was nice to hang out with someone who just saw me as Allie, even if it was only for a few days."

"I still see you just as Allie," I say. Behind her, Teacake shuffles toward us. Her lips open and close quickly and soundlessly, like a muted movie scene. "You really don't need to apologize for not telling me. It's not my business, anyway. It's totally fine."

Allie raises an eyebrow at me. "Really? 'Cause you look like you're about to overdose on awkward right now."

"Do I? Sorry. I'm really sorry." I rub the back of my neck. "I just, I don't know how to act around sick people. Not that you seem sick! You seem . . ."

"What? Normal? I *am* normal," Allie says fiercely. "It's not like I'm an invalid, despite what everyone thinks. Mum wouldn't even let me out today. She thinks I'm having a nap right now. Calum distracted her with some boring story about wildlife photography while I snuck out the back door. Hence the pajamas; we were in a bit of a hurry."

"She's going to kill me when she realizes you're gone."

Calum appears in the doorway, a plastic bag in one hand and a packet of custard creams in the other. He rips it open and tosses a biscuit to Teacake. She gives a delighted yelp and scoffs it down in two bites.

"Calm down, Calculus," Allie says, holding her hands out for the packet. "Mum won't notice for at least another hour."

"You know that's not true. I give it five minutes before she calls one of us. Me, probably."

"Calum, how often do you get to hang out with an *angel*?" Allie bites angrily into her biscuit. "I'm not going to spend the whole summer sitting in bed. Besides, what's Mum going to do? Stop your pocket money?"

They start a game of dirty-look ping-pong, flinging scowls back and forth. I watch them, torn between laughing and making an excuse to leave.

And right then, Teacake decides to speak.

"And the moon shines bright, when I rove at night, to muse upon my charmer."

My jaw drops. Calum jumps so high, I'm surprised he doesn't bash his head on the ceiling. Teacake blinks back at us, crumbs all over her lips.

"What did you say?" I can hardly get the words out.

"Did you say the *moon*?" Allie leans over the arm of the sofa, her face lit up. For a moment I can almost make out the little kid she used to be: climbing over furniture in Star Wars pajamas, turning cardboard boxes into rocket ships. "Are you—no, you can't—are you from the *moon*?"

Teacake looks confused. She rubs the crumbs from her mouth. "Gie fools their silks and knaves their wine, a man's a man for a' that."

It sounds like a riddle, but there's something familiar about the words—something that reminds me of school. After a second, it clicks: "That's *Burns*! That's by Robert Burns, we studied his songs in English. Teacake, are you . . . singing?"

Calum bursts out laughing. Allie laughs along, but her face has flooded with disappointment. It's sort of heartbreaking.

I edge toward her on my knees. "She must have heard it on the radio," I say. "What else can you sing, Tea?"

Teacake chews on her lower lip, then responds with a line from another Burns song. "I'll ne'er blame my partial fancy, naething could resist my Nancy."

This time, we all crack up—even Allie.

"That's unbelievable. For her to be able to produce sounds like that so soon . . ." She shakes her head. "I mean, probably not the songs I would've picked for her introduction to modern civilization, but it's a start."

I try to give Teacake a high five, but she just holds my fingers and smiles, which sets us off again. While Allie finishes sorting out the feathers to repair her wing, I manage to coax a few more half-sung snippets out of her: a few lines of "Green Grow the Rashes," something unintelligible that I think might be Gaelic. Eventually, Calum gets up and goes to the radio.

"Hilarious as this is, if we left it on another channel, she might actually learn something useful." He turns the knob until the music has been replaced with the voice of an older woman with a posh accent. "There, good old BBC Radio 4."

Allie snorts. "Brilliant. She can learn to recite recipes and bits of *The Archers*."

"So what? It's a good way to learn." His usual grumpy tone is gone: Calum's eyes are bright, his face flushed with excitement. "We could be on the edge of something here, you know. She might actually be able to give us some answers."

FIFTEEN

WHEN I GET BACK TO OUR FLAT THAT NIGHT, I FIND DAD IN some sort of frenzy: scurrying around the living room, snatching up papers or reading a few lines of a book before leaping onto his laptop to type up some notes. Newspaper clippings cover the carpet like fallen leaves, and the sofa is practically buried under library books. Rani watches him from the doorway, twirling a lock of hair between her fingers.

"What's going on?" I ask.

She shrugs. "Dunno." She looks a bit put out. "Can you make us some dinner? I'm starving."

There's nothing left in the kitchen, so I help myself to twenty quid from Dad's wallet and head to the pizza place downstairs. Fifteen minutes later, Rani and I are sitting on our bedroom floor with two cans of Diet Coke and an extra-large Hawaiian pizza between us. Rani props her phone against the leg of the bunk beds and starts streaming a clip from an American news channel.

"There was another Fall in Oman last night," she says. "Eighty-seven now."

Eighty-eight, I think, with just a hint of guilt. Two photos flash onto the screen: one shows the scratched, silvery face of a Being; the other a smiling woman in an embroidered gold-and-green veil. An American woman talks over the images.

"When Tariq Al-Farsi went online to check his emails yesterday afternoon, the last thing he expected to see was a photo of his late wife, Esraa, who died of ovarian cancer last year. On second glance, however, the pretty, dark-haired woman on-screen wasn't Esraa at all . . . but a Being, the eighty-seventh to fall, landing outside a shopping mall just thirty miles from the couple's home."

The film cuts to a shot of a young man sitting at a computer, tears pouring down his cheeks. Tariq Al-Farsi talks to the interviewer in rapid-fire Arabic; the news anchor reads out the English translation.

"They're telling me it's a coincidence, or that I'm imagining things, but it's her. This Being, this angel . . . she's my wife, come back to me."

He spins the computer toward the camera. Esraa on the beach, squinting in the bright sunlight. Esraa reading in the garden, a small smile on her lips. The resemblance to the Being really is astonishing: they have the same Roman nose, the same thick lips, matching dimples in their chins. Apart from the silvery skin tone and the mangled wings, they could have been twins.

"I don't know what it means," Tariq sobs. "I don't know what to think. I only just lost her, and now this . . . this is like losing her all over again."

There's a dull pang of pain in my chest. "Is that what Dad's so excited about?" I ask Rani.

"Maybe," she says through a mouthful of pizza. "He's barely talked to me all day."

The newsreader moves on to a story about an LA actor who's been jailed after being caught drunk driving for the third time, and we slip back into silence. I keep imagining Tariq Al-Farsi browsing online, catching sight of his wife among the news stories. The way his heart must have skipped as he watched her fall from the stars; the fear and confusion, the tiny hint of hope that she might land safely. Then the inevitable crash, bringing with it a second wave of despair.

This is why hope is dangerous: if it's taken away, you're left with even less than you had before.

My appetite's gone. I throw my half-eaten slice of pizza back into the box. Rani chews on her piece of Hawaiian.

"Remember how mad Mum used to get when I ordered this?" she asks.

I grin. " 'Pizza is supposed to be Italian! What's Italian about Hawaii?' "

" 'Fruit and meat and cheese together? It's an abomination!' "

We laugh. For a few seconds it feels good, and then there comes the tipping point: that moment where I can feel my mouth start to quiver, and I have to fight to stop the tears from coming. I close my eyes and take a long sip of Coke, until my eyes have stopped prickling. When I open them, Rani is watching me.

"You never talk about her." She picks a fallen chunk of pineapple from the box and nibbles at it. "Neither does Dad. Sometimes I feel like I'm the only one who thinks about her."

"Of course I think about her." Until we came here, she was pretty much all I thought about. Even sleep couldn't give me a break: she appeared in most of my dreams, all of my nightmares. "It's just . . . hard."

Rani picks up another slice of pizza and chews it slowly. When she speaks, her voice is even smaller. "What happened that day, Jaya?"

My veins turn to ice. It starts in my hands and creeps up my arms, around my neck and down my spine. For a few seconds, I can't move. I can't think. The dizziness swirls through my head, and all I can see is rushing water, and rocks, and panicked birds fluttering through the trees.

"You know what happened, Rani. We were walking in the glen. It was an accident," I say, though that has never seemed like the right word for it. Spilling tea on your laptop is an accident. Breaking your leg skiing is an accident. Your parent dying shouldn't be in the same category.

"Yeah, but—"

"Yes! Yes, yes, yes!"

Dad's voice booms through the walls, saving me from answering. Rani runs through to the living room, her pizza slice drooping in her hand. Dad is standing over a semicircle of maps and notes, his fists raised in the air—a mad god surveying his creation.

"I've got it! I think I've got it!" He strides over to the door, picks Rani up, and twirls her into the air. "I think I know where it's going to fall!"

"No way!" Rani slides onto her knees, dropping her slice of Hawaiian onto the carpet. "Where? How did you work it out?"

Dad kneels beside her. He spreads his notes out like a hand of cards. "Right, let me show you . . ."

My stomach feels queasy, and not just from the cheese curdling in my gut. Dad, on the other hand, looks . . . alive. His eyes are bloodshot from lack of sleep and that soup stain is still on his T-shirt, but he looks more alert than I've seen in months. He leans back onto his heels and slaps his knees.

"First of all, I tried looking at the longitude and latitude of each of the Fall spots, both globally and on a country-by-country basis. There didn't seem to be any relation whatsoever, at least not mathematically."

He's talking so fast I can barely keep up. He pulls a map of Edinburgh from the pile. There are seven *X*s drawn in yellow highlighter: four in the city itself, and three a few miles outside it.

"I tried dozens of other theories—the elevation of the places, how close they were to water—but nothing quite fit. Then *somebody* had the great idea of looking into the history of the spots, rather than just their location."

He gives Rani a little bump on the shoulder. She looks so pleased she might burst.

"So?" I ask, taking a step into the room. "What did you find?"

"Well, I did a lot—I mean a *lot*—of reading about the city, and I discovered that all the spots are connected to religion. The cathedral is an obvious one, but the others weren't nearly so clear." He points to the crosses one by one. "I found some records suggesting baptisms took place in the Water of Leith. The golf course where number fifty-eight landed is built on the grounds of an old priory. So, from that, I managed to narrow down the possible locations for the next fall."

"That could be tons of places, though," I say. "I mean, religion is everywhere. It could be a church, a synagogue, a mosque . . ."

Instead of getting pissed off at my picking holes in his theory, he actually seems pleased. "Exactly! But once I knew a bit about the history of the spots, I was able to narrow potential locations of future Falls to just three places. I managed to rule out two of them based on other factors, which left me with . . ."

He draws a mark on the map. I step forward to take a closer look, and my heart leaps. He's drawn an *X* on Arthur's Seat—right on the ruin where I hid Teacake after I found her.

"It's called St. Anthony's Chapel," he says. "I went there yesterday. It's just a few walls now, but it used to be a proper little church. No one's sure how old it is. Some say it could date back to the 1300s."

I can't speak. He may not have found the exact spot where Teacake fell, but he's come *really* damn close—less than a kilometer away. For a few seconds, I actually believe he's somehow managed to crack the code. He's really managed to predict the next Fall.

And then it crumbles. This isn't a theory; it's wishful thinking. For one thing, linking spirituality and coordinates together makes no sense whatsoever. He hasn't considered what's *making* the Beings fall, and anyway, even if his algorithm did work, it doesn't take into account when or where Teacake landed, so he wouldn't get the right result. It's really damn weird that he came so close to hitting the spot where she fell, but then the city isn't that big—most coincidences aren't actually that unusual when you look at their probability. Dad's just seeing what he wants to see. Believing what he wants to believe.

I can't tell him that, though. Not, I realize with a sharp pinch of guilt, when I'm partly to blame for the flaws in his equations.

"That's amazing, Dad." The way he grins, so happy to get my approval, you'd think I was the parent and he the child. "So, how are you going to catch her?"

Rani glances up at me. "Her?"

I feel the blood drain from my cheeks. "Uh, or him. I just have a feeling she'll be a woman."

Dad smiles at me. Not his usual distracted twitch of the lips, but a real smile. It feels like the first time he's properly looked at me in months. I'm starting to understand why Rani puts so much effort into this Being stuff.

"That's funny . . . I do, too." He pulls a notebook toward him. "It's difficult. You were right in a way, Jaya, when you said no one could survive a fall that fast."

He writes an equation that's more letters and symbols than numbers—nothing I can understand. "This calculates the velocity that an item would fall from a certain height, so we can estimate the speed using a Being's average weight," he says. "Of course, that doesn't take into account air resistance. Though most of the Beings have had both wings broken, they still seem to be able to move them, so in reality their descent isn't quite as fast as we'd imagine."

"Plus, the Being could have one functional wing," Rani chimes in, "like the one in Alaska the other day. That would slow it down even more."

I think back to Teacake's landing on the hill. At the time, it had felt impossibly fast; there were only a few seconds, maybe ten or eleven, between my spotting that pinkish light in the sky and the thump when she'd landed in the tree. Compared to some of the earlier Falls, though, it was practically in slow motion.

Dad pulls a detailed blueprint from his pile of papers. "Remember the other enthusiasts I went to meet in Perth? Well, one of them came up with the idea of using a large apparatus—a sort of giant fan, I guess—to slow down the Being's descent. One woman's an electrician, and another guy is a welder, so between us we have a pretty good team."

A giant fan? That's their big plan? These people are clearly as deluded as Dad is. "Right. Um, cool."

I force a smile, and he beams back. He clearly thinks I'm finally coming around to his way of thinking, when really it's only guilt that's stopping me from telling him how ridiculous his plan is. Rani claps her hands like an excited seal. If she's realized how little sense all this makes, she doesn't show it.

"You're going to be famous, Dad!"

"I don't know about that," he says with a laugh. "That's not what this is about, anyway. I just really think I'm onto something here, though, girls. I have a feeling."

He pulls Rani into a hug with one arm, leaving the other open for me. I go toward him, and for a moment I feel like I can't breathe. There is only one thing in the world that my father wants—and I have her hidden downstairs, sleeping on a table and listening to Radio 4. He would hate me if he knew. He would never, ever forgive me.

SIXTEEN

"VIKING, NORTH UTSIRE, SOUTH UTSIRE. NORTHWESTERLY four or five becoming variable three or four, then southeasterly five or six later. Showers, rain later. Good, occasionally poor later."

Teacake beams. After three days of listening to Radio 4 non-stop, she's managed to memorize a few sentences . . . of the *Shipping Forecast*. She might as well have learned to recite *War and Peace* in the original Russian, for all I understand. Still, she looks so pleased with herself, we have to give her a round of applause. She grins and snatches another biscuit, her sixth of the morning.

"Brilliant, Teacake," Allie says as she stitches a feather onto her damaged wing. "You'll be presenting *Desert Island Discs* in no time."

Calum glowers at her. "Don't encourage her, Allie."

He sighs and flicks through the *100 First Words* book lying open on the coffee table. While Allie fixes Teacake's wing, Calum and I have spent the past few days going through ESL textbooks and

YouTube tutorials, trying to coax a few sentences out of Teacake. Her progress has been strange. She'll reel off parts of songs or long paragraphs about fracking or French politicians, random things she's heard on the radio. She'll even parrot things we say, with a hint of a Scottish accent and everything. But when we try to point out things around her, like "sofa" or "biscuit," she responds with nothing more than a blank look.

"How about this, Teacake?" Calum holds up his cup of tea, a large mug with mushrooms on it. "Come on. You know this one."

Teacake sighs and shuffles on the coffee table. Her wings keep twitching—not in greeting this time, but like she's itching to get away. It reminds me of when I was little and Mum started teaching me Tamil. Some days, if she sang a song or found a video for me to watch, I'd sit and pay attention; others I'd just squirm in my chair until I could go and play again.

Teacake stares at the cup for a moment, as if she might find her fortune there.

"There are warnings of gales in all areas," she says. "Except Biscay, Trafalgar, and FitzRoy."

Allie bursts out laughing. Calum grits his teeth. His patience has gone from thin to threadbare. I don't know why he's demanding so much of Teacake so quickly. It's like he thought he could read her a few chapters of *English for Beginners* and unlock the secrets to the universe.

"Calm down, Calcium," Allie says. "She's trying."

His expression is stormy. I change the subject before another argument can break out.

"I think we need to decide about moving Teacake," I say. "We've only got two days before Shona comes back. Even if we manage to fix your wing before then, we don't know if you'll be able to fly on it, Tea."

This is taking longer than any of us thought. Allie was too ill to come over yesterday, and the process of attaching the feathers to Teacake's wing is super fiddly. I thought Allie could just douse them in superglue, but instead each one has to be individually attached with surgical thread: they have to be able to bend and twist or they won't allow for forward movement. It looks beautiful—a landscape of soft browns and silvery grays, broken here and there by a dash of bullfinch red or kingfisher blue—but she's only managed to attach half the feathers so far. It's going to take a least three or four more days to finish.

"You're right," Allie says, her shoulders sagging. "Where to, though?"

We throw out idea after idea, but each one has a fatal flaw. Our flat is out for obvious reasons, and Allie and Calum's house is too small. I suggest their school, but apparently the building is used for summer activities during the holidays. Hotels are an option, but between us we'd only have enough cash for a night or two.

Eventually our ideas peter into silence, filled by the sound of the radio and the theater group outside performing a scene from *Angels in America* to the tourists. After a while, the news comes on. The first item is about a Being who fell in South Africa last night.

"Small feminine Being . . . landed in an abandoned mine near the city of Kimberley . . . quickly spotted by tourists and stripped of its feathers . . ."

Allie takes her purple notebook from her bag and writes a few notes on a new page. Teacake twists around to see what she's doing; her wing knocks the book out of Allie's hand, sending it flying straight into Calum's lap. Allie throws out a hand toward it, but he's already squinting at her handwriting.

"What is this?" He flicks through the pages. "Ksenia . . . Rayyan . . . Who are these people?"

"Give that back." Allie lunges toward him, but he holds the notebook out of her reach. "Calum, come on!"

"This is all just . . . names," he says. "Why are you writing down names?"

Allie pushes her hair behind her ears. The edges have turned pink. "Look, I know it sounds stupid, but I . . . I name all the Beings."

"That's it? That's your big secret?" Her brother's face falls. "Well, that's massively disappointing. Why wouldn't you just tell us that?"

"You'd think it was stupid," she says, snatching the notebook back from him. "Like a kid naming their cuddly toys or something."

I hold my hand out. "Can I see?"

After a pause, Allie sits back down and hands it to me. Each page is dedicated to a single Being, with a first name written in bold letters and details of when and where they fell: *Cheng. Landed in Shanghai, China, on 7 December . . . Valentina. Landed north of Rincón de Valentín, Uruguay, on 19 January . . . Ewan. Landed in Sighthill, Edinburgh, on 16 March . . .*

Below the date, she's written the color of their eyes, how tall they were, if they had birthmarks or scars, anything to distinguish them from the others. There are even a few notes about what sort of person she thinks they might have been.

Strong, athletic. Probably into team sports, if they have them. Grumpy at times, but the kind of guy who would look out for his friends no matter what.

She didn't look scared at all as she fell. I think she must have been a soldier, something dangerous. Something that required a lot of courage.

There's something about him that looks kind . . . nurturing, even. I can imagine him surrounded by a flock of baby Beings, helping out his neighbors and relatives.

"I just don't want them to die without names—even if they're made up, even if no one knows them but me," says Allie. "I mean, it's bad enough that the papers just call them 'Being number one,' 'Being number two,' but the thought of them dying anonymously, with no one to remember who they were . . ."

She trails off, quietly turning the pages of the notebook, reading the names to herself one by one. Calum's smirk has been wiped away. Teacake looks from him to Allie, biting her lower lip. She may not be able to understand our language, but she can pick up on changes in mood and atmosphere. She is as real, as human, and as complex as any of us.

"It's not stupid," I say to Allie, handing the notebook back to her. "You see them as people."

She smiles. It's just a quick movement of her lips, but it reaches her eyes. For a few seconds, it all fades away: Shona's flat, the crowd of umbrellas lining the street outside . . . even Teacake. All I see is Allie. Almost too fast to catch, her gaze flits to my mouth; she shifts on the carpet, moving her knee a few millimeters toward mine.

"You see them as people," Teacake says, a wobbly echo of my

voice. "Cromarty, southwesterly five to seven, decreasing four at times."

Her voice breaks the moment. I remember Calum's still in the room and quickly get up to make some tea, my cheeks burning. Allie laughs, a nervous sound that blends into a cough. She thumbs the corners of her notebook, pauses, then stares at a page somewhere near the middle.

"Wait a minute." She turns to Calum. "Is McEwan Hall still closed?"

"Yeah, till September or something. They've stopped building while the Fringe is going on—" He looks up at Allie, his eyes wide. "Er, *no*. No fucking way."

"But it's perfect!" Allie leans over and clutches his arm. "It's empty right now, since all the workers have left while the building's stopped. It's not far from here, plus it's huge—Teacake would have space to practice flying!"

"Wait, where is this place?" I ask as Calum shakes his head.

"It's one of the university buildings," he says. "Our dad's company is working on it at the moment. There's a problem with the roof or something; it's been under construction for a couple of months."

"No one'll even notice we're there," Allie says. "There are tons of Fringe venues around there, so it's always packed. You'll be able to sing as loud as you like, Teacake."

"Is it safe, though?" I ask. "Like, the ceiling won't fall in on us or anything, would it?"

Calum scratches the back of his neck. "Well, no, it's just the exterior that needs repairs, but that's not the point. If Dad finds out, he'll kill us." Allie opens her mouth to argue; Calum cuts her off, all flustered. "Look, Al, even if we could get the keys, how are we going to get her across town with *that* going on?"

He raps his knuckles against the window. The Royal Mile is chaos: performers dressed as robots or soldiers or caterpillars, musical theater students in matching T-shirts, and of course the Wingdings, the fake angels, the tour guides mingling with the yearly influx of show-goers. The streets won't be quiet until four or five in the morning—I could hardly sleep last night with the racket outside. Calum's right. We couldn't make it across the street to Starbucks without getting caught.

We throw out a few more suggestions, but that glimmer of hope is fading fast. Sensing the change in mood, Teacake arches her back and spreads her wings. "Tiree Automatic, south-southeast five, twelve miles, one thousand and eleven, falling slowly."

I smile. "It almost sounds like she could be talking about the Beings. A guide to the Falls."

Suddenly, Allie's eyes light up. "I've got it!"

She pushes herself off the sofa, runs to the kitchen, and starts rummaging in the drawers again. When she comes back, she's holding a roll of tinfoil, an old council tax bill, and a black Sharpie. She writes *ANGEL TOURS* on the back of the letter and holds it up to Teacake's chest.

"We'll pretend you're a guide, Tea!" she says. "We'll put tinfoil over your wings, so they look fake, and a bit of makeup or whatever on so it looks like face paint. You'll look just like another tour guide!"

Teacake takes the piece of paper, her nose wrinkling in

confusion. "You'll look just like another tour guide," she repeats, staring at Allie's makeshift sign. Calum stares at her.

"That's either totally stupid or totally genius."

"It's kind of brilliant, actually," I say. "No one would expect an actual Being to hide in plain sight like that."

Allie beams and grabs my hand. "Ooh, we can make flyers, too! You're not doing the Fringe unless you're bombarding people with flyers."

"That's if we can nick Dad's keys," Calum says. Allie opens her mouth, but he puts his hands up before she can start to argue. "Look, fine, I'll try tonight. But if we get caught, I don't know anything about this. I never even *saw* Teacake. Okay?"

"Fine, fine. You worry too much." Allie gives him a light punch on the arm. "It'll be fine, Cal. What's the worst that can happen?"

SEVENTEEN

MAYBE I'M IMAGINING IT, BUT WHEN I GO DOWNSTAIRS THE
next day it feels like Teacake understands that her time in Shona's
cramped little flat is almost over. She's so cheery: hopping over the
furniture, echoing our sentences, quoting an entire interview with
Julianne Moore she heard on the radio. Even our forcing her into
leggings and a sweater can't spoil her mood.

Allie and Calum, on the other hand, have been grouchy all
morning. They keep bickering about everything: Teacake's costume, the route we should take to McEwan Hall, the fake flyers
Allie is drawing up. Eventually they explode into a full-blown argument: something about her being selfish, him being a martyr.
All the shouting sets Perry off, barking so loud I'm scared Dad and
Rani will hear her through the ceiling. I slap the coffee table with
my fist.

"Guys, come on! We don't have time for this."

Teacake chimes in, "In forty-five minutes here on Radio 4, the *Food Programme* looks at the future of strawberry production. But first, the news."

Calum mumbles a reluctant apology. Allie rolls her eyes and finishes Teacake's costume in grumpy silence. The makeup we use to cover her shimmering skin makes her wrinkle up her nose in disgust (she keeps shouting snatches of radio quizzes: "Bzzz! Time's up!") and the tinfoil refuses to stick to the wings until we wrap an entire roll of tape around it. The costume is ridiculously cheap and totally unprofessional, but that's perfect: she looks just as inauthentic as the sprayed and feathered guides who stalk the Mile.

"Ready?" Calum shoves his hands into his pockets. The keys to the hall jingle beneath his fingers. "Let's get this over with, then."

We usher Teacake through the door and down the stairs, Allie and I on either side of her and Calum leading Perry on the leash. It's the first time that Teacake's been out since she fell. She tilts her head toward the sky, today a pale gray with darkening clouds to the south, and takes a long, deep breath. A wide smile spreads across her face. It's not home, but it's the closest she's been to it for a while.

"Sorry about all that with Calum," Allie says quietly as he strides ahead with Perry. "He's not always such a dick. He can actually be quite fun when he's not convinced I'm about to drop dead."

"Is that what this is about? He thinks—"

"He thinks I'm doing too much. He thinks that I should stay at home and let you guys look after Teacake until this infection's gone." She rolls her eyes. "Our parents are worse. They treat me like I'm a house of cards. Like the slightest movement could make me crumble."

"It must be hard for them," I say. "Seeing you . . . you know, not well."

"Well, you'd think they'd be used to it by now."

Her voice sounds sharp, even a little bitter—not like Allie at all. Teacake peers at her, her eyebrows raised in concern.

"And, of course, you won the Oscar for your incredible performance in *Still Alice*," she says, the interviewer's crisp English pronunciation sounding almost robotic in her voice. "How did you prepare for the role?"

Allie laughs. "Don't worry, Tea. I'm fine."

Outside, the Royal Mile is mobbed: a current of hundreds of people flows in both directions, forming whirlpools around the performers and fake Beings. For the first time, I notice how much noise there is. Even behind the sounds of the shows, I can hear a kid laughing, a couple arguing, a car alarm whining in the next street. Perry joins in with a few excited barks. Teacake tenses beside me.

"It's okay," Allie murmurs, squeezing her hand. "This won't take long. Just keep walking, okay?"

I hold on to her arm and edge slowly down the street, past magicians and mime artists and countless tourists. I'm amazed at how well our plan is working: in her tacky wings and makeup, Teacake blends seamlessly into the chaos. A few people point or raise their cameras in our direction, but their attention is soon tugged away by other sights and sounds.

But as we reach Starbucks, Teacake comes to a halt. Something in her face changes, bewilderment giving way to horror. I follow her stare: on the other side of the street, footage of the Edinburgh

Falls is flickering on the huge LCD screen. No. 13 falling toward the harbor at North Queensferry; No. 70 slumped across a garden lawn; No. 8 crashing through the roof of St. Giles' Cathedral.

My heart sinks. "Don't look, Tea," I say. "Don't—"

I tug on her hand, but she pulls out of my grasp and staggers through the crowd toward the screen. She reaches for the image, where a male Being is tumbling through a bright blue sky. Calum and I have shown her a few YouTube tutorials for learning English, but we couldn't tell if she understood that the pictures weren't just shapes and colors on a screen—that they corresponded to something living, something real.

But now there's no mistaking the horror creeping over her face. She knows. She understands what she's seeing. The footage keeps playing over and over: Beings falling, spinning, flailing, screaming, over and over, No. 8, No. 33, No. 42 . . . Only to her they were never numbers. They are her people, and she is watching them die.

"Come on, Tea," Allie begins, but it's too late. A low, guttural cry spills from her mouth. One of the Wingdings spots her; a group of them start to swarm around us, most with smartphones in their hands. They film Teacake as she puts her hands to her cheeks, digging her fingernails into her skin. Her knees start to buckle. I grab her under the arms, and a piece of tinfoil slips from her right wing; the feathers beneath glow bright pink in the flashes of the phones.

Allie shoots me a panicked look. The crowd is pushing forward as more and more people try to see what's happening. Perry yaps, straining on her lead. But then Calum steps forward, spreading his arms in front of Teacake. He bows and thrusts handfuls of Allie's fake flyers toward them.

"Ladies and gentlemen, this is a preview of our new play, *The Way We Fall*." He clasps his hands together and gives a wide smile. "See us at, um, the Playhouse. Next Thursday. At four p.m."

Some of the audience begins to clap; others let out a sigh of disappointment. As the crowd disperses, Calum and I grab one of Teacake's arms each and haul her along the street. She's properly crying now. Tears run down her face, revealing streaks of skin below the foundation.

"We have to move, Teacake," I say, tugging at her hand. "Please! We have to keep going."

Slowly, her feet start to move. She sobs all the way along George IV Bridge and across the road to the university. McEwan Hall is half-hidden behind scaffolding, but I remember the building next to it: a student union with Gothic windows and lots of turrets. Mum and I went to see a crappy musical here last time we came down for the Fringe. I fish for the memory, but my head is too busy with Teacake; it sinks into the mire and disappears.

Heads turn as we usher Teacake through the crowd. The square outside is almost as busy as the Mile. Allie pushes flyers into the tourists' hands to distract them. Most end up on the ground: her shaky illustrations of falling angels litter the pavement.

Calum points to the road on the right. "This way. Quick, before anyone sees."

But the screech of tires makes us all spin around. Four vans are pulling up on the other side of the road, just outside the student union. The doors slide open, and dozens of people pour out: women in scruffy, ripped clothes, with matted locks and greasy skin; pale, gaunt men with downturned mouths and dull eyes.

"Shit," Calum says. "It's them."

Allie clutches at my sleeve. "Oh my God, this is perfect! Hurry, let's go while everyone's distracted."

I hear her footsteps scuffle down the road, but I don't follow. I can't take my eyes off the Standing Fallen. Passersby are already starting to surround the building. A few seem to be calling 999, but most are just getting ready for the show to start. Two of the members hold a long ladder against the wall; the others climb onto the roof of the student union, surprisingly nimble for being so frail.

There are dozens of them, more than I've ever seen—so many it's a wonder the ceiling doesn't cave in. They line the gable and ridge of the roof, squashed shoulder to shoulder. Either the Edinburgh group has doubled in size since the day we arrived, or they've joined up with another chapter—Glasgow, maybe, or Aberdeen.

That's when I see her. Treading the slate-gray tiles, her arms stretched out for balance. Tattered jeans, a stained gray hoodie.

Leah.

EIGHTEEN

THE GIRL ON THE ROOF ABOVE ME IS A SMUDGED SKETCH OF the Leah I knew. She's lost a ton of weight—she was always quite curvy, but now her jeans hang loose on her hips—and her once-sandy hair is mousy with grease. There's an angry spattering of acne across her cheek, and her clothes look as if they haven't been washed in months. To her left is a young boy, the same kid I saw on the rooftop opposite our flat the day we arrived. On her right, her frail arms wrapped around one of the roof's turrets, is Leah's mother.

After four months of trying to make sense of it, the situation finally comes into focus. This is the reason they left so suddenly; this is the reason Leah hasn't been in touch since April. She and her mother were never in Stirling, staying at her aunt's house. They were with the Standing Fallen.

"Jaya!" Allie shouts. She's standing by the entrance to McEwan

Hall, staring at me with a bewildered look. "What are you doing? Hurry!"

For a few seconds, I'd forgotten all about them: Allie, Calum, Teacake in her tinfoil and blue leggings. The Edinburgh chapter leader starts to scream into his loudspeaker, the usual rant about sin and death and doom. Allie hurries over to me and gives a sharp tug on my sleeve; I stagger forward, head spinning. Before the roof disappears from my view, I take one last look back. Mrs. Maclennan's eyes are closed, but Leah stares straight ahead, barely flinching when a gust of wind sends her staggering to one side. She doesn't look scared. There's no expression on her face at all.

"Come on!" Calum is waiting by the side entrance to the building. "Quick, before the police get here."

He glances over each shoulder, then ushers us through a narrow passageway in the scaffolding, toward a door with a sturdy metal padlock and a NO ENTRY sign. His fingers tremble as he tries each of the keys in the lock.

"Shit, shit, shit," he keeps mumbling. "Dad's going to kill me."

Behind him, Teacake is still sobbing quietly. I reach for her hand and realize I'm shaking all over. The sirens are growing louder beyond the rooftops: their screams swell in my head, pushing out all thoughts but Leah. She's in the Standing Fallen, and she's *here*. She's in Edinburgh, and so am I. That doesn't feel like a coincidence.

Calum finally finds the right key. He pulls the padlock off and gently shoves Teacake through the door. We pile in after her—I almost trip over a toolbox that's been left on the floor—and slip under the network of scaffolding lining the back wall. The door clicks shut and Calum deflates, the tension seeping out of him.

"Nice one, Calzone," Allie says, patting his shoulder. "You can breathe now."

Perry tugs the lead out of my hand and goes racing into the hall. As we follow her into the space, Teacake's sobbing trails off. Her head falls back, and she stares around the room. She's seeing the absence of Shona's low ceiling and narrow walls. She's seeing the golden afternoon sun pouring in from the skylight, the domed roof above her and the wide space beneath it.

"What do you think, Tea?" Allie says softly. "Better, right?"

Outside, the sirens are getting louder. I can hear the Standing Fallen leader still ranting into his loudspeaker, but his voice is muffled to a murmur behind the thick walls of the hall. Anxiety is crawling all over my skin. I take a step toward the door, holding up my phone.

"I just need to make a call—"

As I turn to leave, Teacake beats her wings together, so quickly the gust sends Calum and me stumbling back into the wall. Before we can stop her, she bounds across the tiles, beats her wings, takes a huge leap up—

And stays up.

For a few seconds, all other worries slip right out of my mind. Teacake soars toward the organ, her back arching as she sweeps upward. Scraps of tinfoil fall to the floor, like winter leaves falling from their tree. She's a little shaky, but she's doing it. She's flying.

But when she beats her wings a third time, the right one refuses to move properly. She starts to quiver, and all three of us rush forward, holding our arms out to catch her. She beats them again and veers to the right at an awkward angle, wobbling toward one of the stone pillars. She swings her legs up and pushes off with her feet, but instead nose-dives into an unused scaffolding tower, leaving it rattling from top to bottom.

None of us moves. It's like playing Jenga—that slow moment when you don't know if the tower is going to fall. But the structure stays standing, and Teacake pushes herself to her feet. She staggers a little, then gives us a huge, lopsided grin.

"And at the end of that round, it's fourteen points to Team A," she quotes, "and sixteen points to Team B!"

The others burst into applause. I'm too overwhelmed with excitement, relief, and worry that someone outside has heard the commotion to join them. The chapter leader's shouting has stopped and the sirens have cut out, but Leah has crash-landed back into my head.

"Now for round two: Medieval History," Teacake says. Calum laughs and pulls another long strip of tinfoil from her wings.

"Maybe take a break first, Tea," he says. "You don't want to overdo it."

Allie gives a dry laugh. "Where have I heard that before?"

Unsurprisingly, Teacake doesn't listen. She takes a short run-up, makes a wobbly takeoff, and turns in jerky circles around the skylight. Calum takes the stairs to the first set of wooden seats to get a better view of her flight, and Allie holds out her hand to me.

"Coming?"

My stomach flips. Allie knows about Leah—I mentioned something about a sort-of ex-girlfriend while we were hanging out at Shona's one afternoon—but for some reason, I can't bring myself to tell her that Leah is *here*, outside, standing on the roof of the next building. Not until I know what's going on.

"I've got a missed call from my dad," I say. "Be two secs."

I sneak through the exit, making sure no one spots me, and run to the courtyard outside. The cult has vanished: the roof is empty, there are no broken bodies on the ground. I hurry across the square and toward the road, hoping to spot one of the vans. No sign of them, either. The only clue that anything unusual happened is the police officer taking a statement from a middle-aged couple in matching Roots Canada hoodies. I consider asking the police-woman what happened, then decide against it. Given that I've just done a bit of breaking and entering, drawing attention to myself probably isn't a good idea.

Instead, I try to call Leah. It goes straight to voice mail, just as it has the past thousand times I've phoned her. I try again, just to listen to her voice on the recording. Hearing it makes my eyes sting. With everything that's been going on, I'd forgotten how much I've missed her.

"Are you okay?" Allie asks when I come back inside. "You look a bit shell-shocked."

"I'm fine. Just glad we got Teacake here okay. That was a bit stressful." I force a smile. "Are *you* okay?"

It's only once I've asked that I see how ill she looks: her skin has a sickly yellow tinge to it, her eyes are bloodshot, and there are beads of sweat on her forehead. Another flush of guilt creeps over me. She should really be in bed, not trekking across Edinburgh on angel-hiding escapades.

"I'm fine," she says. "I probably just need some stronger meds. I've got an appointment at the hospital tomorrow, so I'll speak to my doctor about it then."

We lapse into silence, watching Teacake make short flights around the room. Her movements are shaky, like a bottle tossed on the waves, and she can't stay up for more than a few seconds. Still, it's kind of breathtaking to watch. Perry races after her, enchanted by the giant sparkly bird sweeping overhead.

"I have to admit, this place was a good call," Calum says, calmer now that he's realized their dad isn't going to burst in and catch us trespassing. "She seems so much happier here."

Looking around, I finally notice how incredible the building is. The front wall is decorated with colorful Italian-style frescoes bending into a wide arch below the roof, with a huge wooden organ taking center stage. The ceiling is a vast dome split into thin strips, each one decorated with a figure representing a different subject: a woman with a small lute for music, a man holding a scale for medicine. It's almost like a church, but instead of biblical figures, the characters on the walls represent research and knowledge.

"Our cousin did her exams in here last year," Allie says when I sit down beside her. "I don't know how she managed to concentrate. Beautiful, isn't it?"

She shuffles in her seat toward me. Her little finger is just a millimeter from mine. A few hours ago, I might have slid my hand into hers, if I'd been feeling bold enough. But now I can't concentrate on anything except the memory of Leah standing on the rooftop outside. It was just a few seconds, barely a glimpse of her—but that's all it takes for everything, once again, to change.

. . .

By five o'clock, Allie is starting to wilt: her cough sounds horribly painful, and she's so tired she needs help walking down the stairs. Nonetheless, she still manages to get things organized ("boss us around," as her brother puts it) before they head home. She gets Calum to set up a living area for Teacake with some pillows, blankets, biscuits, and a radio she's taken from home, while she splits our days into shifts: tomorrow morning she and I will keep working on Teacake's wing, then Calum will join her to look after Teacake in the afternoon.

"I think it'll be easier if we do it in twos, or on our own," she says. "We won't draw as much attention to ourselves that way."

I nod as she reads out the rest of the week's schedule, but I still can't focus. I try calling Leah again on the way home, though I know she won't pick up. There are a few small articles online about the Standing Fallen's appearance, but nobody seems to have noticed that there were members from other chapters there, too. The thought makes me nervous. It feels like they're planning something.

When I get home, I hear a half-familiar voice coming from the living room. It takes me a second to place it: Shona. *Shona?* She's not supposed to be back until tomorrow.

"My Buddha is still there, thank goodness, and my grand-mother's jewelry," she's saying. "All that's missing is food and some of my clothes. I don't see what anyone would want with those; they're hardly Golce and Dabbana."

She's sitting on the sofa, wearing a long purple dress and clutching a cup of tea. Her eyes are red from crying. Rani and Dad are nodding along, making sympathetic sounds, but their eyes keep being pulled away, hers to her phone and his to the laptop. I catch a glimpse of Dad's screen: footage of the Fall in South Africa the other day, metallic-brown feathers and dark gold blood.

Shona gives me a watery smile as I step into the room. "Hiya, hen. Sorry, I'm bringing awful negative energy into your living space here—I just got home and my flat's been burgled. Nothing of value, thankfully, but still, quite upsetting."

"Oh no." My insides feel like they've been tied into knots. "That's awful. I'm really sorry."

"It's just so odd." There's a pause as Shona blows her nose. "My mattress was on the living-room table, goodness knows why."

Dad scrolls down the page, pauses at a photo of a teary-eyed white man clutching a handful of matted red feathers. "Maybe just someone looking for a place to stay the night," he says absentmindedly. "That'd explain the food and clothes going missing."

Shona nods. "Aye, the police did say it could have been a couple of homeless people. You didn't see anything while you were watering my bonsai, did you, hen? Nobody dodgy hanging around?"

"No, no one," I say. "I went the other day. Everything looked fine then."

Rani looks at me, her eyebrows knit into a frown. Even Dad glances up. For a moment it looks like he's about to say something, but then the laptop makes a pinging sound and his head swivels back to the screen. Shona sighs and takes a long sip of tea.

"It must have happened today or yesterday, then." Her lipstick leaves a mulberry smudge on the rim of the cup. "You know, in a way it's a blessing I wasn't there. I might have socked the poor sods with one of my elephants and spent the rest of my life in jail."

She stays a while longer, mulling over possible explanations. My pulse is racing. If we hadn't moved Teacake a day early, Shona would have caught us right there, feeding her biscuits to a real-life Being. She may be a bit of a hippie, but I wouldn't trust her to keep Teacake safe. I wouldn't trust anyone with Teacake, except Allie and Calum.

As she gets up to leave, Shona squeezes my arm.

"Those gemstones are working wonders on you, hen. Your aura's much lighter now, a lovely bright orange."

The amethyst and quartz are still lying under my bunk bed, untouched since she brought them to me two weeks ago.

"Oh yeah, thanks. They helped a lot," I say. "I'll bring them down to you tomorrow. And I'll help you tidy up then, too."

I don't know what makes me say that. Guilt, probably. It's not like we left her flat in a state on purpose, though: I had every intention of popping in tomorrow to tidy up the mess before going back to McEwan Hall.

"I'll come, too," Rani says. "It'll be faster with three of us."

I stare at her. She smiles sweetly at me as Shona tells Dad what nice, thoughtful daughters he has, then goes back to browsing Wingpin on her phone. My heart is still thumping after Shona leaves. That was way too close.

And judging by the look on Rani's face, we're not out of danger yet.

NINETEEN

WE LEFT MORE OF A MESS IN OUR WAKE THAN I'D REALIZED.
There are biscuit crumbs and dried tea bags on the kitchen counters,
streaks of makeup around the edge of the coffee table. Even the
ornaments and picture frames that Teacake knocked over are still
lying on the carpet. I really don't know why we didn't pick them
up. I guess tidying just doesn't seem that important when you're
hanging out with a living Being.

"Whoever these folk were, they were obviously raised in a barn,"
Shona tuts. "Would you look at the state of my settee!"

I nod in agreement and scrub at a Coke stain on the carpet. I
keep expecting Shona to spin around, yell, "*J'accuse!*" and thrust
her finger toward me like a lawyer in a cheesy American drama. It
doesn't happen. It genuinely doesn't seem to have occurred to her
that the *stranger* who had her *spare key* is so obviously the guilty
party here. She might be able to see auras, but she can't see that.

Rani does, though. Rani sees everything.

I've felt her gaze following me around Shona's flat since we arrived. I wish she would just come out and ask me something so I could deny it; I'm a shit liar, but I'm even worse at pretending nothing's up. My guilt is in every movement, every mumbled response.

"They could have at least put their rubbish in the bin," Rani says, fishing one of Allie's Kit Kat wrappers from underneath the table. "It's so rude."

"You're no' wrong, hen. Not like you two, eh? So nice of you both, helping me oot like this." Shona puts her hands on her hips and surveys the room. "Well, I think that's us just about done. Take the cushion covers off, will you, Jaya? I'll pop them in the wash."

I pull them off and spot a hint of pink on orange—one of Teacake's feathers, lodged down the back of the sofa. My heart leaps, but luckily Rani's busy rubbing a foundation stain off the coffee table and doesn't notice me shove it in my pocket.

This was all far, far too close.

It's ten o'clock by the time we're done tidying up. According to Allie's schedule, I'm supposed to be at McEwan Hall for our turn looking after Teacake now. We say good-bye to Shona, politely declining her thank-you gift of some yerba mate soap, and head outside. I send Allie a quick text to say I'll be late, then tell Rani I'm going out to meet some friends, trying (and probably failing) to keep my voice light.

"I'll be back in a few hours," I say. "We can go to the dungeons or something after, if you like."

This time, she doesn't beg to come with me. She just smiles and skips up the stairs, like she's totally lost interest in whatever we're up to. "Okay. See you later."

I wait until I hear the door close, then hurry downstairs and slip into the crowd. For once, I'm grateful for the mob outside; if Rani does try to follow me, it'll be easy to lose her in the swarm of tourists and Wingdings. Just to be on the safe side, I take a detour via South Bridge and pop into a supermarket to stock up on snacks. I scan the streets before I cross the road toward the university, but I don't see Rani. Maybe she actually *has* lost interest—maybe she figured I was just using Shona's flat as a hangout, or maybe the Fall in South Africa or Dad's plans were more important to her than whatever I'm up to.

It's twenty past by the time I get to McEwan Hall, but Allie hasn't arrived yet. Calum gave me the key to look after last night, so I undo the padlock and slip into the hall. Teacake is perching on top of the organ, posed like a cat about to leap on a mouse. She smiles, her wings twitching in greeting, then leans toward the edge. My stomach lurches.

"Teacake, no!"

My eyes squeeze shut. In my mind, I hear a branch snapping, a faint "oh" of surprise. I see rushing water and a hand grasping at thin air. I feel my breath catch in my throat, my head start to spin.

But this time, the crash doesn't come. When I look up, Teacake is gliding smoothly through the air, her legs locked and her arms spread wide as her wings. For a few moments, she is a ship riding a wave, a bird in a sea breeze: all peace and grace, exactly where she's supposed to be.

I sink into a wooden chair beneath the organ. My legs are shaking, and it takes a few seconds for my pulse to stop racing. I don't think I'll ever get used to seeing something like that.

"Looking good, Tea," I call in a shaky voice. She comes hurtling back to the floor after just a few seconds, but at least she doesn't crash-land into the scaffolding this time. I clap, laughing at the way she beams at me. She takes off again, giving a word-perfect recital of a poem by Emily Dickinson as she flies, arching so high the edge of her right wing brushes the ceiling. It looks much better than when she first fell: stronger and straighter, even if there is still a large gap where Allie hasn't attached the rest of the feathers yet.

My phone buzzes. *Leah*, I think. I pull it out of my pocket, but it's from Allie, telling me she's feeling too ill to make it over. The disappointment stings. Except I can't work out if I'm disappointed because she's not here or because Leah still hasn't been in touch.

Though I still feel dizzy with confusion when I think about seeing Leah on the roof yesterday, things have started coming back to me, too. There was the time Marek was making fun of the Standing Fallen and Leah snapped at him to shut up, that "at least they believe in something." Another time, when we were having a debate about where the Beings came from, she walked out without an explanation, standing up so fast she knocked her chair to the ground.

There were clues. I can't tell whether I didn't see them or if I chose not to.

Part of me is itching to call Emma and tell her about what I saw yesterday, but I hold back. Emma's got a huge mouth, and Leah might come back to her normal life one day. If she does, she probably won't want half of Scotland knowing about the months she spent living with a cult.

Another secret I'm keeping for her.

After a few more flights, Teacake makes a wobbly landing on the wooden barrier in front of me. "We have Thomas from Auchtermuchty on the line; tell us, what are your thoughts on wind farms?"

"Nice work!" I beam at her. "You'll be home in no time."

My heart pangs at the thought. It's all we've been working for—getting her well enough to leave—but watching her go . . . that's going to hurt. She leans against the stone pillar, and we open a packet of tea cakes. She eats them the same way Allie does: biting off the chocolate shell, then licking out the marshmallow inside.

"Listen," I say, wiping the chocolate from my mouth, "I wanted to talk to you about yesterday. About what you saw on the TV screen."

She replies with a quote about disability benefits. I try to spell it out in shapes as I talk: a rectangle as the TV screen, my falling hands for the Beings we watched tumbling to earth, fingers drawing tears on my cheeks. Teacake's expression doesn't change, but she comes toward me, leaping up and balancing on the back of a chair.

"It's not your fault. I don't know what happened. I don't know why they fell or why you did," I say. "And maybe you feel guilty that you survived and they didn't . . . but listen, they wouldn't have felt anything. It was over before it could hurt."

I swallow and realize that there's a lump in my throat. My eyes start to prickle.

"You have to know that," I say. "You couldn't have done any-thing. So don't feel guilty, okay? Don't blame yourself."

The wings twitch. Teacake takes one of my hands in hers; it feels like sand brushing over my skin. She opens her mouth and starts to speak: an advert for the Bank of Scotland and the chorus of "Call Me Maybe."

I laugh. I laugh until tears roll down my cheeks. Teacake joins in, a weirdly musical noise that sounds a bit like water pouring out of a bottle. There are a billion songs that she could have quoted from, that I could have read something into—"Nothing Compares to You," maybe, or "Bohemian Rhapsody"—but not "Call Me fricking Maybe." It doesn't matter, though. Like everything she does, it's kind of perfect in its own weird way.

We're both still laughing when the door opens. I look around, still grinning, expecting to see Allie or Calum walking toward us. Instead, a blast of shock makes my head spin.

"Rani?"

My sister is standing in the doorway, staring right at Teacake. I swear under my breath: in all my panic about her following me, I must have left the door unlocked. Teacake yelps and falls off the chair and over the wooden barrier; with a beat of her wings, she freezes in the air, just a meter above the floor. My sister's jaw drops. In an instant, my shock turns to anger.

"What are you doing here?" My footsteps echo as I storm across the hall. Rani shrinks back, her hands pressed against the door. "How did you find us?"

"I took your phone—you were in the bathroom, I saw your messages . . ." She trails off. Her eyes are fixed on Teacake, who's scrambling to her feet, a half-eaten Tunnock's Tea Cake in one hand. "That's a Being. That's a *Being*, Jaya."

My throat is tight. "I know, genius."

This is it. This is the end. She's going to tell Dad. He'll march right over here, snatch Teacake from us, and sell her to the highest bidder. She'll be paraded around the country like a circus freak, or experimented on in some awful lab. She'll never be free again, not even to hang out with us, eating biscuits and listening to the radio. She'll never get to fly.

"Ran, you *can't* tell him," I blurt out. "You have to keep this a secret, okay?"

But Rani looks like she's actually frozen, her eyes buglike behind her glasses. Teacake's wings finally give out and she lands on the tiles with a bump.

"What's she doing here?" Rani's stammers. "Where did—Jaya, how is this—"

I'm scared she might pass out from the shock, like she did when the policewoman told her what had happened to Mum. My anger evaporates. I take her hand and lead her into a seat, then make her eat a biscuit and drink some water. Teacake comes to join us. Her head swerves from Rani to me and back again, as if connecting the dark brown eyes we got from Mum, the long noses we got from Dad.

"This is my sister," I tell Teacake. "Rani."

Her fingers shaking, Rani holds up one hand in a wave. Teacake blinks at it for a second, then slaps her own hand against it. I burst out laughing; she's finally figured out how to high-five. Rani's mouth opens and closes, opens and closes, but it's a full minute before she can speak again.

"Where did you find her?"

I tell her everything. I don't hold anything back. I don't think I could—I didn't realize how much this secret had been weighing on me. The story bursts past the dam and comes pouring out, details and plot points getting all tangled up in the rush. For once, Rani doesn't interrupt. She listens to the whole unbelievable tale, her eyes growing wider by the minute, until I reach the point where we are now: hiding in McEwan Hall, with no real idea as to where we'll take Teacake next.

Rani bites her lip. "We have to tell Dad," she says.

I knew she'd say that. But instead of making me mad, it just hurts. I wish she'd take my side for once. It was different when Mum was still here. If she and Dad wouldn't let Rani do something, I'd always back Rani up. When our parents were arguing, she'd come to my room and we'd make a duvet fort and watch stupid YouTube videos to take our minds off it. Us against them. We were a united front.

"This isn't about Dad," I tell her now. "We have to do what's best for Teacake, and that's helping her get home. You should have seen her when she fell—her wing was a total mess, she couldn't stay in the air for more than a few seconds. Allie hasn't even finished fixing it, and she's already so much better."

As if to demonstrate this, Teacake springs off the barrier. She floats toward the skylight, spins through the dusty shafts of light, then swoops past us. The edge of her left wing brushes Rani's cheek. My sister gasps and lets out a nervous giggle.

She hasn't given up yet, though. "But Dad could help," she says. "He knows more about the Beings than anybody, probably."

"*No*, Rani!" I run my hands through my hair, tugging at the roots. "Sorry, but it's not your secret to tell. Or mine, even."

She argues, of course—Rani can never take no for an answer. Even when she realizes that I'm not going to give in this time, she doesn't let it go. She's like Dad that way.

"How about this?" she says. "If she can fly back before the end of the summer holidays, we won't tell Dad. But if she can't, or if anything goes wrong, we'll ask him for help."

Crap. I hadn't even thought about what we'll do when we have to go back to school. I don't even know if Dad's planning on taking us home—I suppose he is, seeing as he thinks his Being will have landed and made him his fortune by then. Either way, we'll need to think of a more long-term solution for when the summer ends.

"Fine," I say, just to get Rani to shut up. "If it comes to that, we'll tell Dad. But not until I say so, okay?"

Reluctantly, she shakes on it. I spend the rest of the morning filling her in on the little we've learned about Teacake, trading thoughts on where she might have come from. It actually feels good to share all this with her. Now that one part of my secret has been removed, I can breathe a little easier.

By the time two o'clock comes around, Rani's nerves around Teacake have worn off. Calum comes in for his shift to find her skidding left and right across the stone floor, giggling and trying to follow Teacake's bursts of flight around the room. His eyebrows rise when he sees her, but he doesn't react with the anger I'd expected.

"What's going on?" he asks, his voice gruff. "Who's this?"

I start to explain who Rani is, and that she's not about to run off and tell our dad, but Calum barely seems to listen. He looks exhausted: almost as pale as his sister, with bags under his eyes and mussed-up hair.

"How's Allie doing?" I ask him as he flops into an empty seat. He pulls *A Dance with Dragons* out of his backpack and shrugs.

"You saw her yesterday," he says. "How do you think she is?"

His tone is so sharp, I actually flinch. He kicks his legs up on the seat in front of him and opens his book. After a few seconds, he sighs and lets it drop to his lap.

"Sorry. She's okay. I think it just caught up with her. All the running around, all the stress." His eyes drift across the room, where Rani is now deep in a one-way conversation with Teacake. "In a way it's good your sister's here. Allie'll probably be out of action for a few days."

He goes back to his book, sinking low in the seat so half his face is hidden behind the cover. When Rani and I leave an hour later, he barely glances up. But he also hasn't turned the page.

TWENTY

MRS. SCOTT DOESN'T LOOK LIKE EITHER OF HER CHILDREN. Her hair is ash blond, streaked with gray, and her cheeks are plump and ruddy. When she smiles, though, she reminds me of Calum: a slight, forced smile that doesn't quite fit with her cheery coloring. I wonder what Allie's told her about me. Maybe her mother blames me for all her recent disappearances. It's starting to seem like her brother does.

"Alison's really not well. I'm not sure if she's up for visitors," Mrs. Scott says when I ask if I can come in. "Wait here. I'll see if she's awake."

She turns and goes upstairs, leaving the front door open. I creep up to the top step and take a peek inside. There's a heap of trainers by the door, and jackets piled over the banister. I can hear the TV playing somewhere in the house—an advert for car insurance— and the washing machine churning in the kitchen.

I feel a sudden pang of homesickness. It's all so *normal*. Our house hasn't looked normal since before the Beings fell. After that, it was all dirty dishes and microwave meals, sliding over Dad's notes or tripping on stacks of books on our way out the door.

On the wall by the stairs, family photos hang in wooden frames: holidays and birthdays and trips to the beach. In a few of them, Allie's wearing her oxygen tube. In another, taken when she was eight or nine, she's in a hospital bed with a plastic mask over her face. Calum's sitting cross-legged at the foot of the mattress, and they're playing Uno. Allie's arms are thrown into the air; Calum's slapping his forehead and groaning in defeat.

The choice of pictures strikes me as a bit strange at first. Allie looks so weak in some of them; her parents are bag-eyed and pale, their smiles lukewarm and tired. It's quite a contrast to the posed professional photos that hung on the walls of Leah's house, or even the Polaroids of me and Rani that Mum, a fan of anything retro, stuck on the fridge.

But in a way, I like it. They haven't tried to gloss over what's obviously a huge part of their lives. They're not pretending to be some perfect catalog family, or that life's all sun and roses. Despite the frosty reception, it makes me think a little more highly of Mrs. Scott.

"Ugh, don't look at those." Skinny legs in Aztec-pattern pajamas appear at the top of the stairs. "Don't want you seeing evidence of my awkward preteen years."

Allie leans over the banister, grinning. My smile wavers: she looks exhausted. She's wheezing slightly, and she looks thinner and paler than usual.

"Hey," I say. "Sorry for turning up like this—"

"Don't apologize! Seriously, I've been dying of boredom." She tilts her head toward the landing. "You want to come up to my room?"

I slip my shoes off and hurry up the stairs so she doesn't have to walk any farther. Mrs. Scott lingers on the landing, her hands curled over the banister.

"Not too long, okay, Allie? You're supposed to be taking it easy."

"What, are you imposing visiting hours now?" Allie rolls her eyes. "Relax, Mother. I think I can handle talking for an hour or so."

She points me toward a door at the end of the corridor. Her bedroom is a bit like her: little and noisy and really, really busy. There's a guitar in the corner, a violin and a clarinet gathering dust on a shelf. There are watercolors and pencils scattered over her desk, ice skates lined up with her shoes, a third-place trophy from a tap-dancing competition sitting on the windowsill. There's even a fishing rod propped up against the wardrobe.

"Wow," I say. "It's like the National Museum of Hobbies in here."

Allie laughs. "I know. I should charge a fiver for entry."

She climbs onto her bed, sinking back into a pile of pillows. I can't stop gazing around me, at the tennis rackets and kites and games consoles . . . a lifetime of pastimes. I pick up a wooden artist's model off her desk and stretch his arms out like wings.

"How do you find the time to do all this stuff?"

"I don't anymore. Most of my hobbies only lasted a few weeks. I was just trying to find my 'thing.'" Allie picks a turquoise ukulele off the shelf above her bed. "Like Calum with his photography. Something I had a real knack for. Something to make me exceptional."

She strums a few chords. They don't sound bad, but she stumbles a bit as her fingers move across the strings. "I never found it, though. A lot of it was really fun, but I didn't have a real gift for anything."

"You still could find something," I say, sitting on the edge of her bed. Her duvet is dark green with hundreds of tiny white roses. "There must be a few instruments you haven't tried. Musical saw, maybe?"

Allie grins. "Nah, I'm all right. I've had enough music lessons to last me a lifetime." She coughs a couple of times, then wipes her mouth with a tissue. "Anyway, how's Teacake getting on?"

I take my phone out and show her the video that Rani and I took this morning. On the screen, Teacake takes a run-up across the hall's floor, curving in a slight arch the way high jumpers do before they're about to make their leap. Her wings beat, the tips meeting before they sweep back to the floor, and she floats toward the ceiling. She makes three wide, neat loops before she has to land on top of the organ.

"That's amazing!" Allie says. "Twelve seconds—that's so much better!"

"All thanks to you," I say. "You're the one who fixed her wing."

We smile at each other. There's the tiniest hint of pink on her cheeks. But then, on the video, Rani starts to cheer. Allie's smile vanishes.

"Whose voice is that?"

"Um . . ." Shit. I assumed Calum had already told her about Rani following me to McEwan Hall. Allie's eyes widen as I tell her the story—repeating, before she starts to panic, that Rani has promised to keep our secret and won't tell my dad. Allie presses her lips together.

"Well, I guess we've got no choice but to trust her." She doesn't look convinced, but I can tell she doesn't have the energy to argue, either. "Maybe she's got some Wingdinger insider info that could help us out."

There's still that edge of disdain to her voice. It irks me a bit, her judging my sister without ever having met her, but I can't really blame her for being suspicious.

"Yeah, she knows her stuff. She might be able to help us communicate with Teacake," I say. "Calum and I weren't having much luck."

"That's his fault. He's so demanding," Allie says. "It's weird—he can stay still for minutes on end, trying to get a good shot of a bird taking off or waiting for the sun to leak through the leaves at just the right angle, but he's got no patience with people."

I remember the way he snapped at me yesterday. "Is everything okay with him? He seems a wee bit off lately."

Allie flaps her hand dismissively. "Calum's always tormented about something or other. Don't worry about it."

Her eyes wander to a print on her wall: a large black-and-white photo of her and her parents walking on the beach. Allie's pushing a lock of hair out of her face and saying something to her dad, who has his arm slung around her shoulder. He's looking over the top of her head toward her mum, both of them smiling. Behind them, a wave is crashing onto the sand, sending its white spray toward the gray sky; two seagulls are battling against the wind, each one buffeted in a different direction; but the three of them walk on, oblivious.

Allie's gaze softens. "I know it must be hard for him. It's not easy, having a sibling who's sick," she says. "I just wish he wouldn't let it consume him so much."

I've tried to imagine how I'd feel if it was Rani in the photos downstairs. The idea makes me feel nauseous.

"Allie . . ." From the way she looks at me, I know she can tell what I'm about to ask. "How bad is it?"

There's a pause, and then Allie pats the duvet. I scoot toward her, copying her cross-legged position so our knees are almost touching. My stomach fills with butterflies.

"Remember I told you I had a double lung transplant?" she says. "Well, now they think I might have something called BOS, bronchiolitis obliterans syndrome. If I do, it means my body's rejecting the new lungs."

The bed seems to tilt underneath me. "*What?* How can it do that?"

"Oh, rejection is really common," she says. "Everyone experiences it to some degree. I was responding pretty well to the drugs at first, but now they don't seem to be working as well as the doctors had hoped. BOS is hard to diagnose, though. They've upped my antirejection meds, so there's a chance I might start to improve with that. But there's also a chance that I won't."

I swallow. "And what if you don't?"

No answer. Downstairs, the news begins playing on the TV, and

163

Mrs. Scott starts up the vacuum cleaner. Allie flops onto her back, her hair falling in chocolate swirls across her pillow.

"You know, when I was diagnosed, my life expectancy was seven years old." She counts the ages on her fingers. "Then it was eleven, then fourteen, and now . . . who knows? My whole life has been in the conditional tense, Jaya. I've learned to live with it."

"What if you don't improve?" I ask again, because *I* haven't—I haven't learned how to live with that.

Allie tilts her head to look at me. Her lips are so pale. A bit like the color of some of Teacake's feathers, but without the sheen.

"If I don't get better, then maybe I'll have a few years," she says. "Maybe one. Maybe five. Maybe less than that. Or maybe they'll find a cure tomorrow and I'll live until I'm a hundred! I just don't know. But neither does anyone else."

She's right. Things happen. Cars crash, buildings collapse, terrorists blow themselves up in airports or on street corners. Healthy people die all the time. I, of all people, know that—I've seen it happen. But it's different when those threats have a label and a definition and a time limit. It's different when the person is only seventeen.

My head is spinning. I feel like I might throw up, but I can't get any words out. I don't know what to say. There is nothing to say. Allie coughs, wipes one tissue on her mouth and another over her forehead. She squashes them between her fingers, forming a crumpled white rose just above the one tattooed on her wrist.

"Why a rose?" I ask, when I can speak again.

She smiles. "Say 'cystic fibrosis.' "

It takes a couple of tries before it clicks. "Sixty-five roses?"

"Exactly. I know, it's a bit corny. I usually really hate soppy tattoos. Like those couples who get a key and a padlock, or two jigsaw pieces—so cheesy."

She props herself up on one elbow, so she's looking down at me, and rests the back of her hand on my hip. The petals look darker in this dim light: smoky blue.

"But I have to admit, I do kind of like what this represents," she says. "Roses aren't any less beautiful because they don't live long. No one looks at them and thinks, man, what a tragedy they'll only be around for a little while. You just appreciate them while they're there. Or if you don't, you're missing the point."

I trace the outline of the rose on her wrist, feeling the soft bump of the tendons beneath the skin. "I like that," I say.

A nervous smile flits across her face. "I thought all sixty-five would be pushing it. Transplant patients have to be really careful getting tattoos, and the artist obviously knew I wasn't eighteen. It was hard enough to get him to agree to do even one, but I dragged the oxygen in and coughed a lot. He probably thought it was my dying wish." She cackles.

I try to smile, but my lips won't move. "How can you laugh about it?"

"What do you expect me to do? Sit around moping?" she says. "I was so lucky to get my lungs—a lot of the time, people die before they find a match. I've been lucky to get those years. I think about my donor all the time. Every day."

She presses her index fingers to the corners of my lips and pushes them into a smile. I brush her hand away, blinking away the prickling in my eyes.

"Don't get me wrong, Jay. There are days when it feels so unfair

I can hardly breathe." She slides her hand into mine. Her fingers are clammy, but warm. "But it's going to happen one way or another. It just makes me more determined to make the most of the time I do have."

For a while we're silent, listening to the muffled sounds of the TV downstairs, the odd hum of a car turning onto her quiet street. I think about Mum. She was only thirty-seven when she died. That's longer than a lot of people get, but it wasn't enough. Nothing can convince me that it was enough.

"Calum's right. You shouldn't push yourself so hard," I tell Allie. "Don't make it worse than it has to be."

"I know, I know. It's just hard. I don't want to miss out on a minute of Teacake." Her free hand sweeps across the room, over all the instruments and art supplies and sports equipment. "All this . . . it was fun, but since the transplant, I don't really care about being good at something. I'd rather just *be* good. Do good."

I remember the first time I saw her and Calum, outside the restaurant with her leaflets and the homemade placard. I think back to all the hours she spent in Shona's flat, painstakingly sewing feathers onto Teacake's wings. I remember her telling us to talk *to* Teacake, not about her, and her list of the Beings' names.

Allie is exceptional. So exceptional. I want to tell her that. I just don't know how to say it.

But maybe I don't need to, because now she's tilting her head toward mine. She's looking at my lips, the way that only Leah and a handful of boys at parties have before, and part of me is thinking this shouldn't be happening, not right now, when she's not well, but a larger part of me doesn't think it matters, and now I'm leaning ever so slightly closer, and I can feel my heartbeat in my throat, and then—

And then my phone starts to ring.

"Shit. Sorry." My cheeks burn. I grab my phone from my pocket. "That'll be my dad."

I go to turn it off, but then I see the caller ID and pause. It's an unknown number, an Edinburgh one. I don't know anyone who'd be calling me from a landline. Unless—

"I have to take this."

I hurry out of her room and into the corridor, leaving Allie blinking behind me. My fingers tremble as I slide the green button across the screen.

"Hello? Hello?"

There's a long pause. There's static on the line, and behind it car horns, a pedestrian-crossing beeping. It's someone calling from a phone box.

"Hello?" I'm clutching the phone so tightly, my fingers start to cramp. Then I hear her voice, and everything inside me somersaults.

"Jaya." Another pause. I can hear her breathing, quick and shallow. "It's me. It's Leah."

TWENTY-ONE

CALTON HILL IS HEAVING WITH PEOPLE. THE FRINGE HAS spread, like a sea creature stretching its tentacles, out of the Old Town and toward the monuments overlooking the city: there are dancers in orange leotards leaping over the grass, a choir singing "Oh Happy Day," an actor performing a one-man *Hamlet* to a crowd of silver-haired tourists. As I hurry up the steps, I realize that's why Leah told me to meet her here. Among the tour groups and performers, the laughter and camera flashes, she can hide.

She's sitting at the foot of the National Monument, a towering line of Greek-style stone columns. A group of foreign exchange students buzzes around her, almost shielding her from view, but she stands up as she sees me coming. It's like watching someone you know acting in a play: it's undeniably Leah, but not the way I knew her. Her shoulders are hunched, and she tugs anxiously at the hem of her hoodie. As I move closer, I can see how ill she looks. Her cheeks curve inward, and there are scabs around the corners of her mouth.

Still. She's here.

We meet in the middle of the path. For a moment, we just stare: me at Leah, Leah at the ground.

"You came," I say, stupidly, as if I'm the one who called her here.

Her eyes dart from my shoulder to the blue sky above us to a man walking his dog. Anywhere but my face. My arms twitch forward, but I hold back from hugging her. I may not know exactly what the Standing Fallen believe in, but I'm pretty sure they wouldn't approve of our sort of relationship. Leah had enough trouble accepting it before she left; I doubt four months in a religious cult has helped.

Then a thought hits me: maybe that's why she's here. Maybe that's what this is about. Maybe she's trying to save me.

"If you're here to convert me, you're wasting your time," I say. "I'm not interested in all that redemption crap."

She flinches; I blink. Both of us are taken aback by the venom in my voice. For months I've been rehearsing what I'd say to Leah if I ever saw her again. That wasn't it.

"No, of course not." Her teeth are a sickly yellow. Leah, the girl who'd get her toothbrush out in the toilets at lunchtime. "That's not why I'm here."

"Why, then? How did you even know I was in Edinburgh?"

She looks up, toward a couple posing for a selfie. "I saw some photos you posted on Instagram. One of you and Perry, about a week ago."

"And you couldn't have sent me a message?" I try to stop myself from shouting, but anger is pulsing through me: anger at her leaving, anger at being left. "I've called you about a thousand times, I sent you all those emails. I went to your house—"

"Jaya, *please.*" Leah cringes and shakes her head, tresses of greasy hair falling across her face. "Seeing you . . . it's the only thing that's kept me going."

I take a step closer. She cowers back, shrinking into herself. "Tell me, then," I say. "Tell me how this happened."

For a moment, I think she's going to cry—her lip wobbles and she tilts her head back, blinking rapidly—but she takes a breath and carries on in a shaky voice. "I don't think I can. I don't even know how it happened."

The foreign exchange students begin to pour past us, matching red backpacks bumping against our arms. We move away from them and find a free bench overlooking the Old Town. Leah's hands are shaking; she presses them between her knees to hold them still. For a few minutes, she doesn't say anything. She keeps glancing over her shoulder, scanning the hillside for some invisible threat.

"Remember the first time the Standing Fallen were on the news?" she says at last. "We were coming out of school, and Sam showed us the video?"

I'd forgotten all about that, but the moment comes back to me: Sam pushing through a crowd of first years, muffled audio leaking out of his phone. On the screen, six or seven people were standing on top of a building somewhere in the United States. Most of their speech was drowned out by sirens and chatter, but you could make out a few words: "destiny," "mankind," "dragons" . . . Leah made a joke about it, saying the guy must have picked up *Game of Thrones* instead of his Bible.

"Mum wasn't well. She'd had a few bad episodes in the past, but nothing like this. The Falls . . . they messed with her head," Leah says. "When I got home that day, she was watching the video on repeat. Dad said something about them being a bunch of nutters and told her to turn it off. She did as he said, but I noticed her watching it again the next morning. She seemed . . . enthralled by it.

"Remember how fast it spread? Videos starting popping up from Tokyo, Moscow, Paris . . . then suddenly the London chapter was on the news, and then Manchester and Edinburgh and Glasgow. She was careful not to let Dad find out, but I kept catching her watching them, or looking at their website or forums. I think she liked that they were taking the Falls seriously, as a message from God. Most people had started shrugging them off or ignoring them, like my dad. She thought the Standing Fallen could give her answers, or a purpose. Whatever she was lacking."

I think of Dad, lost in his labyrinth of notes and hopes and theories. For once, I feel grateful that his obsession wasn't something darker.

"Then one night, I woke up to hear Dad shouting," Leah says. "Mum was packing her stuff. She'd decided we were all going to sign up, all three of us. Dad wasn't having any of it, obviously, but I told Mum that if she waited until the end of the week, I'd go with her. I managed to get her to agree to that, to give us more time to sort things out.

"I was hoping she'd calm down after a few days, realize what a mistake she was making. It might have worked, but a few days later Dad tried to talk her into going to a hospital to get some help. Mum panicked and ran out of the house—I didn't want to let her go on her own, so I got in the car with her. I didn't even take a change of clothes."

A man dressed as a hobbit wanders past, talking loudly on his phone. Leah and I fall silent, watching the traffic crawl through the city below. It's strange how much Leah's voice has changed. It still has the same high pitch, the same light Highlands accent, but all the confidence that made it hers has gone.

"So you joined the Edinburgh chapter?" I ask once the hobbit has left.

Leah shakes her head. "Glasgow."

My stomach flips as I remember the video of the Glasgow display I saw on the BBC website a few weeks ago, the same night Teacake fell. If my phone hadn't cut out, I might have spotted Leah on the roof with the rest of them.

"What was it like?" I ask.

"It was . . . tough. Boring, too. We were staying in an old farm-house outside the city, thirteen of us sharing a room. The food is really basic, just soup and bread. We only get to wash once a week. They don't let us have any entertainment, no laptops or phones—I had to steal one every time I wanted to check up on you or my dad. Regretted it when I got caught, mind."

I wait for her to elaborate. Instead, she pushes the sleeves of her hoodie up. I let out a gasp. Her fingers are red and calloused, the edges of the nails black with dirt, and there are bruises all over her arms: some fresh purple, others yellow with tinges of pink.

The anger feels like hot coals at the back of my throat. I want names, I want to call the police, I want to storm over to the cult's base and kick the crap out of whoever did this—but I can tell from the way Leah's anxiously tugging her sleeves over her fingers that she's already regretting showing me. Instead, I close my eyes and take a breath.

"What are you doing in Edinburgh?" I ask, trying to clean those purplish stains from my memory.

"We're staying at the base here. There are rumors—"

Leah breaks off as a couple of women, one in a cream head scarf, another in green, walk past to take photos of the skyline. She waits until they've gone before answering.

"There are rumors that a Being fell here, but that it was caught before word got out," she says, lowering her voice to a whisper. "Damien, the leader of the Edinburgh chapter, wanted extra members to help out with the search. I persuaded my mum to volunteer us a couple of weeks ago."

My blood runs cold. "Have you found anything?"

She shakes her head. "Not that I've heard. Apparently the leaders are talking to some people online, people who say they found some feathers. Has your dad heard anything?"

"No, nothing." I take a deep breath, hoping she can't hear the tremor in my voice. "Nothing at all."

Somewhere in the Old Town, a clock strikes six. Leah gets up sharply and, though it's not raining, pulls her hood over her hair.

"I should go. If they find out I was talking to you, they'll . . . they won't be happy."

"You're not serious," I say, following her across the grass. "Why did you even bother phoning me if you're just going to go back?"

Her eyes dart around the hillside for a moment, but finally she looks at me. Her eyes haven't changed—the same pale blue I remember—and yet they're completely different, too. They seem duller now. Lacking.

"Because I needed to see you," she says. "I've had a lot of time to think, since we left, and . . . I was awful to you. You were going through so much, with your mum's accident, and then your dad . . . and I was just worried about people finding out about us, what they might think if they did. I should at least have told you where I was going. I should have said good-bye."

There have been times over the past four months when I've wondered if I've been overreacting about Leah's leaving; that whatever we had clearly didn't matter that much to her, if she could leave so suddenly; that my mind might have warped a few meaningless encounters into something resembling a relationship. When Leah finally says those words, I know that's not the case. It was real.

It only lasts a moment, and then she's running across the grass. I chase after her and catch her sleeve.

"Leah, come on! You can't go back there—look at yourself, look at what they've done to you!"

She pulls away from my grip. "It's not that easy. I can't just walk out."

"Why not? You don't owe them anything." I follow her down the steps, weaving through the group of tourists ambling upward. "Look, let's go to the police. They'll help you; you'll be safe—"

"I can't!" She spins around to face me, eyes wild. "What do you want me to do? I can't just leave my mum, Jaya."

The words are like a punch to the stomach, so hard it brings tears to my eyes. I know it's not about me, not some judgment on the fact that I couldn't save my own mother, but that's how it feels. It feels like she's telling me that I didn't do enough. Leah sighs and swears under her breath.

"I didn't mean it like . . . Jaya, that's not what I was saying."

When I blink, fast, hot tears roll down my cheeks. As I reach up to wipe them away, Leah throws her arms out and hugs me. My eyes close for a moment. Just a second. And for a tiny moment, though her hair doesn't smell like coconut anymore, and I can feel bones I never could before, it's just like it used to be.

"I'm sorry," she says. "About everything. I really, really am. But I didn't come here for you to save me."

I look up just in time to catch a flash of dark blond hair disappearing into a group of Wingdings. I run after her, shoving through the tourists dawdling at the foot of the steps. But I'm too slow, and by the time I reach the road, she's slipped away from me all over again.

TWENTY-TWO

IT TOOK FOUR MONTHS, TWO NEW FRIENDS, AND A BEING TO finally empty Leah from my head, and one twenty-minute conversation to fill it up with her again. That night I sleep only in fits and starts, each one interrupted by flashes from our meeting on Calton Hill. The way she flinched when I came toward her; the dull look in her eye when she described how they'd treated her. I don't understand how they broke her so quickly. It doesn't fit with the girl I knew.

She's still in my head as we eat breakfast the next morning. I nod through a conversation with Dad, my cereal tasting bland in my mouth, as he says something about going to Glasgow to meet his Wingding friends; they have a few last-minute touches to make to their plans. He kisses the top of my head, grateful that I'm not making a fuss this time about having to keep an eye on Rani.

"Not long to go, pet," he says as he shrugs his jacket on. "After tomorrow, things can start getting back to normal. I promise."

Tomorrow. He thinks the Being is going to fall tomorrow. I feel a faint stab of dread that the day has arrived so soon, but it's dulled by thoughts of Leah.

As soon as the door shuts behind him, I turn to Rani. "Let's go and see Teacake."

It's not even eight o'clock: Calum is supposed to arrive at ten, and then we'll take the afternoon shift, but I need something to take my mind off Leah. If I stay here I'll just keep staring at my phone all morning, hoping for—and dreading—another call.

Before we leave, Rani goes through Dad's books. She squashes a dozen or so into her backpack, all hardbacks with titles like *Rembrandt's Angels* or *Celestial Creatures in Islamic Art*.

"I've got a plan," she says, grinning. "Something to get Teacake talking."

Now, as Teacake soars above us, Rani opens the books and spreads them across the floor of McEwan Hall. Some of them I recognize, like Raphael's bored-looking cherubim. Others I've never seen before. There's one of three angels with musical instruments surrounding the baby Jesus; a vivid drawing of four winged beings attacking a pair of demons beneath a line of neat Arabic script. Rani flicks through the books, telling me about Rossetti, about van Eyck, about Klee, about artists and movements that I haven't even heard of.

"If the artists were right about what angels looked like, maybe they were right about where they were coming from. Look at this." She points to a colorful picture of a man in a gold crown and patterned clothes, with sharp wings of red, blue, and green feathers protruding from his back. "That was painted in 1590 in the

Mughal Empire, what's now India and part of central Asia. And this one . . ."

She grabs another book and opens it to a painting of the angel Gabriel presenting himself to the Virgin Mary, though she's suspiciously white for someone from the Middle East. "This is by Fra Angelico, painted in Italy in 1426. They're more than a century and thousands of miles apart, but look how similar the wings are— the colors, the shape."

There are some similarities, but I don't see how they're as alike as she says: the colors of the first angel are so vivid, his wings angular and the feathers thick as organ pipes; the Italian Gabriel's are softer, the neat lines of pastel blue and harvest yellow complementing his salmon-pink robes. Like Dad, Rani's only seeing what she wants to see.

"I know you could say it's a coincidence, or that the artists were just copying religious stories or other paintings." She runs her finger over the page, tracing the form of the wings. "But surely, if so many people had such similar visions, it must have come from something real."

Before I can answer, Teacake lands beside us. Rani pushes the first of the books toward her and begins telling her about the paintings, the biblical scenes some of them represent. I can't believe she knows so much. A year ago, Rani's main interests were trampolining, gummy bears, and an iPad game about flying koala bears. She seems too young to be obsessing about all this.

She turns to a photograph of a Baroque church. Its ornate ceiling is decorated with a twee mural of angels and saints chilling on clouds; there's even a Jesus figure balancing on a rainbow.

"Do you recognize anything?" she asks Teacake. "Does it look like this where you came from?"

Teacake looks at the pictures with interest, her eyes widening when she realizes the white or colored shapes on the page are meant to represent wings. But she doesn't nod, or shake her head, or point at the clouds and start gabbling excitedly. Soon Rani pouts and turns to the next book, and then the next. After an hour we've gone through six of the titles, but with no reaction from Teacake other than to parrot our words back to us and recite the first scene of a radio play about selkies.

"I don't think she's following, Ran," I say gently as she turns to *Rembrandt's Angels.* "We might never know."

Her head droops to her chest. When she looks up, she's crying. "Jaya, did Mum kill herself?"

My heart leaps. "What? No! Ran, no, how could you think that? It was an accident. You know it was an accident."

"I don't know *anything,*" she says. "You still haven't told me what happened. I miss her so, so much."

The last few words are swallowed by sobs. For a split second I hold back from hugging her—there's been such a gulf between us, for so long—but then I remember who I am and who she is and pull her close. My throat gets tight. I shut my eyes and see rushing water and crumbling rocks and her yellow scarf, snagged on a branch.

Don't think about it. I focus on Rani: the small pressure of her sobbing body, the tears soaking into my T-shirt. I nudge her so she looks up.

"Hey. Remember that time we went to the Black Isle for a

picnic," I say, "and a seagull yanked her sandwich right out of her hand?"

Rani gives a bubbly laugh. "She chased it halfway down the beach! It's hardly like she would have eaten it afterward." She sits up, wipes her eyes. "Remember when you were wee and she bought that really expensive lipstick and—"

"And I colored both our faces in with it!" There's a photo of that somewhere: six-year-old me and Rani, just a baby, both beaming, MAC Ruby Woo smeared all over our cheeks and mouths. "She didn't even yell."

My eyes start to prickle. It makes me almost dizzy, talking like this. Though I think about Mum so often, I never speak about her out loud. But I can tell Rani needs it.

So we talk. We talk about the songs she played in the car, the lullabies she sang when we were tiny. We swap her favorite jokes and worn-out film quotes, the Tamil sayings she'd inherited from Ammamma, all vague and strange in her literal English translations. We talk about her cooking: her milky eggplant curry, her pad Thai, her *parippu*, her mac and cheese; how the kitchen smelled of bacon on Saturday mornings and cinnamon or nutmeg when she'd been baking on Sunday afternoons.

We talk about the things we miss most. There are so many: her hugs, her screeching laugh when she was on the phone to Ammamma or her friends in London; the way she'd absentmindedly braid our hair while we did our homework; the way she smelled of earth and roses after she'd been gardening. We talk about the things that bugged us, too, like how she'd always start vacuuming just as we'd sat down to watch TV, or how she'd barge into our rooms when our friends were over and start panning through the mess for dirty clothes . . . only now we can't imagine how those things annoyed us at all. Now we miss them, too.

And as we talk, long-trapped memories come floating to the surface. Mum grinning at a lopsided snowman with an orange scarf; her hands peeling a mangosteen in a market in Nuwara Eliya; singing along to a Take That song in the kitchen, a wooden spoon for a microphone. But with each story, I feel the lack of another: another moment or day that could have awaited her, and now never will.

It's just so fucking unfair. I only got sixteen years of her, Rani even less. We should be having this conversation in fifty years' time, with decades' more memories to add to the list: birthdays, weddings, holidays to France or Sri Lanka or New Zealand. One tiny moment wiped away that future and blocked out much of her past. I'll never be able to ask her what she might have become if she hadn't got pregnant at twenty, or if she would have been okay with me being gay. I know she would have—she never asked me about boys or girls, but she not-so-subtly bought me *The Miseducation of Cameron Post* last summer—but I would have liked to talk to her about it.

Eventually, we slip into an easy silence, watching Teacake spin slowly beneath the roof. I count how long her flights last: seventeen seconds, twenty-two, nineteen. Her movements are much smoother now, no wobbly takeoffs anymore. She's made so much progress.

"I wish Mum was here to meet her," Rani says. "She would have loved her."

"I know," I say, slinging my arm around her neck. "Me too, Ran."

There's a creak behind us. Calum is in the doorway. He's not supposed to be here for another half an hour. I feel a jolt of worry, then another of fear, as I think about Allie.

"You're early," I say. "Is everything okay?"

"Aye, grand." Calum's voice is a monotone. He dumps his jacket on the ground and walks toward us, squinting at the books. He taps one with his toe. "What's all this?"

"I was hoping Teacake might recognize something," Rani says as Teacake comes gliding back to the floor. "If the Beings look so like the way people paint angels, maybe heaven does, too."

There's a glint in Calum's eyes. He drops to his knees and begins turning the pages of the nearest one. He stops on a painting called *The Ascension*, one of the first few that Rani showed Teacake.

"Look. See these clouds?" he says to Teacake. "Where you're from, is it beyond there? Why can't we see it?"

Something in his tone makes me feel uneasy. Teacake stares at him blankly. Rani starts to tell him she's already asked Teacake all of this, but Calum cuts her off.

"You just need to nod, Teacake. Yes or no."

He goes on and on, machine-gun quick, demanding answers to impossible questions. What's heartbreaking is that I can tell Teacake is really trying. Her eyes follow his hands as he turns the pages, blinking as images of clouds and angels flash past. Occasionally she'll start to say something and Calum will pause, but she'll splutter a few song lyrics or a radio jingle and he'll groan and turn to the next page.

Soon Teacake's wings start to twitch: she's bored of being

questioned, or maybe she senses the manic edge in Calum's voice. She beats them together and bends her knees to spring off, but Calum grabs her wrist. Teacake lets out a strangled cry.

"Just say it!" he shouts. "Tell me where you fell from!"

"Calum! Let her go!" I grab his arm and wrench it away from her. Teacake leaps into the air and flies toward the roof, where she lands in the alcove above the organ. Rani runs up the stairs, calling after her. My hand is still clutching Calum's arm. He pulls away and kicks at the books, sending one sliding across the floor.

"Calum—" I flinch as it thumps against the wall. "It's okay, she just—"

He paces toward the door, his arms above his head and his fingers clutching at his hair. "It's not okay," he snaps. "You don't get it. You don't understand anything."

"What do you mean?"

He spins around. His eyes are bright. "You know what Allie wanted to be when she was little? An astronaut. A bloody *astronaut*." He laughs coldly. "Can you imagine somebody with CF, who has a hard enough time breathing down here on earth, being sky-rocketed into space?"

I don't get what he means. What six-year-old doesn't want to be an astronaut? "Well, no, I suppose," I say. "What's that got to do with Teacake? What's your point?"

"My point is, she acts like it's nothing." Calum's hands clench into fists. "She had a *lung transplant*, Jaya. Don't you get how serious that is? She was in a coma for two weeks. She almost died twice. She shouldn't even be going out at the moment, not with this infection—but you, you've just waltzed into our lives and you expect her to be able to keep up with the rest of us."

The unfairness of this takes my breath away for a second.

"That is *not* true! I haven't forced her into anything. You guys were protesting Beings' rights before I even found Teacake. You know how strongly she feels about this." When his scowl doesn't fade, I echo what Allie herself has told me, so many times. "Besides, it's her life. She should be free to choose what she does with it."

Calum's mouth twitches. For a second I think he's about to shout at me, but instead he turns his head to the ceiling. The scholars gaze back, their books and instruments clutched to their robes.

"You're right. I can't stop her doing what she wants. Hell, she could give up altogether if she wanted." When he looks down again, his eyes are cold. "But you can't expect me to sit back and watch as she puts her life in danger. She's not going to be the one left behind when it ends, and neither are you."

I open my mouth to reply, but the weight of what he's said hits me, and I just stand there gaping.

It must hit Calum, too, because he swears and looks at the ground, his hands dug into his pockets. I can tell he's trying not to cry.

"Maybe you should take the day off," I say. I glance up at Teacake. She's still hiding behind a pillar near the second set of seats while Rani tries to talk her down. "We'll cover your shift."

"Whatever." He throws his hands up and turns on his heel. "It's over, anyway. She's never going to give us any answers."

As he walks away, I realize what was bothering me about his voice. His tone is just like Leah's when she left me yesterday, the same desperation, the same fear. He's being pushed to the edge, too, and I don't know what his next step will be.

TWENTY-THREE

IT'S A BEAUTIFUL DAY FOR CATCHING ANGELS. QUITE WARM outside, according to my phone, and not a hint of a breeze. From the bottom bunk, the slice of sky I can see is so bright it looks like it could burst. I almost wish it would. Maybe there are hundreds of Beings hidden behind the blue, waiting to tumble down into Dad's arms and make all his dreams come true.

Not likely.

It's eight o'clock. According to Dad's calculations, the Being is going to fall today at around 10:54 a.m., give or take ten minutes. We need to be at the foot of Arthur's Seat at nine to help everyone set up. He assumed I'd be coming, too, and I felt too bad to tell him otherwise. This is his big day, after all. This is what his months of stressing and obsessing have been leading up to. I know it's going to be a disaster, but I'll only make things worse if I refuse to go at all.

I can't quite deal with it just yet, though. I roll over and check my phone for messages. The past few days have been like the first few weeks after Leah left: constantly glancing at my phone, checking Instagram, refreshing her online profiles. There are no missed calls on the screen, no texts. It's like our meeting on Calton Hill never happened.

As I'm about to get up, a WhatsApp from Allie appears.

Bad news—my mum/prison warden is off work with a cold, so I'm not going to be able to sneak out to hang out with T. Gutted . . . it's been way too long since I've seen her. Or you.

There's a flutter in my stomach, and a knot of guilt in my chest. I can hardly stop thinking about Leah, and yet I still wish I'd kissed Allie before running out of her room the other day. She's funny and brave and pretty and smart, and she's so thoughtful and caring around Teacake. I like the way she throws back her head when she laughs, and the cute way she fiddles with her earrings when she's thinking, and . . . yeah. I really, really like Allie.

But I really, really liked Leah, too. And I don't quite know what to do with that.

I text Allie back, then reluctantly roll out of bed and get dressed, bracing myself for high-octane excitement from Dad. Instead, I find him sitting on the edge of the sofa, brows furrowed as he and Rani watch a video on his laptop. On the screen, a neatly coiffed white guy is standing on a quiet hillside, overlooking a valley dotted with rustic Mediterranean farmhouses.

"This is Manosque, in the French region of Alpes-de-Haute-Provence," he says as the camera pans across the valley. "A quiet town with a population of twenty-two thousand, it was perhaps best known as the birthplace of writer Jean Giono—until five forty-two this morning, when it became the Fall spot of the eighty-ninth Being."

The film cuts to a school courtyard, where a dozen flustered gendarmes are pushing back a pulsating crowd of Wingdings. If this were my plan rather than Dad's, I would take that as a bad sign: it's unusual for two Beings to land in one day, and even more so for them to be relatively close together. If one's already fallen in the south of France, there's very, very little chance that a second will turn up in Edinburgh on the same day.

Rani has made the same connection. "Remember the twelfth of June?" she says. "Three Beings fell that day: one in the Philippines, one in Canada, and one here. It happens all the time."

Dad nods. "Good point. It's certainly not unheard of." He jabs the red button on the remote control, then slaps his knees and stands up. At this stage, his confidence is like a brick wall; it'll take more than a few bumps to knock it down. "Right, then! Let's go catch this Being, shall we?"

My insides feel as if they're being tossed around like lottery balls. I sense Rani's gaze flick toward me, but I don't look at her.

"Yep," I say, copying his neon-bright tone. "Let's do it."

His Wingding friends are already waiting for us when we arrive at the hill ten minutes later. They're not wearing tacky T-shirts or plastic halos like some of the tourists you see around town, but I can pick them out instantly. There are people of all ages and races, dressed in everything from suits to football tops, *Doctor Who* T-shirts to floral dresses. What else would bring all these people together, if not the Beings?

Dad parks near the edge of the road and grabs a box of tools from the boot of the car. A couple of the Wingdings wave, and the *Doctor Who* fan lifts a cigarette in greeting. Behind them, two people are working on a strange contraption of metal and plastic. Its base is a little like a giant four-poster bed, only with metal wheels for feet, waist-high handles meant for pushing and pulling, and a large steel hook linking it to the back of a pickup truck. Attached to the top is a huge metal contraption not unlike the engine of a plane, only much bigger: a giant metal sphere encasing eight enormous propellers. It looks a bit like a fan, just like Dad said it would, only twenty feet tall and as wide as a bus.

"That," he says proudly, "is what we've been working on up in Perth."

"Wow, Dad!" Rani looks up at him and beams. "It looks amazing! It's huge!"

A few of the Wingdings come over to greet us, all handshakes and high fives. Others look over from across the lawn, where they're dragging lumps of bright blue plastic from the boot of a car. Dad introduces us, but I can't keep up with the names: there are about twenty-five of them in total, more than I'd expected. Rani makes a beeline for the machine, where a black woman in green overalls is fiddling with a huge tangle of wires, while a lanky Nordic-looking man climbs a ladder to attach something to the frame. Rani begins to bombard them with questions.

"We didn't have much time to put it together, but it's incredibly powerful," says the woman, who introduces herself as Maya. "It rotates at around the same speed as an aircraft, but we've modified the propellers to allow for greater resistance. Look, I'll show you."

She reaches up and presses a button on the side of the machine. The fan makes a roaring sound like a jet taking off; a couple of crows get caught in its airway and are blasted into the sky, so fast some of the feathers are ripped from their wings.

The man, Lars, points to a row of dials just below the button. "These let us control the power and the speed. So the idea is, we'll direct the machine toward the Being, use the fan to break its Fall, then slowly lower the pressure, letting it make a safe descent to earth."

I barely know anything about physics, but all of this seems quite amateur to me. Lars tells Rani—who's now questioning their credentials—that he's a maths teacher, and that Maya has a PhD, so they must know their stuff. I suppose it's just hard to make calculations when we don't know much about the most important variables: how much the Being weighs, the angle and speed he or she is going to fall at, when it's going to happen . . .

Dad claps me on the shoulder. "Right, you two," he says, grinning from Rani to me. "Let's get to work."

The lumps of blue plastic that the Wingdings were pulling from the car turn out to be inflatable mattresses to cushion the Being's fall. Rani and I spend the first hour helping a chatty Glaswegian called Amir unfold and inflate them using an electronic pump, then help Lars and Maya practice moving their machine across the grass. It's quite tiring, but at ten o'clock Evelyn, the *Doctor Who* fan, starts handing out ice creams—nobody questions having dessert for breakfast—and we sit on the grass, chatting and licking our sticky fingers.

To my surprise, I'm kind of having a good time. Having a task is distracting me from the guilt of letting Dad carry on with this farce, but also, the Wingdings' happiness is sort of infectious. They seem so convinced that the Fall is going to happen, all talking of "when" rather than "if." Some are planning what they'll buy when they get their share of the reward money; others have long lists of questions they want to ask the Being.

"I'm no' looking for proof of the afterlife, mind. I have my faith—dinnae need anything else, ken whit I mean?" Amir says. "But there's other things I'd like tae know . . . aboot what's going on up there that's making them fall."

Evelyn nods. "I know it won't be straightforward, that it all depends on how fast the Being learns English." (I bite back a smile at that—if only they knew.) "I just want them to tell me if I'll see my Daniel again. That's all."

She wipes the ice cream from her mouth and goes to help Maya and Lars with the machine. Her words leave a lump in my throat. *That's all.* As if it's not too much to ask, instead of the biggest question going.

By half past ten, a crowd has started to gather around the machine. There are dozens of Wingdings from other countries, all taking photos and asking tons of questions. Shona pops down and waffles on about positive energy and the moon being in Scorpio as Rani gives her a grand tour of the site. There's even a journalist and a cameraman wandering around.

"Should we do a countdown?" Amir asks at 10:53.

Dad scoffs, "It's hardly going to be on the dot! You know there's a ten-minute margin on either side." But after a moment, he shrugs. "What the hell. Let's do it."

The audience buzzes. Some people look on with genuine hope and excitement, but most with ironic interest or even outright cynicism—half the crowd is clearly here out of curiosity alone. Lars flips the switch again, and the propellers start to whirl. The noise is deafening; even with more than a hundred people shouting, I can barely hear the numbers over the roar of the engine.

"Ten . . . nine . . . eight . . ."

The voices grow louder. Somehow, I find myself joining in. All these people, together, all focused on the same purpose, chanting the same words: there's power in that, even if the numbers themselves are meaningless.

"Seven . . . six . . . five . . . four . . ."

Just a few meters from me, Rani is standing beside Dad. Her eye catches mine. There's an expression there I can't quite read. After a moment, she looks away.

"Three . . . two . . . one!"

We wait for a speck of light. We wait for the streak of gold or silver or copper, the things that we've seen in the YouTube videos. We wait for an answer.

It doesn't come. Some of the Wingdings throw up their arms in mock defeat; others start to laugh. The crowd looks around, confused by this countdown that has led to nothing. Dad grins and waves his hands.

"Don't worry, it'll still be coming! Our calculations were never that precise." He grins at Rani, who gives him a weak smile in return. "Would have been a nice dramatic touch, though, wouldn't it?"

It would have been more than that. It would have been a

miracle. But we've already had eighty-nine of those. This time, another one really would be too much to ask.

People talk about the stages of grief as if it's something you complete; a training program with a printout certificate at the end. I'm not sure where I'm supposed to be, eight months since Mum died.

It changes every day. There are moments when I think I'm starting to accept it, but then there are times when I'll see someone on the bus with an expression like hers or read something that would have made her laugh and I can't believe—like, physically *cannot* believe—that I'll never see her again. It all feels like a sad, slow dance, and I'm being passed back and forth between different partners: denial, anger, bargaining, depression, over and over and over again.

That morning, I see Dad go through all the stages. Only this time, it's not Mum he's mourning. It's money. It's fame and fortune and everything that a Being could have brought him. It's the purpose that the hunt has given him, all gone.

The shock doesn't last long. Just a few minutes of blinking at the bright blue sky, a quiver in his smile as his ten-minute margin slips past—then he claps his hands and slides smoothly into denial.

"Must have been a wee bit off with the timings," he says, laughing weakly. "Let me go over them again . . . Don't worry, it can't have been off by more than an hour or so."

But an hour turns into two, then three, and there's still no sign of a Fall. The audience has long since wandered off; Shona remembers a drum-circle practice and scurries back up the Mile. Dad's denial starts to turn to anger. He yells at the engineers about the noise the fan is making, as if that could be keeping the Being away. He snaps at another Wingding for suggesting they come back tomorrow. A journalist asks him for a comment on his "failure"; Dad turns so red I'm worried he's going to punch the guy in the face, but he just spits a string of swear words at him instead.

Rani trails after him, tugging on his sleeve. I follow close behind, terrified she'll crack and tell him about Teacake if I'm not there to stop her. She keeps repeating the same few platitudes: it could still happen, don't give up yet. Eventually, Dad jerks his arm away and glares down at her.

"Just shut up for five minutes, Rani! I'm trying to think!"

For a second, she looks as if she's about to cry. Instead, she tugs on Perry's leash, storms down the hill, and sits on a rock, her arms crossed tight. The area is quiet now, just a few walkers and late-comers looking on. I realize that we haven't had lunch and go to the ice cream truck to buy us each a Fanta and some crisps. By the time I come back up, even the Wingdings are starting to leave.

That's when Dad reaches the bargaining stage.

"Guys, come on, it could still happen! Amir . . . Amir, just wait another hour, will you? I'll cut you a higher percentage of the reward."

Amir squeezes Dad's shoulder and shakes his head. Maya hugs Rani and me; Lars gives us a sad smile and climbs into the driver's seat of a red Toyota. No one bothers to take the fan with them, or the tower of inflatable mattresses. Whatever spell had convinced them that this ridiculously, laughably improbable feat might actually happen has worn off. Now they just look dejected and a little sheepish.

Maybe Dad was the spell. Maybe his blind faith was what kept them going all these months. It's not enough now. And so he starts bargaining with something else.

"Please," he keeps muttering. "Please. Just give me this. I've worked so hard for this. This is all I'm asking for."

We try to talk to him, but he barely seems to hear us. The afternoon drags on: Rani is getting weepy, Perry keeps whining to be fed, I'm starving and grumpy and anxious to get back to McEwan Hall—my shift started hours ago. Eventually, it's my turn to snap.

"It's not coming, Dad! It's not going to happen!"

He keeps scanning the sky, as if looking for a detail that he might have missed before. But his shoulders start to sag, and soon he's staring at his feet instead.

"Fine," he says, his voice quiet and flat. "Fine. Let's go."

We drive home in silence, an atmosphere like a summer storm brewing in the small car. Back in the flat, Dad goes straight to the kitchen and pours himself a large whiskey. He downs it in one, fills the glass again, and walks into the living room. The maps and notes and bulletin boards already seem like a museum exhibition: proof of some bygone folly, maps of a flat earth.

He slams his glass on the table; Laphroaig slops over the side.

"You idiot," he says. "You bloody, useless idiot. What the hell did you think you were doing? Waste of time—"

He tears the world map off the wall. He rips his notes in half. He pulls the pages from library books, crumples Post-its in his palms. Rani and I try to stop him, but he shrugs us off and keeps storming the room, destroying days and nights of research, weeks and months of planning. And even though I've resented every minute of it, it's painful to watch it come apart.

"Bloody . . . delusional . . . moron . . ."

He slumps onto the sofa, his head in his hands, surrounded by a snowfall of paper scraps. Rani goes to make him tea and toast, though we both know he won't eat. I tiptoe around him and sweep up the paper into a bin bag. Even when he falls asleep, the sadness wafts off him, potent as the whiskey.

As I carry a handful of ripped-up equations into the kitchen, Rani catches my wrist. She's crying. "We have to tell him. *Please*, Jaya."

Though I shake my head, a small part of me is actually tempted to do it. He'd be angry, yeah, but the shock and the joy would cancel that out. The relief, too, and the vindication.

I could give him all that. But I'm still choosing not to. Right now, Teacake still comes first.

Rani sniffs and wipes her tears on the hem of her T-shirt. "Look how upset he is. You're being so selfish!"

"Rani, come on. You promised you wouldn't say anything."

"That was before—"

I cut her off with a sharp look. "I'm serious, Rani. If you tell him, I'll just deny the whole thing."

"Fine." She sniffs and takes off her glasses to wipe the tears from her eyes. "But don't blame me when he finds out and hates you for it."

By the time I finish cleaning up, it's past five: I should have been at McEwan Hall over three hours ago. It takes me ten minutes just to cross the road—there are a thousand Spanish kids running riot, plus a squad of break-dancers gyrating on the cobbles—but the chaos is a welcome relief from the atmosphere in the flat.

When I reach Bristo Square, I see something that makes my heart skip: Allie, crossing the road toward McEwan Hall. She looks pale, tired, and tiny in her oversized cardigan and skinny jeans, but her face lights up when she sees me. Man, she's pretty.

"Guess what? Prison Warden Scott went out to Aldi," she says, grinning. "God bless their unbeatable deals."

She reaches up to give me a hug. The heavy feeling that's been sitting in my stomach all afternoon starts to lift instantly. I let my arms linger around her just a little bit longer than friendly.

"How are you feeling?" I ask. "Are you sure you're up to being out?"

"Aye, I'm much better," she says, but she's interrupted by another bout of coughing. She gives me a wry smile. "Okay, not *that* much better. I probably shouldn't stay more than half an hour. I just figured it was worth it."

We smile at each other, then both break eye contact at the same moment. I fill her in on the day's events as I rummage in my bag for my keys. Part of me thinks I should finally tell her about Leah, too, but I'm not sure how to bring it up. I mean, how do you tell the girl you like that your sort-of ex is in town and that you might still have feelings for her and that, oh yeah, she's also part of a huge international cult? Where would you even begin?

"I'm glad you're here," I say instead. I double-check that nobody is watching, then turn the key in the lock. "My dad had a bit of a meltdown after the Fall—well, the lack of the Fall. I could do with something to take my mind . . ."

The words dissolve in my mouth as we step into the hall. Rays of evening sun seep through the skylight, leaving a circle of pink-tinged light on the wooden floor. Calum's black backpack lies open by the organ, *A Dance with Dragons* poking out behind the zipper.

But Teacake's not there.

Teacake is gone.

TWENTY-FOUR

THERE'S NO SIGN OF A STRUGGLE. OTHER THAN CALUM'S backpack and a crumpled Twix wrapper in one corner, there are no clues that anyone has been here at all. Allie's fingers dig into my arm.

"Where is he? Calum? Calum!"

There's no answer. I scan the murals and the ceiling, stupidly hoping that Teacake might be hidden somewhere among the scholars and angels—that this is all just a horrible joke. But then I look down and see three feathers by my feet: one blackbird, one sparrow, and one a glittering pink.

"No, no, no . . ."

My head swirls with unwanted images: blurred figures storming the hall, grabbing Teacake's wings, pulling Calum's hair. She's gone. She's actually gone. Allie sees the feathers and freezes.

"Shit. Shit." I can see her mind filling up with the same pictures that are spinning around mine. Her hands shake as she pulls her phone from her pocket. I hear it ring three, four, five times, then go to voice mail. She swears and throws her phone into her bag.

"They must have t-taken them," she says, stammering a little on the words. "Someone must have followed them here."

"Who, though?" I ask. Allie doesn't answer. There are too many possibilities: the cults, researchers, any of the thousands of Wing-dings milling around the city center. If I hadn't spent the whole day with him, I might even have counted Dad among the suspects.

A jolt of nerves flashes through me. The Standing Fallen—they know there's a Being in Edinburgh, and according to Leah, they have dozens of members on the hunt for her. If we're looking for suspects, they're at the top of the list.

Before I can mention this to Allie, she gets to her feet, her knees shaking so much she has to put her hand on my arm to steady herself. "Come on. We have to find them."

She pulls me toward the door, not bothering to stop and lock up behind her. There's nothing left to protect now, anyway. She leads me down the road to her car, a silver Renault parked outside the art school.

"Where do we start?" I ask as I slide into the passenger seat.

"I don't know!" Allie pushes the key into the ignition. "I have no idea. Let's just *go*."

We couldn't have picked a worse time to lose a boy and an angel in the middle of Edinburgh: the city center is crammed full of traffic, and Allie keeps having to stop for pedestrians stumbling out into the road. I look out for pink feathers, hoping for a bread-crumb trail to lead us to Teacake, but the pavement is hidden beneath thousands of pairs of shoes. Just a week ago we'd been racking our brains for even one spot to hide Teacake. Now this relatively small city has multiplied, a knotted labyrinth of endless nooks and crannies.

We drive past the stalls outside St. Giles' Cathedral, double back toward the university, crawl in and out of streets with names I don't recognize. Eventually, we realize we'd be quicker going on foot and park around the back of the train station. We check alleyways and hidden gardens; we glance in pubs and run into cafés, knowing that we won't find them there but too desperate to pass them by. All the while, images of the Standing Fallen bursting into McEwan Hall flit through my head. I see them grabbing Teacake, tying her up, stripping the feathers from her wings . . . Over and over again, so vivid they make me feel sick.

Something doesn't quite fit, though. Why would they take Calum, too?

The adrenaline keeps Allie going for a while, but soon I can feel her starting to flag. By the time we end up back on the Royal Mile, an hour or so later, she's wheezing and has started to cough again.

"Let's stop for a sec," I say. "Just till we get our breath back."

I steer her onto Cockburn Street. We sit on the step of a bright red door, away from the torrent of tourists. Allie pulls an energy bar from her bag and offers me another. I shake my head. I feel too sick to eat, too nervous to sit still.

Now that the worst has happened, it seems ridiculous we ever thought we could keep Teacake safe. We should have found somewhere more secure. We should never have left her alone, not even for a few minutes. There are thousands of people after her, organizations with more money and power than we could even imagine—and we left her in a room with one measly padlock on the door.

Suddenly I realize how Dad felt, coming home to see his months of failed research on the walls: it was never, ever, ever going to be enough.

Allie tries calling Calum again, and then her mum, but neither of them answers.

"What if they've hurt them?" She keeps turning the phone in her hands. "I know I moan about Calum, but I don't know what I'd do if anything . . ."

Her voice wobbles. I take her hand and squeeze it tight. I'd be tearing my hair out if this were Rani. And for all of Dad's faults, even after everything he's put us through over the past eight months, I'd fall apart if anything were to happen to him.

It's then that I remember the deal I made with my sister: that I'd ask Dad for help if anything went wrong. We're just a couple of minutes from our flat. I could run up, tell him the truth. . . . His anger would be a small price to pay if it helped us get her back. And if anyone knows who might have taken her, it's Dad.

I swallow. I know Allie's not going to like it, but it may be our only option.

"Listen, I think we should—"

The sound of a siren drowns out my voice. I flinch, the way I always do when I hear the high-pitched squeal. That sound means accidents, blood, guilt.

And sometimes, that sound means the Standing Fallen.

I spin around on the step, trying to pinpoint the noise. The sirens are getting louder. Closer.

"Come on." I hold my hand out to Allie and pull her to her feet. "I know somewhere we can try."

We cut through the arcade and hurry down North Bridge, toward Princes Street. As we draw closer, people begin climbing out of one of the top windows of the Balmoral Hotel. They scramble over the building's domes and turrets, clutching at its chimneys: fifty, sixty, seventy of them, multiplying, like an infestation of ants.

The traffic is backed up to the end of North Bridge. Pedestrians spill into the road to take photos, ignoring the drivers furiously honking their horns. I drag Allie through the crowd and scan the building for Leah. As we turn the corner, I see her. She's climbing through one of the windows high above the main entrance to the hotel, helped up by her mother and a very tall, bald man.

"That's her." My voice comes out as a croak. "That's Leah. My ex."

Allie stares at me, her eyes wide. I wait for a barrage of questions to come, but instead she just holds my hand a little tighter. We watch as a short, fat woman with lank black hair slowly climbs to the spire at the top of the building. Clutching the barrier, she fumbles with the button on the loudspeaker and begins to speak into it.

"Sinners! For eight months now, angels have fallen from the skies. Not for two millennia has the Creator . . ."

Her voice shakes as she stumbles through the speech. I search the members on the roof: the young boy and girl I saw the day we arrived in Edinburgh are up there, but the bearded man who leads the chapter isn't. I think back to the Standing Fallen displays that I've seen on TV. It's always the same person who gives the speech, and it's almost always a man. Today, for some reason, they're using a stand-in.

Allie's fingers press into the back of my hand. "Oh my God."

I follow her gaze, toward the Duke of Wellington statue on the other side of the road. Standing beneath it, looking up at the Standing Fallen with his arms crossed tight over his chest, is Calum. He blinks and glances around, that way you do when you feel you're being watched. His eyes meet his sister's.

After that, I don't need an explanation. The look on his face is enough to tell me what happened.

Allie drops my hand and pushes through the crowd. I run after her, shoving people out of the way, red spots of anger blurring my vision. Calum backs up against the wall, shaking his head. I could hit him. I actually want to punch him in the face, but Allie gets there first. She storms up to him and whacks him over the head with her satchel.

"What the fuck did you do?" she screams. "Where is she? What did you do with her?"

Calum cowers, his arms wrapped over his head. "I didn't mean to! Allie, just listen!"

Tears are pouring down her cheeks. Seeing her so upset stills my own anger, at least for a moment; I catch her wrists and gently lead her behind the statue, away from the onlookers staring at us. Calum follows, his hands held palms up.

"I swear, it was a mistake." His voice breaks. "I never meant for them to take her . . . I just showed him the photos . . ."

"You showed someone *photos* of her? How fucking stupid are you?"

"Who?" I ask. "Who did you show?"

He looks up at the roof of the Balmoral. My insides lurch. The inkling I had back on Cockburn Street becomes a full image. I was right. The Standing Fallen have Teacake. The Standing Fallen: the people who think the Falls are a sign of their god's wrath, who probably think Teacake is some demon, something tainted and unworthy of heaven. Only it wasn't their horde of volunteers who handed her over—it was Calum.

His voice is trembling. "It was after Jaya mentioned someone had found Teacake's feathers. I looked it up online and saw they were offering a reward for more information. I emailed the guy asking how much he'd pay for some photos." He looks at his feet, wincing. "He said he'd give me ten grand for them. I didn't realize it was them, I swear—I thought it was just some random rich Wingding."

A blast of a horn makes us all jump. Two fire engines are trying to edge toward the building, but the crowd is moving too slowly for them to get through. I try to focus on Calum's voice, but my attention keeps being drawn to the people standing on the roof.

"The guy didn't believe they were real. So yesterday, I sent them a video." He wrings his hands together, as if he could squeeze the guilt out of his skin. "I was so stupid, I didn't think how easy it would be to find her. But they came this morning. I opened the door, thinking it would be Jaya . . . There were three of them; there was nothing I could do."

On top of the hotel, the speaker continues her rant. Leah stares straight ahead, over the rooftops and toward the horizon. On one side of her, her mother is chanting along with the leader's speech; on the other, the tall man bows his bald head in prayer.

"So that's it," Allie spits. "You sold her for ten grand."

"Not even that." Calum's voice breaks. "They never gave me any money. They just took her and left."

The black-haired woman is reaching the part in the speech about redemption and responsibility; usually the point where the speaker's voice swells, rising in a thundering crescendo, though this time the words are stilted and unsure. Allie starts to pace, her hands balled into fists.

"I can't believe this. I can't believe this." She spins back to face Calum. "What the fuck do you need that much money for, anyway?"

Calum's eyes flit to me, then drop to the ground. "For you," he says. "For stem cell treatment."

All the anger drains out of Allie's face. She puts her face in her hands and groans. "Oh, Calum. You idiot."

His lower lip is wobbling. He opens his mouth to say something, but a squeal from the loudspeaker cuts him off. The firefighters' ladders have finally reached the roof of the building. Some of the members scurry away, slipping into open windows or lowering one another toward the balconies.

But not Leah.

Leah is still standing beside the bald man, at the very edge of the roof. Her mother has climbed up to the gable; she's screaming at her daughter to hurry, but Leah doesn't listen.

Leah takes another step forward.

Screams explode into my head, but when I open my mouth, no sound comes out.

I can't see this again, this can't be happening again—

I close my eyes. A split second later, a body hits the pavement.

TWENTY-FIVE

THE SCREAMS COME LIKE A TIDAL WAVE, ROARING OVER THE crowd before sweeping back into a horrified quiet. Police officers push through the scrum, yelling at everyone to get out of the way. The crowd staggers backward, sending me stumbling into Calum. My eyes are shut tight, but there's an image behind the lids: small body, arms at odd angles, the ground spattered red.

But when I finally look up, Leah is still standing on the roof of the hotel. She, her mother, and several other members are staring down at the pavement, some crouching to clutch at the tiles. The black-haired woman drops the loudspeaker as she scrambles past the chimneys; it slides down the roof and catches in the rain gutter.

"What happened?" I ask. "Who jumped?"

"You didn't see?" Allie's voice is shaking. "That man, the one standing right beside Leah. He—he just stepped off the edge."

The ground dips and the sky spins toward me, but I push past the people telling me to take it easy and run toward the hotel. The cult members are pouring out of the hotel doors now, wading through the crowd toward the vans parked illegally outside the train station. Some of them make it; others are caught by police officers, like reeds snagged on river rocks, and dragged away.

As I rush forward, I catch a flash of gray slipping past an elderly couple by the pedestrian crossing. The two kids make it to the van, followed by the black-haired woman: she stands by the door, screaming at the others to hurry up. As she passes, I lunge forward and catch Leah's arm. Her mouth falls open when she sees me.

"The Being," I say. "Do you know where she is?"

"What? What do you mean?"

Frustration rushes over me, but I can tell from her expression that she's not lying. "I'll explain later," I say. "I need you to take us to the Standing Fallen's base. Now."

"*What?* I can't, Jaya. I told you . . ." She looks over her shoulder. One of the vans revs and jerks backward into the road, sending tourists scattering. "I have to go, I have to go back to the base—"

"No!" She tries to pull away, but I tighten my grip on her arm. "You have to get away from them! I saw you up there, you were going to—"

I stop myself from saying it, but Leah fills in the blanks. Her face crumples. She looks so weak, so devastated. And the worst part is, I don't know if that's because she was pushed to the edge, or because she didn't step off it. I don't understand—she won't walk away from the Standing Fallen without her mother, but she was ready to throw herself off a building to escape? It doesn't make sense.

"You don't know what it's like," she whispers, as if she's read my thoughts. "You don't understand the kind of power they have."

I try another tactic: guilt.

"Please, Leah. You owe me this." I grab her hands, tug on them until she looks up at me. "My mum's gone, you disappeared . . . this Being, she's my friend. I don't want to lose her, too. Not like this."

Slowly, something in Leah's expression changes. It hardens. She sniffs and rubs her sleeve across her nose.

"What do you need me to do?"

As I start to tell her, I see the black-haired woman look toward us. She takes a step toward Leah, but she's blocked by a policeman saying something about "trespassing" and "breach of peace." Before Leah has a chance to change her mind, I grab her hand and drag her across the road, back toward Allie and Calum.

"Quickly! Let's go, now!"

"This way," Allie shouts. "I can drive us there."

We follow her down the road, weaving in and out of the buses lined up on Princes Street. Allie is wheezing heavily now, her pace dropping, but she keeps going. She leads us through Waverley Station, up the escalators, and onto Market Street. It's only when we reach the car that I realize Calum's followed us all the way here. He pushes past a group of tourists and sprints toward the car, beating Allie to the driver's seat.

"I'm coming with you," he says. "Please. I want to put things right."

The anger I'd put on hold outside the hotel comes searing

through me. "No way. All of this is your fault! You practically handed Teacake over to them. You as good as sold her."

He winces. Allie pulls open the door to the passenger seat but pauses before she gets inside. She shakes her head. "Jaya's right, Calum. Teacake won't be able to trust you now. You'd just make things worse."

I usher Leah into the backseat and climb in beside her. Calum half chases after the car, even as Allie pulls out of the parking spot and starts off down the road. I watch as he grows smaller and smaller in the rearview mirror, until we turn a corner and he disappears altogether.

It's strange having Allie and Leah in the same place. They both look pale and tired, both clearly shaken up after what happened outside the hotel, and yet they're so different: Leah sits in the backseat, her knees pulled to her chest, nervously grasping at her hair; Allie's hands are steady on the steering wheel, and her expression is calm and determined as she wheels us out of the city. My life in Edinburgh has collided with the one I was living a few weeks ago, and it's just . . . surreal.

Awkward, too. Allie is one of the most talkative people I've ever met, but even she doesn't know what to say to someone who was contemplating throwing herself off a building just a few minutes ago. When I close my eyes, the scene repeats itself behind my eyes: the swarms of people, the noise, the crashing sound as the man's body hit the earth. And Leah, ready to follow him.

Just remembering it makes my heart race and my eyes prickle. But now isn't the time to talk about it.

"Where are they staying?" I ask her instead as the car crawls through the Old Town. "Where's the base?"

"I don't know, I don't know!" She gives a sharp tug on her hair; several strands fall away in her hands. "It's an old power plant, maybe half an hour from the city, but I don't know where. They didn't tell us."

Allie tilts her head up to meet Leah's eyes in the rearview mirror. "Does it have two huge chimneys outside it? Near the sea?"

"Yes! That's it."

"I know where that is. It's going to be demolished soon." She looks down at the dashboard. "It's only ten miles or so, but it'll take us an hour in this traffic."

"You need to tell me what's going on," Leah says. Her hands are shaking so hard she can barely attach her seat belt. "What are you looking for?"

This really isn't the time for another shock—she's just seen someone she knows throw himself off a rooftop, for Christ's sake—but I don't have a choice. I tell her everything, from finding Teacake to losing her. From the way Leah stares at me, you'd think I was describing being abducted by aliens. Her expression doesn't change until I take out my phone and show her the videos that Rani and I took of Teacake flying around McEwan Hall.

"So that's what all the commotion was about." She falls back in her seat, shell-shocked. "We weren't supposed to do a demonstration today, but a few hours ago Damien and Ross, the chapter leaders, rounded everyone up and ordered us out. The whole thing was a

212

mess. Normally they spend weeks preparing. Telling us to go some-where so public, with no planning . . . It's not surprising there were so many arrests."

The car edges onto South Bridge and through Newington. We eventually leave the traffic jam and move onto country roads, the atmosphere in the car thick with nerves. Allie puts the radio on to fill the silence: there's a brief mention of the Standing Fallen on the news, but nothing about their discovering a Being. If we were to call the police now, they'd think it was a prank. We're Teacake's last hope.

Eventually the power station looms into view. It's enormous; a characterless chunk of gray and black, stark against the pink tinge of the evening sky. Parts of the wall have been ripped away, reveal-ing an inner skeleton of girders and pipes, and the land around the building is littered with scrap metal, rusted tools, disused machines.

"You've really been living in here?" Allie can't keep the disgust out of her voice. "Jesus."

One of the Standing Fallen's vans is parked just outside the building, but there's no sign of the other three yet. Allie parks behind a public toilet around the corner, a hundred meters or so from the car park. We're at enough of a distance to avoid raising suspicion—if anyone notices the car going past, they'll think it's someone popping into the loos—but hopefully close enough to sneak in unnoticed.

"So . . ." I give a nervous cough. "What's the plan?"

More silence. Allie rummages in the glove compartment, pulls out a crumpled brown bag and a Sharpie, and passes them to Leah.

"Can you draw us a plan of the building?"

Her hands trembling, Leah flattens the paper and begins to sketch a rough outline of the power station. It's more complicated than it looks from the outside, with open stairways and overlapping walkways that make it easy to see from one side of the building to another.

Allie and I exchange a look. This isn't going to be easy. The only things giving us a slight advantage are the lack of electricity in the building and the arrests made outside the hotel. Some of the members will be taken into custody and won't be released until long after our arrival at the base. We just have no way of knowing how many, or if it'll make any difference.

As Leah draws, the realization of what she's being asked to do sinks in. She lets out a sob and curls in on herself, her face pressed into her knees.

"I can't do this! I can't, I can't." Her fingers grab at her matted hair. "They'll take it out on my mum, they'll go after my dad—"

"They won't," I say feebly, because I have no way of knowing that. I really don't know what these people are capable of.

Leah shakes her head and reaches for the door handle. "No. No. I have to go back. If I go back now, maybe they won't realize that I came with you—"

"You just need to help us get in and find Teacake," Allie says. "How about this—if we get caught, you can say you have no idea who we are, and you were trying to stop us. We'll back you up, I promise."

Leah presses her lips together. I want her to say no, that she'd never hand me over like that. Instead she gives a small nod.

"Okay. I'll try."

There's a long silence as we look up at the building. I'm starting to feel like an extra on the set of an action movie, thrust into the role of the hero with no clue what the lines are.

"Okay." I take a deep breath and unclip my seat belt. "Let's go."

My stomach keeps flipping and I feel like I might throw up, but somehow we make it across the yard and past the heap of scrap metal. Leah points to a rectangular hole in the wall where a door once stood. Before we can move, a few figures walk past the windows on the third floor. We wait until they're out of sight, then slip inside.

The gap leads into the underbelly of the power station, a large, cold labyrinth of huge metal pipes and rusted equipment. There are a few rubbish tags spray-painted over the generators, and cigarette butts and broken bottles litter the ground, but the place clearly hasn't been used for some months.

Though it's warm outside, a shiver runs over my skin. I follow Leah's quiet footsteps over the cement floor. At the end of the room is a stairway, a larger version of the fire escapes you see on buildings in New York or Montreal. When she points toward it, my stomach flips. It's even more exposed than I'd imagined: should anyone leave the rooms upstairs, they'll be able to see us instantly.

"Is there no other way?" Allie asks, eyeing the stairs nervously.

Leah shakes her head. We tiptoe up, wincing at every creak of our feet on the steel. Allie stifles her coughs with her sleeve, but to my ears they rumble like thunder. Leah pauses at the top of the second flight, then leads us over a walkway and toward a large locker room. It looks much like the ones we have at school, only there are ragged blankets laid out over the cold, hard floor tiles.

I wonder if this is where Leah's been sleeping. The thought makes my heart throb with sadness.

"We'll go through the turbine hall," she says. "Less likely to bump into anyone there."

She leads us through more bleak hallways, past half-dismantled machinery and abandoned tools, dust and rusted nails littered at our feet. A couple of times we hear voices above us and draw back into the shadows. As we step into another large room lined with pipes, Leah lets out a gasp. A redheaded woman in black jeans and a ripped woolen sweater is walking down the stairs toward us— her mother.

"Shit! Quickly, hide!"

There's not enough time for us to go back downstairs, and little to hide behind but a huge cylindrical green tank in the corner of the room. Leah shoves us behind it: it's wide enough to shield the three of us from certain angles, but if Mrs. Maclennan comes this way, she'll definitely spot us.

"Anyone there?"

Her voice bounces off the walls and high ceilings. Allie's hand finds mine. I lift it to my lips, muffling a scared yelp with the back of her hand. This is it. We've failed. It's over.

Until Leah steps out from behind the pillar.

TWENTY-SIX

AS IF HER MOTHER WERE A LOADED GUN, LEAH'S HANDS FLY toward the ceiling.

"It's just me, Mum! I was—I dropped something. My hairband."

Mrs. Maclennan comes into my view. She looks terrible: her collarbones poke above the low collar of her sweater, and her lips are lined with cold sores. The past few months have left her with creases around her mouth and a stony look in her eyes that wasn't there before, but her face floods with relief when she sees her daughter.

"Oh, thank the Lord. I thought you'd been picked up by the police," she says, rushing forward to hug Leah. "How did you get back so quickly?"

"I tried to get back to the vans, but they both left before I could, so I—I got a bus."

Her mum's hesitation only lasts a second, but it feels like forever. "A bus? How did you pay for it?"

"Didn't. Snuck on with a big group of tourists." Leah's hands twitch, like the truth is bursting to get out of her. She tugs her sleeves over her hands. "Mum, do you know where Damien is, or Ross? I've got something important to tell them."

"About what?"

Leah doesn't reply. Her mother's eyes narrow. "They're in the control room. Leaders' meeting. They've been there all day."

"No, Mum, really, I need to speak to them. It's important." Mrs. Maclennan puts her hands on her hips, ready to argue, but Leah cuts her off. "Please! Believe me, they'll want to hear this. Can you get them for me? They'll be pissed off if I interrupt, but they respect you."

Mrs. Maclennan presses her a little more, but something in Leah's tone convinces her; she eventually turns and walks up the stairs. For a moment, I wonder if Allie and I are what Leah plans on showing the leaders—if we'll end up stuck with her in this miserable place, forced to pay or jump our way out. But as soon as her mother's footsteps fade away, she hurries toward us.

"I'll distract them," she says. "I'll take them downstairs—they won't be able to hear anything from there. Wait until you hear the door close, then go to the control room and get the Being."

Allie and I gawp at her; Leah stares back, as shocked by this rush of courage as we are, and for the first time in months, I feel like I'm looking at the girl I fell for last year. I pull out the paper-bag map and memorize the route to the control room: up two more flights of stairs and along a long passageway to the left. "How long do you think you can hold them off?" I ask.

"Probably not more than a few minutes. You'll need to be quick."

"What are you going to tell them?"

Leah bites her lip. "I don't know," she says. "I'll think of something. It doesn't really matter, as long as it gives you time to get her out."

"But—"

There are a dozen ways this could play out. The scenarios flash through my mind, each one ending with more of those deep purple bruises on Leah's arms—but before I can put any of them into words, a door above us slams open and footsteps creak across the metal walkway. Leah blanches and scurries away.

"Leah?" says a voice, a man with a Glaswegian accent. "What's this about?"

He walks slowly down the stairs: I recognize his strawberry blond hair and cauliflower ears from the video of their last display. The stocky, bearded man in charge of the Edinburgh chapter comes next, with Mrs. Maclennan close behind them.

"Come on, then!" says the Glasgow leader. "We've no' got all day."

"I need to show you something." Leah's entire body is trembling, but she manages to keep her voice steady. "Downstairs. Please. It's about . . . It's about the Being."

The three adults blink in surprise. My phone buzzes. My heart leaps, but the noise is muffled inside my pocket.

"Show us," the man snaps at Leah. "Now!"

She nods and shuffles toward the staircase, both men and her mother following in rushed steps. Allie and I shrink back behind the pillar, but Leah's gaze flits toward us as she turns onto the stairs. That sudden flare of the old Leah has already faded—she looks so scared now, so fragile—but she leads them downstairs and away from us.

As soon as we hear the door close, I grab Allie's hand and hurry up the stairs, toward the control room marked on Leah's map. The door is unlocked, but it's pitch-black inside. I take out my phone and switch on the flashlight. The room is a large oval, its walls lined with bright green control panels covered in complex buttons and gauges and levers. In the middle of the space, tied to a computer chair, is Teacake.

Relief explodes onto her face when she sees us. Her cheeks are streaked with tears, and there's a smear of metallic blood across the right side of her jaw. She begins babbling, a mix of our own words and ones snatched from the radio. "Thundery showers, moderate or—Calum, what are you—so don't feel guilty, okay?—every little helps—"

The wings are strapped together, so tight some of Allie's carefully stitched feathers are coming loose. Teacake's arms have been pushed behind her back, and her ankles are tied to the base of the chair. I rush forward, gently shushing her, but she keeps babbling, her words tangled in her panic. Just as Allie starts to undo the knots, there's a sound from outside: footsteps creaking on the metal stairway.

They're coming. It's only been a couple of minutes. I feel a sickly blast of fear for what that means for Leah. Allie's fingers grapple at the ropes, but I put a hand out to stop her.

"If we untie her, they'll know we've been here. We need to hide."

There's a space opposite, leading behind some of the switchboards. One of them has a metal panel missing from the back:

cables and wires sprawl out from it like guts, but I push them back to make space for us to hide. I swing the light of my phone toward Allie. She's holding Teacake's face in her hands and is saying something, her voice quiet and slow. On the stairs, the footsteps are growing louder.

"Allie, quickly!"

"I'm coming." She crawls through the missing panel of the switchboard. She has to pull her knees to her chest to give me enough space to sit, and I have to tilt my head so my chin is by my collarbones, but we just fit. Behind us, Teacake keeps moaning. Allie calls to her softly.

"Just do what I said, Tea. Remember what I said."

Before I can ask what she means, voices come floating along the walkway. I switch the flashlight off on my phone and drop it into my lap. The door opens, smacking against the wall with a bang.

". . . too much of a coincidence," the Glasgow leader is saying. "We find the thing, and then the girl claims to know something about it? There has to be something in it. We should interrogate her."

"She doesn't know anything, Ross." The Edinburgh leader's voice, loud and so close it sets my nerves alight. "I don't know what she's playing at. We'll discipline her once this is all over, find out what she's up to."

He clicks a button, and a beam of light sweeps across the room. The leaders fall into silence. There's a dull groan of plastic on tiles as Teacake shifts in her chair. I can feel Allie's breath on my shoulder, shallow and warm. My pulse is so loud, I'm amazed they can't hear it.

"Jesus Christ. I still can't believe this." A light scratching sound, followed by a whimper from Teacake. I picture the Edinburgh leader running a finger over her face, touching her wings, and my chest tightens with anger.

"We need to make a decision," he says. "We've wasted enough time as it is."

Ross grunts in agreement. "Aye. It's gonnae get out of hand if the followers catch wind of this."

They're divided. Ross is torn between contacting "administration" to tell them about Teacake—"the thing," as he calls her—and selling her to a research center, splitting the reward between them. For a while the Edinburgh leader, Damien, keeps quiet, listening to Ross talk through their different options. But then footsteps move across the room. There's another long moment of silence, broken only by a tiny whimper from Teacake.

"We should destroy it," Damien says. "Break its wings. Throw it off the roof."

The beam of light sweeps from right to left. "Are you mad? If administration finds out we had a Being and *killed* it—"

"Administration are crooks. They're frauds," Damien says. "If we tell them, they'll just ship it off to America for testing anyway. We won't see a penny of it."

"Let's do it ourselves, then," Ross says. "Now, before they can find out. That center in California is offering a reward of—"

"Who gives a shit about some reward? I'm talking about *power*." Damien's voice begins to pick up pace. "There are over a hundred believers here. We could have more, if we bring the Newcastle and Manchester chapters up. Imagine it—all those people, hundreds of them, all standing together—and then this thing, this demon in our midst, falling through the air, breaking apart on the concrete. Do you not see? This thing is evil—Christ, it must be, if it's been pushed out of heaven. We'd be the ones to send it falling down to earth! That makes us closer to the Creator than anyone else alive."

He goes on and on, describing how they'd appear on every news channel in the world, how converts would flock to them from all over the globe, how they'd outsize the London and New York chapters in a couple of days. I squeeze my eyes shut, but the images he's describing swirl behind the lids. Allie keeps muttering, "Come on, Teacake, please," below her breath. Whatever she's willing her to do, Teacake doesn't comply.

Then my phone starts to buzz.

The men's chatter cuts out. "What's that?" says Damien.

One of them takes a step. Toward us.

That's when I stop thinking.

I leap out from behind the control panel, snatch the flashlight from Damien's hand, and throw it across the room; it smashes against one of the control panels and shatters, leaving us in darkness. One of the men lunges for me, but I kick him in the shins and push him to the ground. "Get her, Allie! Go!"

Swears and bumps fill the darkness. Allie grabs the back of Teacake's chair and pulls her through the door, scrambling to untie the ropes as she does so. Another hand grabs my sleeve, but I slip out of my hoodie and follow Allie through the door. I slam it shut and jam the chair, now empty of Teacake, under the doorknob. It won't hold long, but a ten-second head start could be all that we need.

"Go, go!"

We turn toward the staircase we came up. Before we can run back down, we see a cluster of Standing Fallen members, all ashen-faced and slow, ambling up the stairs toward us. A few of them look up, their jaws dropping as they see Teacake. The kids from the rooftop are among them; the little girl clutches the boy's arm, her dark eyes huge and unblinking.

I spin around and push Teacake in the opposite direction, toward a second staircase leading upward. After just a few steps, the door to the control room bursts open and the two men spill out, their heads twisting in all directions. Damien sprints after us. Ross leans over the barrier and shouts at the members staring slack-jawed up at us to move.

My legs have never worked so fast. I leap up the stairs three at a time, one hand holding Allie's and another pushing the spot between Teacake's wings. I'm too scared to look back, but I can hear the men's footsteps drawing closer, their heavy breathing just a few feet behind us. I bound forward and push open the fire escape door at the end of the final staircase. We stumble out, tripping over one another—

Onto the roof.

There's nowhere to go. Only forward, toward the edge. No wall to hold us back, no barriers. Up here the evening wind feels icy on my bare arms, and strong—strong enough to pull us from the rooftop and drag us into the sea beyond. My head starts to spin, but I grab Allie's hand and follow her and Teacake toward the edge. Ross and Damien come running through the doorway. Other members hurry after them, eyes wide and mouths gaping.

"Stay back!" Allie shouts. "If you come any closer, she'll jump. Her wings are still weak. There's no way she'd survive the fall."

It's a risky lie—they've seen Teacake zipping around McEwan Hall—but in the confusion of the moment, it stalls them: they might want Teacake to die, but only in front of an audience. Damien holds the others back.

"That's not your choice to make," he shouts to us. "That thing is a fallen angel, a manifestation of evil. It's not up to you to decide what becomes of her."

"It's not up to you, either—" Allie begins to shout, but a sudden gust of wind sends us staggering sideways, knocking the breath out of me. Damien and Ross rush forward. This is it. This is the end—

But then Teacake begins to speak.

"You're wrong about God. You're wrong about everything."

Her voice is soft and lilting, almost carried away by the wind, but the men slam to a halt. For a moment, I forget about the crowd surrounding us, about the wind and the fact that we're on a rooftop fifty feet above the ground. *This is it. She's learned to talk. She's going to tell us her secrets.*

But then I see Allie nodding, and it clicks: these are the words she whispered to Teacake down in the control room. Even with the Standing Fallen leaders just a few feet away, I find myself beaming at her. I would never have thought of that.

"Go on," she says, loud enough only for Teacake and me to hear. "You can do this, Tea."

Teacake closes her eyes and begins, in her strange, musical voice, to repeat Allie's words.

"You're wrong about everything," she says again. "Choosing to sleep on a dirty floor doesn't make you a purer soul. Risking your life climbing onto buildings doesn't make it any more valuable, and you're not going to save anyone screaming through a loudspeaker. I know you're scared, but use that fear for something good—tackle the greed and destruction you see in the world, make it better for people who suffer from it the most. Go back to your homes and your families and get to work, because this isn't the way to the afterlife. It isn't the way at all."

Teacake opens her eyes. Dozens of the gaunt, tired faces stare at her, the wind whipping through their hair or ruffling their scruffy clothes. There's shock in their expressions, confusion and fear— and in some cases, anger. But only Damien reacts.

"No. No." He shakes his head. "You're lying."

This time, when he steps toward us, only a few people follow. The other members simply look at one another. Some run their hands over their protruding ribs or examine the fraying hems of their clothes, blinking, like they're emerging from a dream. A skeletal woman slides her arm around the young boy and his little sister, pulling them close.

But Damien hasn't given up. With a few stone-faced followers behind him, he charges toward us.

Before I have time to react, or even to feel fear, Teacake loops one arm around my waist. She slips the other around Allie and takes four steps backward.

Together, we fall from the roof.

TWENTY-SEVEN

THE GROUND ROCKETS TOWARD US. THE ROAD BENEATH US swells, hurtling upward at an impossible speed, until all I can see is tarmac and moss and cigarette butts. I hold my breath and close my eyes, waiting for the blast of pain—but then Teacake throws her body backward, flipping head over heels, and sends us spiraling into the air. Sky and concrete and the almost-full moon loop across my vision; the people on the rooftop spiral in and out of sight, smaller with each rotation.

For a few seconds, I am frozen with shock. It's only when Teacake beats her wings and regains her balance, gliding some two hundred feet above the ground, that fear snatches my breath and turns my blood to ice. Beneath us the sea is blue-gray and restless, its waves smashing on the shore.

"Put me down!" I scream, thrashing in Teacake's grip, kicking my legs as if I could swim back to land. I can't focus on the wind in my hair or the feeling of gliding birdlike above the sea; all I think about is the biting waves below, and our bodies being swallowed up by them. "Please, please, I need to get down!"

Her voice almost snatched away by the wind, Allie shouts and points toward her car. Teacake lands a few meters away from it, dropping us from her grip: Allie goes rolling across the dirt, while I skid toward the pavement. The gravel chews through my jeans and bites at my thighs, but I hardly notice. Our crash landing has sent dust billowing into the air: Allie hides her mouth behind her sleeve, but her face is already turning red.

Everything is happening too fast. Dark figures move behind the station's windows: Damien and the handful of followers who obeyed his instructions, hurrying down the stairs toward the exit.

"Get Teacake into the car!" I tell Allie. "Quick!"

Without thinking, I grab a beer bottle on the side of the road and smash it open on the curb. While Allie and Teacake rush down the road to her car, I race toward the two gray vans parked at the opposite end of the building and stab the bottle into their back tires, wiggling it into the rubber until I hear a hiss of air.

As I sprint away from the vans, I hear Leah shout my name. She comes scrambling over a pile of junk, her jeans snagging on scrap metal and old wires. More people are beginning to pile out of the building, looking from us to Leah to the members still standing on the roof. Leah tears across the road, running faster than I knew she could, and reaches Allie's car just as I do. We leap into the backseat, our arms and legs becoming tangled with Teacake's.

"Go, go, go!"

Allie slams her foot on the pedal. She skids in a semicircle at the corner to the building, then thunders down the road, scattering a couple of Standing Fallen members chasing after us.

"Teacake, sit down!" she shouts. "I can't see behind me!"

Her wings are blocking most of the rear window. I gently press on her back until she's leaning forward, her head between her knees, one wing spread across Leah's lap and the other over mine. As I glance through the window, my stomach flips: Damien is behind us, climbing into one of the shabby gray vans.

"No, no, no . . ." Leah moans and clutches my arm. "We have to go faster! He's going to catch up!"

Behind the windscreen, Damien's head dips as he jabs the key into the ignition. The van lurches, then comes to a halt. Allie watches in the rearview mirror, her face tense, as Damien stumbles from the car and stares at the wheels.

Allie takes a deep breath. She's still wheezing, and it takes her a moment to speak. "That was so close," she finally says, her voice wobbly and raspy with dust. She meets my eye in the mirror. Though she looks as shaken as I feel, she forces a smile. "Nice work with the vans, Jaya. You're like those badass nuns from *The Sound of Music*."

I try to laugh, but my heart is pounding so fast I can hardly speak. Teacake is still bent forward, her head between her knees. I stroke her hair and she mumbles something—a few lines of an Alanis Morissette song. I turn her head toward me and wipe the goldish blood from her jaw. Her skin is lightly scraped, and there are rusty bruises on her wrists and ankles. Just the thought of those men touching her makes my face hot with anger.

"It's over now, Tea. They're gone," I say, though she keeps

shaking. More than ever before, I wish I knew exactly how much she understands. I keep stroking her hair and her feathers, trying to communicate what the words can't, hoping that being with us is enough to make her feel safe.

"What did you tell them back there?" I ask Leah. For a moment, she can't get the words out: her eyes are wide as the moon, and she keeps glancing through the back window, checking that no one is following us.

"That I'd found a—a Being. I said that I'd hidden it in the basement, but that it had escaped. They knew it wasn't true. I'm not a good liar."

"You did great," Allie says, stifling another cough. "That took some guts, facing up to them like that."

Leah shakes her head. "I shouldn't have left my mum. I really wasn't planning on it." She wipes her eyes on the back of her ragged sleeves. "But when I saw how angry she was with me about lying to the leaders, I knew she'd never choose to leave herself. You guys were my only chance."

"You did the right thing," I say, but she keeps looking back toward the base, even when it's long out of sight.

The towns soon fall behind us, and we find ourselves moving through quiet country roads. I climb into the passenger seat beside Allie, and though there's no one out here to spot her through the windows, Leah stretches her legs over the back to help Teacake squeeze into the space on the floor. Her right wing curls over her body like a blanket; the left pokes up toward the roof, but I hang my jacket over the back of Allie's headrest to keep it out of sight.

"Where should we go?" I ask. "We can't keep driving around all night."

"We can't go back to Edinburgh, either," Allie says. "Someone could have seen Teacake on the roof of the power station, or one of the Standing Fallen members might tell their superiors. It'd be all over the internet in five minutes."

I think for a moment. "How about my house? It's pretty remote, and our garden is lined with trees—you can't see in much. We can drop you off at your dad's," I add, looking at Leah. She nods, her eyes glassy.

"Won't that take, like, four hours?" Allie rubs her eyes with one hand. "Honestly, Jaya, I'm knackered. There's no way I can drive that long. You don't have a license, do you?"

I shake my head. "I won't be seventeen until October."

"I do," Leah says. "I don't have it with me, though, and I'm pretty sure my insurance has run out."

I give a dry laugh. "If we get pulled over, that's really the last of our worries."

Allie's phone rings—it's been buzzing nonstop for ages. I see Calum's name flash onto the screen. Allie pauses, chewing on her lip, then sighs and swipes the call away.

"Let's do it," she says. "I've got enough pills on me for a few days. We'll have to stop for about a gallon of coffee en route, mind."

She types the address into her GPS, selecting a route off the A9 so we can avoid most of the CCTV and speed cameras. We drive through villages and clusters of houses, past fields of sleepy animals and through quiet woodlands dappled with moonlight. Allie puts the radio on, filling our sleepy silence with meandering chatter about the *Great British Bake Off* and a competition to win a holiday to Tenerife.

As the nerves fade, sleep slowly takes over. *We did it*, I think as my eyes droop. We got Teacake back.

Another miracle, after all.

Leah's house looks lonely when we drop her off. It's almost two o'clock in the morning, the deepest point of the summer night; all the lights are off, and the gate to the drive is closed. For a second I think of Peter Pan, returning home from Neverland to find his parents have forgotten about him. Only Leah's the opposite of the Lost Boys—if anything, she's done too much growing up.

She sits in the driver's seat for a moment, clutching her seat belt and staring at the unlit windows. "I don't know what to tell my dad," she says. "What if he's angry that I left Mum behind?"

"Are you joking? After everything you've been through . . . there's no way he'll blame you for this." I give her a little nudge forward. "Go on. Just tell him the truth."

Leah nods, her eyes red and watery. We might have gotten her away from the Standing Fallen, but a 150-mile car ride hasn't magically returned her to the funny, mouthy, slightly cocky girl I knew a few months ago. Then again, maybe she was always full of these insecurities. Maybe the Standing Fallen just stripped away her means of hiding them.

"Okay. I'm ready."

She takes a deep breath and looks down at Teacake, who's tucked up asleep on the floor. Even after spending four hours in a cramped car together, Leah's eyes still fill with amazement when she looks at Teacake; at the huge, shimmering wings wrapped like blankets around her body.

"Tell her good luck from me," she says, nodding at Allie. She turns to me last. "Thanks, Jaya. I really am sorry."

We watch from the car as she opens the gate and walks up the front steps. An upstairs light comes on, and a minute later, the door opens. The Standing Fallen have changed Mr. Maclennan, too: he looks older than I remember, all sharp lines and streaks of gray. It takes him a beat to recognize the pale, gaunt girl standing in front of him, but then he lets out a sob and throws his arms around her. They're still there when Allie climbs into the driver's seat and drives off, slowly swaying in the glow of the streetlight.

Ten minutes later, as we pull up to my own front door, a lump forms in my throat. The house looks smaller than I remember. The red door I've walked through so many times is unfamiliar, the garden wilder in the darkness. I wish I had someone to welcome me home like Leah did. Even if it was Dad. He's called me thirty times in the past few hours, and Rani another twenty. I've texted them to say I'm fine but can't bring myself to phone them back. I've got no idea what I'll say when I do.

Allie switches off the engine and slumps over the steering wheel. "Remind me to never, ever do that again."

I get out of the passenger seat and open the back door. "We're here, Tea." I give her shoulder a gentle shake. She wakes with a start, mumbling a few lines of a car insurance advert and rubbing her eyes, and follows me out of the car.

Her fatigue evaporates the moment her feet touch the ground.

The first thing she does is take a breath. I'd forgotten how different the air feels here, much softer and cleaner than in the city. She inhales and exhales, her shoulders rising with each slow breath, then tilts her head back to look at the stars. I wonder what she sees there: if the constellations spell out ancient stories, like the tales of gods and beasts told from China to Egypt, India to Greece, or if they're simply a map home.

The tips of her wings begin to twitch. "We're here, Tea," she mimics. "Call in now for your chance to enjoy ten days of sand, sea, and sun."

I nudge her forward. "Go. You've got this."

Out here, with only the garden's shadows and the sky's inky blue as a backdrop, her wings look larger and grander than ever. The fibers of her feathers glitter in the starlight: countless shimmering pinks, now mixed with mallard blue and goldfinch yellow. She sprints over the gravel—if the stones hurt her feet, she doesn't show it—leaps over the pond, and rises above the house, looping around the chimney like a curl of smoke.

Allie climbs out from the driver's seat, her yawn freezing into a gape as she watches Teacake glide over the treetops. "What if somebody sees?"

I shake my head. There are a few houses over the hill, but our neighbors are either old or couples with little kids: it's unlikely anyone will be awake to spot her at this time of night. Even if they did, I don't think either of us could deny Teacake this.

We don't rush her, either. We lie on the grass, slipping in and out of sleep, as Teacake rises and dips across the sky, sometimes staying airborne for almost twenty minutes at a time. By the time she's tired herself out, it's past four and there's a hint of orange on the horizon. I find the spare set of keys hidden under the clay hedgehog in the flower bed and unlock the door. Teacake's face crumples when she realizes we're asking her to go inside again, but she follows us up the front steps.

The house feels strange, the way it always does when you come home from a long holiday. I get Teacake settled into the living room, the most spacious in the house. I turn the radio on for her and fish out a packet of Kit Kats from the kitchen cupboard in case she gets hungry in the night.

"Sorry, I know it's a bit small after the hall," I say. "You can go out again tomorrow. As long as you like."

Teacake smiles. "As long as you like," she echoes.

Butterflies start to flit around my stomach as I take Allie up to my room. Everything between us has been put on hold since we began our rescue operation. Now, as I get out a sleeping bag from the bottom of my cupboard, it all comes flooding back: the tension, the almost-kiss. Her silent questions about Leah, the answers I couldn't have given until a few hours ago.

Right now, though, we're both too tired to think about much other than sleep; Allie, in particular, looks exhausted. She sinks onto my bed, too knackered to even kick her shoes off, her hands above her head. From this angle, the falling petals on her wrist look as if they're floating upward.

"How are you feeling?" I ask.

When she answers, I get the feeling it's the first time she's being totally honest with me about it.

"Pretty shit. Really shit, actually. This isn't the stupidest thing I've ever done, but it's probably in the top three." She opens one eye and gives me a watery smile. "Also . . . I kind of lied. I've only got enough meds to last me until tomorrow. After that, I'll need someone to bring me more."

It takes me a few seconds to catch what she means. "Calum."

Her eyes flutter shut again. "I know what he did was unforgivable," she says. "I won't call him unless you say it's okay."

There's no way I can say no. Her treatment isn't optional—and if Calum doesn't bring it, her parents will, and they probably hate me for dragging her up here without telling them.

"What was that thing he wanted the money for?" I ask, sitting on the bed beside her. "Stem cell treatment?"

She nods. "It's being developed as an alternative treatment for CF. It hasn't been approved here, but I've read about a few people who have gone to the Dominican Republic for it. It costs loads. Thousands—much more than Calum's photos would have earned." Her eyelids droop shut. "I guess he's looking for a miracle, in case things take another turn for the worse."

My insides turn to ice. "Why didn't you tell me that sooner?"

"It doesn't make any difference. It was still a shitty thing to do. He shouldn't have gone behind our backs. Besides, he shouldn't be trying to make decisions about my treatments for me." Her hand inches across the duvet, until her fingertips are touching mine. "But I think he deserves a second chance. If that's okay with you."

People make mistakes. I have. I can't judge Calum for doing the same. I nod. "It's Teacake who has to forgive him, not me." I look at my phone. Another ten missed calls since I last checked. "Actually, I think—I think I need to make a phone call, too."

Allie's eyebrows lift. Even in the dim glow from my desk lamp, I see the fear and suspicion and anger flickering through her eyes. "Your dad?"

"I promised my sister I would tell him if we were in trouble. I think it's time for me to trust him," I say. "Plus, Rani will want to be with Teacake, too. She'd want to say good-bye."

Allie's silent for a moment, fiddling absentmindedly with one of her earrings, but then she nods. "Okay. Let's do it."

The sun is coming up now. My mind is fuzzy with fatigue, and my words are beginning to slur. It's far too early to ring anyone, or maybe far too late. But we take out our phones anyway, and we make the calls.

TWENTY-EIGHT

IT HAPPENED ON A MONDAY. IT HAPPENED IN NOVEMBER, IN A place where we weren't supposed to be. I should have been in double math, listening to Mr. Anderson drone on about vectors and tangents. She should have been in the office she'd set up in what was once our guest room, doing her paperwork or responding to clients' emails. Neither of us was supposed to be walking in the glen.

I couldn't face school that morning; I was still recovering from Amy Williamson's party the Saturday before. Part of that was the combination of vodka, Red Bull, and Blue WKD that I'd drunk—my first two-day hangover, and hopefully my last—but most of it was down to the same reason I'd spent all of Sunday in my room, locked in a WhatsApp fight and drowning out the world with music: Leah.

We had kissed three times by then. Once on my sixteenth

birthday, back in October; once on Guy Fawkes Night; and once in the woods on an orienteering trip when we realized neither of us knew how to read a map and got completely lost. Each kiss was rushed, but each one lasted longer than the last. Each kiss was secret, but each one felt like a step toward something bigger. She didn't want a label, but we were building up to something with a name. That's what it felt like, anyway.

But that Saturday, I walked into Amy Williamson's kitchen and saw her kissing Joseph Macrae, and that "something," that thing that I'd thought we'd been building up to—it had crumbled. The argument we'd had afterward, the messages she'd sent saying that this wasn't who she was, that I wasn't who she wanted, that the whole thing had been a phase and a mistake . . . all that had ground the rubble into dust.

"I'm not going in," I told Mum when she came into my room at half past seven on Monday morning. "I'm not well. Got a migraine."

She put her hand on my forehead. When I was little, I tried once or twice to fake a fever by pressing a hot towel against my forehead. This time I didn't even have the energy to fake a headache. It was obvious I wasn't sick, but Mum just swept my hair out of my face and pulled the duvet up to my shoulders.

"You can stay home with me today, then," she said. "Get some more sleep, I'll give the school a ring."

She came back at ten o'clock with a tray of tea and toast. She stayed with me as I took a few bites, telling me about some emails she'd had from an irate customer, then suggested we go for a walk in the glen. "You look like you could do with some fresh air. Clear that headache of yours," she said, grinning.

She'd been going on for months about how important my Highers were, how every lesson counted. I didn't know why she was letting me stay home, but I didn't argue; I was just happy not to have to face Leah, or Emma's questions, or Joseph Macrae's annoyingly handsome face.

I brushed my teeth, got dressed, pulled my hair back into a ponytail. I went downstairs, put my shoes on, walked out to the car. I can't work out at which point things went off course. Maybe if I hadn't paused to put my hair up, she'd still be here. Maybe if I'd forgotten something and run back to my room, she'd still be here. I *know* that if I'd said no, or if I'd gone to school in the first place, she would be.

But I didn't. I got in the car and we drove to the glen, and the unlikely became the inevitable.

Nowadays it's just another bullet point on my long, long list of places to avoid, but back in November, the glen was one of the many spots Mum and I loved to go walking: a little green haven of birch and yew and elm trees, with a beautiful waterfall looking out toward the hills. It was quiet that day, as always, and strangely sunny for November. We walked up the path, talking about school, Emma's latest boy drama, my uncle Dinesh's new girlfriend. I could feel my bad mood start to lift a little, until she brought Leah up.

"Leah hasn't been over for a while," she said as we pushed open the gate leading into the glen. Or maybe it was, "What Highers is Leah doing again?" Like so many things, I can't quite remember. Whatever it was, she was skating around the topic, clearing a path for me to talk about her.

I didn't take it. It felt good, being outside, with the fresh air clearing my thoughts. I'd even left my phone at home so I couldn't check if Leah had sent any more messages.

So I changed the subject. Another time, I decided as I followed Mum up the path toward the top of the waterfall. I would talk to her about it another time.

We left the path, then headed toward the clearing on the east side of the waterfall. It was the best viewpoint in the whole glen: you could see way out to the mountains, topped with a dusting of snow. You had to cross the brook at the top of the waterfall to get there; the water was usually shallow, and there were stepping-stones from one side to the other, past the sharp drop of the water's edge and the rocky pool some ten meters below.

I'd crossed that stream dozens of times, Mum even more. The current wasn't faster that day; the rocks weren't slippery or frosty. There was nothing to suggest that trip would be different from any other.

If she was closer to the edge than normal, I didn't notice. If the rock gave way, I didn't see. But for some reason, she lost her balance. Her right leg kicked out; her arms spun around. She grabbed a branch overhead, and for a second she was still—but then came a snap, and the branch broke off in her hands.

"Oh," she said.

And then she disappeared.

There was a crash: a snap of bones, a splash of water. Noises I've heard echoed dozens of times, each time another Being falls. Sounds that loop over and over in my thoughts, in my nightmares.

After that, all I have are spots of color. Her scarf, bright yellow, ensnared on a branch by the foot of the pool. Splashes of red across the rocks, spilling into the water. A dozen different greens, scratching at my arms and tangling around my feet. Then black.

Allie once told me her life had always been a conditional clause. Since that day, mine has, too. If we hadn't gone for that walk. If I hadn't skived off school. If I'd never kissed Leah on my birthday. If Mum hadn't gotten pregnant with me in the first place.

There are countless cases that could have kept Mum here. For most of them, I'm the only common factor. No matter how you work it out, the answer is the same: it was my fault, it was my fault, it was my fault.

TWENTY-NINE

THE SOUND OF TIRES CRUNCHING ON GRAVEL WAKES ME UP.
I sit up, squinting in the morning sun, and for a moment I can't
work out where I am. Flashes of last night's events come back to me:
McEwan Hall, empty—Leah on the rooftop—untying Teacake—
the long drive north—

Phoning Dad. Telling him to come home now, and not telling
him why.

Key in the lock. The front door opens.

"Oh, shit."

I scramble out of the sleeping bag, trip on the hood, and fall
down again. Allie jerks awake, her hair sticking up in all directions.
I run downstairs: Dad's shoes are lying by the door; Rani's backpack is at the foot of the stairs. The living-room door is ajar. Maybe
he hasn't seen yet. Maybe I still have time to explain, in person,
like I wanted to—

Too late.

For a split second, I see it through Dad's eyes. There is a Being in our house. In our living room. Sitting on the back of our sofa, her wings sharp strokes of pink against our antique cream walls. A Being eating our Kit Kats, grinning a chocolatey smile at our dog.

Perry bounds forward, barking in delight; Teacake lifts her up, giggling as the dog licks at her face. Rani leans against the wall, scratching one leg with the back of her foot, and lifts her hand in a small wave.

"Dad," I say. "Dad, I was going to—"

He looks around. My lower lip is trembling, and my palms are clammy. He's going to kill me. He's going to hate me. I don't know which is worse.

"Jaya, what's going on?" He steps toward me, then turns to Teacake, then back to me again. "I don't understand. What is this?"

"This is . . ." I swallow. "This is Teacake."

Before he has a chance to ask, I tell him the whole story: Teacake's story, or the part I know of it, at least. For a long moment, afterward, none of us speak. In the silence, it feels as if the echoes of my sentences swell, becoming more absurd with each passing second.

Teacake is the one to break the silence.

"Coming up on the show today, we'll be hearing from Russell Tovey about his latest film and sharing a ratatouille recipe that's to die for," she says. "But first, the weather!"

The color drains from Dad's face. He collapses into an armchair, staring at Teacake with unblinking eyes. His head turns from her to me and back again. I can't tell which of us he's more surprised by.

"Why didn't you tell me?"

His voice is so fragile. I can't stand it. He's my dad. He's not supposed to sound like this. Like my words have chipped and chiseled at his bones. Like the next sentence I speak could cause him to crumble.

"Why didn't you tell me?" he says again. His fingers clench; for a moment I think he's about to throttle me, but instead he grabs at his hair. "This is all I've thought about . . . everything I wanted to . . . why the *hell* would you keep this from me?"

I don't know how to answer. Like so many things, it seems ridiculous in hindsight.

"She thought you'd sell her," Rani says. "She thought you were going to give her up for research, or to a cult."

Dad looks at her, his mouth open. "*You* knew about this, too?"

Rani's eyes fill with tears. "She wouldn't let me tell you! I wanted to, but she made me promise!"

"I can't believe this. I can't believe you'd . . ."

He pushes himself out of his chair and begins to pace. Every few steps he stops and stares at Teacake with a crazed look in his eyes. She presses herself against the wall, her wings twitching nervously. For a moment, he's quiet—then he spins around to stare at me.

"You let me go ahead with it." There's a pink flush spreading over his cheeks. "Yesterday. You let me make a fool of myself in front of all those people, when you knew there was no chance of it happening."

The guilt is aching. Tears blur my vision, but I brush them away. "Dad, I'm sorry! I never wanted to lie to you. I had to do what was best for Teacake."

"For *her*?" The pink has turned to red now; the veins at his temples begin to bulge. "What about your family, Jaya? Did you think about what was best for us?"

The last few words come as a shout. Teacake starts and falls backward off the sofa. Rani grabs her hand and drags her out of the living room and upstairs. The lump in my throat has blocked out my voice. I didn't expect it to be like this. I've been angry at Dad for so long: I thought I'd be able to argue back, to stand my ground—the way Allie and Calum stood up to the manager outside Celeste's the time I first saw them. Instead, all I feel is a deep, crushing sadness.

"I didn't know what to do. I should have told you. I should have—" My head is starting to spin. The living-room walls swirl around me. "I saw it happen, I saw her fall. It's my fault. It's all my fault."

The floor tilts beneath my feet. I sink to the carpet, my palms over my eyes. After a moment, I feel hands on my shoulders. Dad slides his arms around my back and pulls me into his chest. I don't know how he knows, but he knows . . . he knows I'm not talking about Teacake anymore.

"Come here, pet," he says quietly. "It's okay. It's okay."

And suddenly, like lightning cracking on ice, something inside me splits and I'm sobbing. Because there's part of the story that I haven't told anyone: not Dad, not Rani, not the police. It's the part of the story that I can only barely admit to myself. And though the words stab at my throat, I force myself to say them now.

"I ran."

I saw her fall, and I ran.

All these months later, I still can't explain it. Logic, rationality, even common decency, they were all swept away by the avalanche thundering through my mind. All I thought was: I'll go back to the house. I'll run back, to before this happened, to half past seven that morning, when she walked into my bedroom, when she still had lunch and the weekend and years and years of life ahead of her.

I ran.

It was only a couple of minutes, just a few hundred meters—but I ran.

Somewhere in the glen, I came to my senses: I had to help, I had to get help. I sprinted back to the waterfall, but even then I couldn't look at her properly: all I remember was the blood blossoming into the water, the jarring yellow streak of her scarf against the bracken. I didn't have my phone on me to call an ambulance, so I ran toward the nearest village and flagged down a couple of hikers. One of them said something about first aid—I followed her back into the glen, but when she got to the pool, the woman turned around and grabbed both of my arms.

"Don't look." That's the last thing I remember hearing, until the ambulance came and the police turned up. "Don't look."

If I'd checked her pulse. If I hadn't run. If I'd taken my phone with me.

More conditionals.

Now the words come spilling out of me. I hardly notice I'm talking until I reach the point where the memories grow murky; where the hiker told me not to look and I knew that Mum was gone.

I keep waiting for the moment when Dad realizes what I've done and pushes me away. Instead, he hugs me tighter with one arm and holds the other out to Rani, who's crying in the doorway. She slides underneath, pressing her damp face into my shoulder. We stay there, the three of us, together for the first time in forever.

After a long while, Dad draws back. He turns my head gently so I'm looking at him. His eyes are red, and there are tears on his cheeks. It's the first time I've ever seen him cry.

"There's nothing you could have done." His voice is soft and fierce at the same time. "The doctors told me. The way she hit her head . . . she died instantly, Jaya. It was over in a second. Even if you'd called right away, darling, it wouldn't have made a difference. There's nothing you could have done to change what happened."

Another wave of pain hits me, and another, as Dad keeps telling me I'm not to blame. They're only words: they don't change anything, and they can't bring her back. But I realize, as another wave of tears well up, that they're all I've been waiting to hear since last November.

THIRTY

"IT WAS NEVER ABOUT THE MONEY."

It's a few hours later, after my tears have dried and his shock has subsided, and Dad and I are sitting on the bench under the Japanese maple, the one Mum and I planted the summer we moved into this house. Allie is still upstairs, sleeping or waiting for Calum's taxi to arrive from the train station. Rani and Perry are chasing Teacake around the lawn in a semi-airborne game of tag, taking care to stay hidden below the trees. But for now, it's just me and Dad.

I can't remember the last time we sat like this, the two of us. It's nice, but also slightly awkward. He keeps slipping into long, thoughtful silences; I can't stop staring into my apple juice, swirling the ice cubes as if I might find something to fill the gaps in conversation in the glass.

"It had nothing to do with the rewards," he says finally. "I can see why you thought that, though. I was obsessed: the stats, the research, the sales. I wanted to learn as much as I could. It was a distraction. But that was never why I wanted to find one. I just thought it was a sign, a message from the universe. Or from Mum."

A lump rises to my throat. I take another long sip of apple juice, trying to soothe it. In all the times he talked at me about his Wingding research, Dad never brought Mum into it. Not once. I knew that her death was tied to the Falls in his mind, just like it was in mine—but he'd never said that was the main reason for his wanting to find a Being.

"I know it sounds daft, thinking the Falls were a personal message just for me," he says. "Selfish, even. But they started so soon after she died. One fell a few feet from the spot where I proposed to her, just outside St. Giles' Cathedral. Can you blame me for reading into it?"

Across the garden, Rani is leaping over the flower bed. She tries to grab Teacake's foot, but Teacake flits out of reach, giggling. As I grapple for something to say, I realize I've hardly thought about what the past year has been like for Dad: losing his wife, leaving his job, being plunged into single fatherhood. I've been so busy hating his fixation on the Beings, I never really stopped to consider its cause.

The few inches separating us suddenly feel like miles. The person I was before all this never would have believed he was capable of giving Teacake up to be tortured or experimented on. But the person that Dad was before never would have led me to believe such a thing.

"I don't know if you could find out, even if you asked her," I say. "We've tried. Teacake has an amazing memory—she can practically recite the entire news word for word—but she doesn't seem to understand much of what she's saying. Maybe she will in a few weeks."

Dad gives a sad smile. "That's too long, though, isn't it? There must be people up there who love her, people she misses. If she can leave now, she should. It'd be unfair to ask her to stay just for us."

Another surprise: I'd never heard him express any interest in what the Falls might mean for the Beings. I didn't think he'd even considered it. There's a lot I don't know about Dad, just like there's a lot I don't know about Mum. But he's still here to help me fill in the blanks. And so are Ammamma and Dinesh, all her friends and family in London and Sri Lanka. It's not enough, and it'll never be the same. But it's something.

We talk for a while longer, slipping back into everyday topics for the first time in months—lunch, the garden, the exam results I'm due to get in a couple of days—until a taxi comes crawling up the drive. Teacake stiffens; I don't know if she's guessed what's coming, or if the car reminds her of being kidnapped by the Standing Fallen. I hurry across the lawn toward her.

"It's okay, Tea. It's just Calum," I say, glancing toward the car. "He's not going to hurt you."

The taxi stops at the bottom of the drive, far enough away that the driver won't be able to see Teacake behind the trees. Calum steps out and slowly walks toward the house, his eyes nervously flitting from me to Teacake and back. Teacake crosses her arms, a habit she's picked up from Allie. Calum stops at the edge of the lawn, his hands deep in his pockets.

"Hey." He looks at the ground, bumps the toe of his trainer against the grass as the taxi drives off. "I . . . I don't know where to start."

"Just speak to her," I tell him. "She's listening."

I don't know if Teacake even knows what he did or if she's just picked up on the tension between Allie, Calum, and myself, but it doesn't matter: either way, she deserves an apology. Calum's cheeks flush, but he looks Teacake in the eye. Her wings bend, then straighten, quickly, like a whip cracking. Calum slings his back-pack off his shoulder and unzips it. It's filled with packets of Tun-nock's Tea Cakes.

"I got you these," he says sheepishly. "I know it can't make up for what happened. I just thought you might like them."

Teacake takes a box. "Our best-ever sofa sale is now on," she says flatly, the usual musical lilt in her voice gone. After a moment, though, she rips open the cardboard. A small grin tugs at Calum's mouth, but he quickly suppresses it. None of us are going to let him off that easily.

"I've expected too much from you. You're not a sign of the after-life or anything like that." His head dips toward the ground, but he forces himself to look Teacake in the eye. "You're just a person. I don't know how I forgot that. I'm sorry."

Teacake eats the biscuit in three bites, leaving smears of choco-late and marshmallow around her mouth. She reaches into the box for a second, then pauses. Instead of unwrapping it, she hands it to Calum.

"Malin: Southwest four or five. Slight or moderate," she says. "Mainly fair. Good."

Calum grins. It's just more of the *Shipping Forecast*, but there's a hint of optimism in her words. He starts to unpeel the foil, then pauses.

"Whatever I did, it wasn't out of greed." His eyes dart to me, just for a second. "I was doing what I thought was best for my family. You get that, right?"

My dad thought he was doing the same. It's funny: Calum prioritized Allie before Teacake, but I picked Teacake over my dad. Maybe things would have been easier if I'd tried to see things from his point of view, or if I'd just trusted him. But I don't think I need to feel guilty about it anymore. I was doing what I felt was best, too.

"I do," I tell Calum. "I get it."

We smile at each other; it's still kind of awkward, but the bad vibe between us is starting to fade. And as we head inside to see Allie, an idea comes to me: a way that Calum really could get some of the money he was promised.

"Ready, Teacake? Action!"

Calum claps one hand against his leg and presses a button on his camera with the other. The sun has just set, and the sky is slowly melting from pink and orange into navy—Calum's favorite time of day for filming or taking photos, and dark enough for Teacake to rise above the trees without attracting unwanted attention.

She dives into the air, somersaults over our heads, then spins in dainty pirouettes toward the clouds. Calum's explanation of how the camera works confused her at first, but now she's showing off for it: darting and dipping, rising in sweeping loops toward the stars, then zipping sparrow-quick toward the ground.

We've agreed we won't share the footage until Teacake has left and we're sure she's gotten away safely. If it comes to that, this video is going to make the internet explode.

"Awesome, Tea." Calum gives her a thumbs-up and tilts the camera toward her with the other. "This looks amazing."

The rest of us sit on the grass and watch her display. Allie leans against my arm, wrapped up in two of my hoodies. She spent most of the day sleeping to make up for yesterday's overexertion. She still looks pale and tired, but her temperature has gone down and she's less breathless than she was last night. It feels like a lucky escape.

Still levitating above us, Teacake starts to pose: she clasps her hands and bends her knee in prayer, a perfect imitation of the images in Rani's art books. Dad laughs and shakes his head, like he still can't quite believe what he's seeing. I don't know if he's fully forgiven me for lying to him about Teacake for so long. That might take a while. But hopefully this, this breathtaking sight that so few other people will ever get to see with their own eyes—hopefully this makes up for it.

As Teacake makes a smooth landing just beside the flower bed, we all burst into applause. She beams and quotes three lines of a Dylan Thomas poem; there was a special on Radio 4 this afternoon. Rani tugs on Calum's sleeve to watch the video.

"How much do you think we could sell this for, Dad?" she asks. "I heard the guy who filmed the first Fall is a millionaire now."

"You'd have to prove it's genuine," Dad says. "You wouldn't believe how much fake footage is out there."

"We'll have one of Teacake's feathers," Calum says. "That has to count for something, right?"

As we're talking, Teacake turns to Allie and drops to her knees. She spins around, facing away from her, and bends her head toward the ground. Like an eagle soaring above the plains, her wings open wide.

Allie's eyes light up. "Oh my God. Teacake!"

The blood drains from Dad's face, but Allie's already climbing onto Teacake's back. Rani helps her sling her legs over Teacake's hips, and then Allie loops her arms around Teacake's neck. Calum abandons his camera and hurries toward her.

"Al, wait! I don't know if this is a good idea," he says. "Last thing I need is for you to break your neck."

Allie gives a dry laugh. "Oh yeah, that would really suck for you." She rests her chin on the curve of Teacake's spine. "Come on, California. You can't seriously ask me to miss this."

Calum runs his hand through his hair and sighs. I can practically see all the terrible ways this could end flicking through his eyes. After a minute, he sighs and throws his hands up.

"All right, fine. Just don't tell Mum, all right? And don't go too high, Teacake!"

Teacake quotes an M&S advert in response, which we take to mean agreement. She takes a short run-up, her legs buckling ever so slightly under the extra weight of Allie, and suddenly she's in the air. Allie lets out a laugh that sounds a little like a scream as they swerve past the house, spinning over the lawn.

"Oh my God! This is amazing!"

Calum picks his camera up and sprints after her, trying his best to hold the camera steady. After a minute, though, his steps begin to slow. He stops by the little brook on the edge of the garden and just watches, with his own eyes, as Teacake carries his sister into the air. They move through the trees, birds flocking out of the branches.

For a few seconds, they slip out of sight, leaving us in silence but for the hush of the breeze. Just at the point where I'm starting to worry, the leaves of two birch trees rustle and Teacake shoots toward us, looping around Dad and landing smoothly at the edge of the pond.

We all burst into applause. Allie slides down, slightly shaky on her feet but beaming. She throws her arms around Teacake, who pats Allie's head with a bemused expression, then stretches her hand out to Rani. Allie pushes her forward.

"Go on, Ran, it's the best!"

Dad's eyes just about pop out of his head. After much cajoling, he eventually lets Teacake take my sister on a gentle trip over the lawn. As we watch them, Allie slides her hand into mine. We drift toward the other end of the garden and sit on the grass, sheltered beneath the drooping branches of the willow tree.

"How are you feeling?" I ask for the twentieth time that day. "What did your mum say when you called?"

If my fretting bugs her, she doesn't show it. "I'm fine. She gave me the Muhammed Ali of bollockings—I'm lucky she and my dad both have work this week or they'd have driven up here to deliver it in person. I suppose I deserve it, though. Believe it or not, I was pretty strict about taking my meds and doing my treatments until you showed up."

My mouth drops open. "I never said you shouldn't—"

"I'm not blaming you!" She laughs. "I just mean, you coming to Edinburgh, bringing us to Teacake . . . it changed everything."

"So you're saying it was fate?" I grin. "That's not very atheist of you."

She bumps her shoulder into mine. "Unlike other people, *I* never claimed to have the answers. But no, I don't think it was fate. I still don't believe in any of that."

I tilt my head in the direction of Teacake, who is now struggling to lift a far-too-heavy Calum into the air. "Even after hanging out with an angel for the past few weeks?"

"My gran used to say that God has his plan, and that everything, no matter how horrible, is part of that." She runs her hands through the flowers, brushing the edges of the yellow and purple petals. "Personally, I think it's random. Chaotic, even. But I don't think that makes it less valuable. If anything, I think it makes it more incredible—the fact that we're here at all, just the happy result of some gas and dust and gravity."

My gaze drifts back to Teacake. Her feathers catch the light, glinting blue-black-pink like oil on water. I don't know if I agree with her, but in a way Allie's right: there's so much magic around us, such breathtaking beauty, that it doesn't really matter where it came from.

"Did you talk to Leah?" Allie asks.

I nod. "She called me on her way to Edinburgh. She and her dad are going to try to get her mum back, and then they want to go down south, or maybe even to France . . . somewhere the Standing Fallen can't follow them."

I'm silent for a moment, remembering our conversation. "Say good-bye to Teacake for me," Leah had said, half shouting over the hum of traffic. There was a pause, filled only by the sound of the cars zipping past. For a second, I thought she might have been about to say something, any of the things I'd wanted to hear for so long. But she didn't, and in that instant I realized it honestly didn't matter anymore.

"Thanks, Jaya. Really," she'd said instead. "You saved us both."

"What are you thinking?" Allie asks. She's gone still. When I look at her face, I realize she's anxious, waiting to hear what I have to say about Leah.

But there's nothing to say. The person Leah was before the Standing Fallen is gone, just like the person I was before the accident is gone. The people we were together have changed, too. I know that a few months away from the cult will help Leah find her way back to herself, and that there'll come a time when I can talk about Mum without my throat closing up. But whatever was between us is over, and it's better that way.

I run the tip of my finger over the rose on Allie's wrist. My eyes skip from her freckles to her eyelashes to the tiny diamonds in her earlobes, before slipping down to her lips.

"I was just . . ." I swallow. "I was thinking it's pretty ridiculous that we've rescued a Being, saved a girl from a bunch of abusive fanatics, and possibly helped bring down an international cult together, but we haven't even kissed yet."

A slow smile spreads over her face. "You're right. That is ridiculous."

"Well, then."

"Well."

It doesn't matter that she has to leave in a few days. It doesn't matter that we live hundreds of miles apart. I put my hands on her face, and I finally kiss her. In those seconds, all that exists is Allie, her lips, her hair, and her hands—and the shadows sliding across our skin as Teacake floats above us, inching ever closer toward home.

THIRTY-ONE

THE GLEN HAS CHANGED SINCE NOVEMBER. ITS WINTER-BARE branches are now hidden behind a patchwork of greens, and the reddish leaves that littered the ground have given way to long grass and wildflowers. Birds flit through the trees: I spot a gray wagtail, followed by a black-headed bunting. Neither of those would have been here in winter. I wouldn't have known their names back then, either.

It's beautiful. But that doesn't still the tight, fluttery feeling in my chest as Dad pulls the car up by the gate.

"Are you sure about this?" Allie stifles a yawn. It's just past five in the morning—early enough that we won't bump into any dog walkers or bird-watchers.

I nod. "This is the place. It has to be here."

It's been six days since we rescued Teacake from the power station. Each one has given me bizarre and beautiful memories. There was seeing Allie finally finish stitching the last feathers to her wing, and Teacake's face light up when she took into the sky afterward. There was Calum teaching Rani and Teacake how to play chess, and the way his jaw dropped when Teacake eventually beat him. There was the stormy night we stayed in and watched *Les Mis* (she was singing "One Day More" for hours on end) and the boiling-hot afternoon we introduced her to ice pops. There was hearing her hum along to Nina Simone, one of Mum's favorites, and seeing Dad's ears prick up when a bulletin about another Fall in Tunisia came on the radio—only to watch him switch it off and turn his attention back to Rani, laughing in a way he hadn't done in months.

After that, there were our exam results. Allie got a full house of As, of course, and Calum got what he needed to get into his photography course. Even my own cluster of Cs and Ds, plus a B in French, was better than I could have hoped for. I actually found myself wondering what I might do with my results, and I realized that I cared. That I still had things to look forward to.

More time with Allie, for one thing. We haven't talked about what's going to happen when she goes back home yet, but we've done more kissing. Quite a lot of it, actually. Calum's started hurrying out of the room every time Allie and I come within less than a meter radius of each other (not that he has an issue with her being bi; he'd do the same no matter who she was making out with), but I don't care who sees. I've had my fill of secrets for one summer.

There's still one left, of course. But I won't have to keep it for much longer.

Now that Allie has finished repairing her wing, Teacake's flights have steadily grown longer. Last night, she disappeared for so long that I started to think maybe she had left for good, without saying good-bye—or worse, that she'd been caught, shot down over the fields like a game bird. When she finally reappeared, something had changed. Her eyes were bright, and she was chattering in her own language, fast and high-pitched; I couldn't understand the words, but the excitement was obvious. She'd seen something up there.

A streak of sadness tainted my relief. It was time.

I half expected to find her gone when I woke at half past four this morning, but she was curled up on the roof where we left her— she'd taken to sleeping up there on dry nights, tucked behind the chimney. This morning, though, she was wide awake and watching the sky, its stars hidden behind a layer of thick blue-gray clouds.

"I know," I said as she twitched her wings in greeting. "I'm ready when you are."

I got Rani and Calum up to say their bleary-eyed good-byes, then asked Dad to drive Teacake, Allie, and me over to the glen. The short journey passed in sleepy silence. Dad kept glancing at Teacake in the rearview mirror, a question—*the* question—forming on his lips. Now, as he parks the car by the gate leading to the glen, he turns around to face her.

"Well, then," he says. "This is it."

He opens his mouth: I can see all the questions in his head spilling onto his tongue, but he swallows them back. Instead, he takes out his phone and pulls up a map of the country to show Teacake.

"Fly north if you can," he says, suddenly businesslike. "It won't hurt if a few people spot you, as long as you're high enough, but best to avoid large towns or cities just in case. Fewer plane routes up there, too."

He says good-bye and leaves the three of us to take the path toward the waterfall. Morning dew brushes against my ankles; the weak sunlight leaves glints of gold in Teacake's hair and feathers. After a few minutes, we enter a small, leafy clearing and the water-fall comes into view. My breath catches at the splash of red in the pool below. It's just the sunrise, spilling its colors into the water, but it sends painful images flickering in front of my eyes.

Allie puts her hand on the small of my back. "Are you sure this is what you want? Teacake can leave from anywhere—"

I shake my head. "I'm fine. It has to be here."

This place is where everything began to go wrong; where my own apocalypse began, even before the sky started to cave in. But so much has changed since then, I feel like I'm coming full circle.

Teacake flies low across the pool, dipping her toes below the sur-face of the water. My heart is hammering. The closer she comes to leaving, the more impossible it seems that we've gotten this far. I flinch every time something rustles in the hedgerow, half expect-ing Damien and a dozen Standing Fallen members to pop up from behind the bushes. The fear that crept up my spine the first few times I heard a car in the distance has lessened with each day that passes, but it hasn't quite disappeared.

Allie says her good-byes first. She hugs Teacake (who shoots me a bewildered look, then gingerly pats Allie's back—hugs are obvi-ously something they don't do where Beings come from), then takes both of her hands. I linger by the bushes, letting them have their moment. Allie walks back to me, wiping the corners of her eyes with her sleeve. Her hand brushes my side as she moves back onto the path, leaving me alone with Teacake.

She sits down on a rock, the lower edge of her wings falling into the water. I watch her, trying to memorize all the things I know will eventually fade from my mind: the musical swell of her voice, the impossible lightness of her skin, the dreamlike feel to the world when she's around.

A sparrow alights on a rock just by her foot. It dips its beak into the pool, ruffles its feathers, then takes off again. I watch it flit above the trees with another jolt of nerves. The sky is so vast, endless. It seems impossible that Teacake could ever find her way home again.

"It's not your fault."

My heart stops. Everything stops. Teacake is looking at me, her eyes solemn. "What did you say?"

"Maybe you feel guilty that you survived and they didn't," she says slowly. "But don't feel guilty, okay? Don't blame yourself."

A lump comes to my throat. She's just repeating my own words—the things I said to her back in McEwan Hall after she saw the videos of the Falls. But the tears spill over, and I let out a sob. She still doesn't know what she's saying. To her they're just sounds, without meaning.

Only . . . they're not. *I* meant them. I meant them when I said them to her. If I could tell Teacake she's not to blame, surely I can tell myself that, too.

I look up, to the edge of the waterfall. The stream keeps rushing over the rocks, oblivious to all it robbed me of that morning.

The same pain throbs beneath my rib cage, no duller than the day Mum fell. But something else has gone: the restless creature wriggling in my stomach and squeezing at my windpipe; the thing telling me it was all my fault.

Suddenly, Teacake is standing in front of me. I hold her tight, pressing my face into her shoulder, my hands against the waxy feathers of her wings. She wipes the tears from my cheeks. Her own eyes are glistening: the whites are pale pink against her deep garnet irises.

"And the moon shines bright, as I rove at night," she says, nodding seriously. "Terms and conditions apply, Jaya."

"Exactly," I say, half laughing and half crying. "Go. Go fly."

This time, there's no dramatic takeoff: she simply pushes off from the ground and rises above the waterfall, slow and serene. A few curious blackbirds loop around her legs, like ribbons trailing from a kite. Her wings make powerful sweeps back and forth, creating gusts of wind that ripple across the water. I close my eyes, feel the breeze on my face and in my hair.

When I look up again, Teacake has floated far past the treetops. Then, quite suddenly, she stops. She glides downward, picking up speed as she tumbles toward the water. I leap forward, my heart in my mouth—but then she makes a wide curve across the pool, splashing me with the edge of her wing, and flies back into the air. She hovers above us for a moment, a peaceful smile on her face, and flicks her wings good-bye.

"Go!" I laugh, though my heart is still pounding. "Get home. Be safe."

I walk back to Allie, who's sitting below a beech tree at the edge of the path. She kisses the tears off my right cheek, runs one hand through my hair. Above us, Teacake rises higher and higher, her wings sketching pinkish curves against the sky. Allie leans against my shoulder, her hair tickling my ear. "It's still hard to believe, isn't it?"

The sun's glare starts to makes our eyes water, but we keep watching as Teacake shrinks into the sky. Soon, she's just a shimmer of movement against the sunrise. Another few beats, and she disappears from view. But not completely.